cook like a chef

techniques, tips and secrets from the professional kitchen to yours

CHRIS KNIGHT

whitecap

As seen on Food Network Canada

Edited by Lesley Cameron
Proofread by Ian Whitelaw
Cover and interior design by Val Speidel
Photography by Mike Tien
Food Styling by Julie Zambonelli
Printed and bound in Canada

Library and Archives Canada Cataloguing in Publication

Knight, Chris, 1960–
    Cook like a chef : techniques, tips and secrets from the professional kitchen to yours / Chris Knight.

Includes index.
ISBN 1-55285-612-7

    1. Cookery. I. Title.

TX714.K54 2004   641.5   C2004-905690-5

The publisher acknowledges the financial support of the Government of
Canada through the Book Publishing Industry Development Program for our
publishing activities.

Table of Contents

Foreword

Welcome to *Cook Like A Chef*. By the time you read this, we'll have shot at least 165 episodes and the show will be on the air in some twenty countries and counting. Routinely, we get mail from viewers in Europe and South America (where the show is dubbed and perhaps the concept is slightly less clear), asking how one might become a student in our cooking school. Hmmm ... now there's an idea ...

Cook Like A Chef is shot in a studio at Cinevillage in Toronto on a huge soundstage. All told, some sixty people work on the series. Thousands of hours, tons of food, crates of ASA, gallons of coffee, cartons of cigarettes (yeah, I know, I know), shredded nerves, greying hair and *beaucoup de* giggles have gone into making *Cook Like A Chef*.

The idea for the series was to try to reinvent the genre of the studio cooking show. Taking nothing away from the other fine shows on the air all over the world, we wanted to do something really different. For me, the fun part of television is coming up with the concept, the idea upon which to hang the series. How do you improve on an already beloved genre that has spawned dedicated channels the world over? If you're interested in this stuff, read on. If not, go to the last two paragraphs of the Foreword. There are four primary creative issues to deal with in designing a studio-based *programme de cuisine*: theme, content, talent and set design.

First there's the theme. Most cooking shows are recipe based. Today we're gonna make such and such. Absolutely nothing wrong with that. But how could we be different? A show driven by techniques, tips and secrets from professional kitchens. The HOW to cook, as opposed to the WHAT to cook. I think the art and the craft of cooking have slipped away from us. In an age of boil-in-the-bag, drive-thru-window, microwaved, salt-laden faux food, we have forgotten how to peel an onion, how to make stock, how to scrape yummy brown bits from the bottom of a skillet.

Hundreds of millions of dollars in marketing and advertising tell us we're wasting our time in the kitchen. Shun fresh and local they say, buy pre-fab and mass produced. "Hey! You're important! Don't waste your time in the kitchen, get out there and watch TV so you can buy more junk and get further into debt and second mortgage your house to pay off the credit cards and get fat and bloated and pretty soon your brain will stop working because of all the sugar and salt and locustbean gum and hydrogenated cancerous bilge we've pumped into you. But you're cool, baby, oh yeah! Listen to our jingle. Buy our stuff! Do you have any idea how much this brightly coloured packaging cost?"... oof ... I'm exhausted ... must lie down ... anyway, you get the idea. Collectively, we have forgotten how to cook. The basic techniques elude us because it has not been part of our cultural heritage. The new world demands new attitudes, and why spend an hour making dinner when there are *Seinfeld* reruns to watch?

What we hoped to do with *Cook Like A Chef* was to remind our audience just how *easy* cooking is. The skills necessary to prepare a killer meal are not beyond the most intimidated novice. And so we eschewed the traditional recipe approach. Think about it. You never see one of our chefs talking about quantities, but they do show you how to fillet that fish, or carve that bird. There are no measuring cups or exact amounts on our show, but yes, here's *mirepoix* and that's how to peel a tomato. The how and not the what.

Next is the content. Take a handful of the best chefs in the country and tell them they get to show off their culinary prowess on national television. First thing they all want to do is fillet a two-ton blue fin tuna and cook everything with fois gras and truffles. Let the big dog hunt. All of us who work on the show love food. It is a constant battle reconciling our enthusiasm for all things exotic and culinary-groovy with the discipline of making the show accessible to everyone. Yes, we wanna do cool things ... and we do them. But we also wanna show how to dice an onion, clean a leek, peel a mango, quarter a chicken, deglaze a pan ... In 165 episodes I think we've covered all the basics. Watching *Cook Like A Chef* will improve your skills in the kitchen, whether you're an accomplished foodie or a novice.

Which brings us to talent. What makes for a great TV chef? Certainly the chef must be articulate, telegenic, enthusiastic, knowledgeable, inspiring, commanding, focused, have an innate ability to make eye contact with the camera (or in our case, cameras plural, because there are four of them with which the chef has to contend), and preferably avoid shakes, jitters, spasms, retching and crying before camera rolls ... you know, all the things you and I are naturally good at. Being a TV chef is a tough gig. It is not fun. Nothing in your life— no news-at-noon-let's-make-turkey-leftovers, no wine and food show demo stage, no riffing in your own kitchen—can prepare you for the gut-wrenching, ulcer-provoking, pupil-dilating mind mess that is big league television. The quality of programming on Food Network Canada (and around the world) is such that viewers demand their TV chefs hit a homer out of the gate. There is no opportunity for "growing" into the job. You have to be as good as everyone else from day one. You have to exude the same ease, the same charm, the same *savoir faire* as the guys who've been doing it for years. And what makes a great chef doesn't necessarily make a great TV host, and vice versa. In fact, some of the best chefs in the world are such fragile introverts that even working the floor in their own restaurants is beyond them, let alone appearing on television. There's a reason why they're in the back of the house. I'll tell you more about the chefs that make up our on-camera ensemble later.

When we designed the show, we wanted to minimize the TV fright and give our guys a chance to do what they do best, namely to cook. But someone who has spent his or her life learning the ins and outs of pots and pans deserves to be on TV. That's why we came up with the "chef interview." Those are the bits coming in from and going out to commercial, where Chef is sitting on a stool and talking about stuff going on in that episode. This technique allows Chef to give us an insight into what's going on without having to look into the camera and read from a teleprompter. It also lets us show a bit of the personal side of chefs' lives, their stories and memories of years in the trenches. Really, all we wanted to do was let a chef cook.

Finally, there's the set design. When you watch the show, you'll notice that everything and everyone works in a circle around the oval table in the middle of the set. Television is all about movement, and we wanted to take our chefs out from behind a counter and let them move about.

You see the cameras because we figured you are sophisticated television viewers and know the cameras are there, and we wanted to allow them to move in and get shots they couldn't otherwise—if they were restricted by the normal rules of television production. The on-air cameras and crew have been the most controversial design element of *Cook Like A Chef*. Some people have said we're groundbreaking, innovative and fresh. Others have been distracted by the fogging cameras, the roving floor director, and the odd camera angles. Either way, it makes for entertaining television.

You will see things on *Cook Like A Chef* that you have never seen before.

Blackout drapes are used so you can see vapour, steam, fat, broth and the angel's share rise from the pots and pans. The lighting scheme is complex and used to dramatic effect. The appliances are suspended in stone walls because we didn't want to pretend we were in someone's kitchen. The prep table in the back of the set has sous-chefs and prep chefs working away because we know you know these things don't happen by magic and we want you to see the entire process.

There is music throughout *Cook Like A Chef* because there are only two cooking sounds—chopping and sizzling—and after a while that gets boring. The graphics and introduction are simple and to the point because we want to get to the cooking.

Acknowledgements

I mentioned there is a bunch of people who work on the show. If you don't blink you'll see their names go by in the credit role. All are talented, wonderful folk who have invested their creative selves in *Cook Like A Chef* to make it a success. There are many comparisons between the TV and the restaurant biz. These people are the *Cook Like A Chef* brigade.

First of all, there's Producer Kathy Doherty who actually makes the show (I just get all the glory). She is an amazing dynamo who can multitask and adapt to new situations on the fly. She is intelligent, opinionated and, occasionally, a royal pain in the soufflé, but without her there wouldn't be a show, let alone this book.

Trevor Grant is the Director. He and I worked on *The Great Canadian Food Show*, and Trevor has made it his lot in life to make me look good. He is a lovely man with the work ethic of a Clydesdale. I think he and I work so well together because the more freaked out I get, the calmer he gets. Love ya, man!

Christine Overvelde has been with me longer than anyone. It is her steady, constant support in running the company that allows me the great indulgence of going off for six or seven weeks to shoot a show like this.

While my beautiful wife, Jennifer, might not be a part of the production per se, without her I would be selling used cars out of a trailer in Belleville. She keeps me grounded and puts up with me. While I'm immensely proud of what we've all done here, it's just a TV show and family is everything. My son, Adam, is the centre of my universe. Lucky me.

All the recipes you see in this book have been tested or developed with the superhuman assistance of Karrie Galvin, who also works behind the scenes on the show itself.

To all of you on the crew—the camera guys, the kitchen staff, the production assistants, the control room gang, the shoppers, the runners, makeup, office staff—a very big thank you.

Finally, there's Karen Gelbart and Eleanor James at Food Network Canada. I hesitate to tell you how wonderful, supportive, creative and all-round great eggs they are. Now you'll go pitch them your own show and I'll end up working the perfume counter at the Bay. *Cook Like A Chef* is a serious departure from the safe middle ground, and they took a chance. I am their humble servant. My feet are like wings.

So that's it. That's the skinny on the show. That's what we're all about.

All in all, we think *Cook Like A Chef* is a pretty cool show. The recipes in this book are all from the show. If you're buying this book, I'm guessing you're a fan of the show. For that, a big fat chocolate-covered thank you. May your capon be big and juicy, your snapper fresh and boned, your produce firm and ripe.

Chris Knight

Some Things You Need to Know About This Book

Read the recipe from beginning to end. Twice.

I learned this one the hard way. The number of times I'd be in the middle of a recipe for dinner that night when I read something like: "And marinate for 24 hours". Yeesh. Besides, by reading the recipes you can visualize yourself actually cooking, much like an athlete zones before a big game.

Preparation ratings.

You'll notice there's a preparation rating at the beginning of every recipe: easy, moderate and difficult. Sometimes we fudge and say prep is moderate to difficult, easy to moderate. That's because the level of difficulty really depends on how good a cook you are and will vary from person to person. Please don't be intimidated by the ones that are rated difficult. For the most part it just means there are more steps involved as opposed to the recipe requiring trick techniques.

Temperatures and times.

Every oven and every stovetop is different. The altitude and relative humidity of where you live will affect baking and chocolate tempering. Convection roast is way faster than regular roast. You get the idea. In a lot of places we've given you visual signposts (e.g., continue to reduce until thick enough to coat the back of a spoon, sweat the shallots till translucent, etc.) instead of exact times.

Do your mise en place.

Roughly translated, mise en place means to put everything in its place and it is essential to the smooth running of a restaurant, and your kitchen. If the recipe ingredient list calls for a diced shallot and a chopped carrot then you really should get that chopping done in advance of beginning to cook. (See my first note about reading the recipe.)

Cooking is an art, not a science (except for baking).

Experiment and explore. Adjust the recipe to suit your cooking ideas and tastes. Make it sweeter or more bitter. Add three times the amount of garlic called for, or none at all. Substitute tequila for rum, veggie stock for chicken stock. Let your imagination and creativity influence the composition of the dish you're making.

Ten Very Opinionated Tips
for Good Kitchenology

1 Buy fresh and local, unless you're buying exotic.

Most big-time chefs these days are making hay out of cooking with local seasonal ingredients. You should too. Local farmers and producers depend on your patronage to make a living. You know that something picked that morning and brought to market is going to taste better than something shipped by truck. There are things that grow or are raised in your little corner of paradise that I can't readily get and vice versa. These things should be celebrated. Okay, so you need some passion fruit or fois gras or truffles or orange roughy ... in that case, see #3 below.

2 Buy seasonal.

I'm sorry, but a tomato in December tastes more like wet newspaper than a tomato. Just because some mega-corp with a greenhouse the size of Prince Edward Island ships you plastic fruit and veggies doesn't mean you have to buy them. You and your taste buds deserve only the best. So do your friends and family. Don't sell yourself short. If it's not fresh, fresh, fresh, walk on by and look for something new in season you haven't cooked with before. The real strawberries will taste even better when their time comes.

3 Get to know a fishmonger, butcher, greengrocer, baker, cheesemonger.

There are many reasons to shop at a mega-grocery store. It is indeed convenient to buy personal hygiene products, patio furniture and a pork roast all in the same place. Except the meat from a supermarket will never ever ever be as good as from a butcher. Same goes for fish, veggies and bread. In your town, in your neighbourhood, there are people who make it their lives' work to specialize in these food items. Seek them out. They want to talk to you. They're full of information and advice, and their selection is always the best. Besides, their kids go to school with your kids.

4 Use only the **best ingredients** you can afford.

Many of the dishes in this book have only a handful of ingredients. Good chefs know you don't have to be fancy-schmancy if you're working with great ingredients. Remember, the dish you make is only as good as the stuff you put into it.

5 Never use **powdered stock** substitutes.

Okay, so you're busy and you've got a life and you can't always (or ever) make stocks from scratch. Fine, no worries. While they won't be as good as your own, there are stocks of all kinds (veggie, beef, chicken, etc.) in the grocery store. They come in cans or those vac-pack things. They are low in sodium (as opposed to powdered, which is huge in sodium) and pretty tasty. Also, check with your local butcher, as more and more of them are selling ready-to-go stock they make themselves.

6 Don't be afraid to **screw up**—it's not a contest.

You have to eat every day ... three times a day. This is a good thing. It should be a pleasant experience. Remember that not every dish is going to turn out perfectly. Big Deal. Professional chefs tinker and putter over dishes before they're ready for the line and the menu. You don't have that luxury. Just jump into the deep end of the pool, baby. I mean, let's face it folks, in the end (and I do mean in the end) it's just food. No need to bust a gut.

7 **Try new** things.

At the time of writing, my son is just five years old. He won't eat anything green. He won't eat anything new. There are people I know (mainly guys) who can cook three things and that's it. They have no inclination to stretch. When it's their turn to cook, it's the same old same old. But that's not you. You experiment. You're interested in new herbs, spices, cuts of meat, types of fish, cooking techniques. You are open minded. You are a rock in the river and new things flow over and around you (sorry, I'm listening to Indian music while I'm writing this). You are a river to your people and you just keep on giving.

8 Cook with **love and passion.**

Not your family, not your dinner guests, not your in-laws, not anyone is going to think anything but good things of a meal you've put your heart into, no matter if it turns out or not. Love and passion are the secret ingredients to all good meals. By the way, it is impossible to infuse a microwave, boil-in-the-bag, freeze-dried meal with hope, let alone love and passion.

9 There is no such thing as **a good bottle of wine** under ten bucks.

Okay, this one isn't about cooking, but what's a good meal without a good bottle of wine? I'm tired of reading wine columns about best buys under ten dollars. There's just no such thing. Yes, there is bottled wine-like stuff that is drinkable in that price range, but it is to be consumed and not enjoyed. Sorry, but nobody lingers over the yummy backwash from a bargain basement wine. The difference between a ten dollar wine and a fifteen-to-seventeen dollar bottle is night and day. Drink less, drink better.

10 Support your **local restaurant** scene.

Hey, you can't cook all the time, right? So go out. Go out often. Go out on a Tuesday night. But whatever you do, make sure you go to a locally owned restaurant. Fagedabout the big-box commercial restaurants in big-box parking lots. Don't even think of a drive-thru or I'll track you down and shoot out your headlights. Find some nice little places where the owners are either in the kitchen or working the floor. I promise you the food will be better and, as with the butcher, grocer, fishmonger, etc., these people live in your neighbourhood and can only survive with your continued support. Tell them Chris sent you.

The Chefs

These lovely people are the heart, soul and face of *Cook Like A Chef*. It is my pleasure, indeed my honour, to call each one a friend. They each have their own style, quirks and craziness. As an ensemble they bring varied opinions and experience to our sound stage, giving *Cook Like A Chef* a depth and texture I don't think would be possible with only one chef/host. They are truly artists. Their canvas is a plate, their art is ethereal and their craft is for consumption.

I'd like you to meet them.

Michael Allemeier

Michael is a big lad with a shock of blond hair and an ear-to-ear grin. When he's in the kitchen he can also be a laser-beam-focused serious son of a gun. Michael's cooking knowledge is prodigious. When I first met him he was Chef at one of Calgary's best restaurants, where we did an episode of *The Great Canadian Food Show*. In that episode we got him to play pool on camera as a dinner bet. He played along like a seasoned vet. We were never sure exactly what colour Michael's hair would be from one season to the next. Chefs, wada ya gonna do? Family is a big deal to Michael. His wife and two kids keep him grounded, keep him centred. Michael is now heading up the Culinary Program at the Mission Hill Family Estate in the Okanagan Valley.

Ned Bell

I first met Ned in New York at a food thing. I think he was like 12 years old and Executive Chef at Senses in Toronto, with a beach bum hair dye job and a cheesy goatee. Ned is like one of those perfect pitch musicians who can play piano at the age of three. You just wanna throttle him for all his natural talent. Ned is now in Calgary as partner and Executive Chef at Marietta's.

Michael Bonacini

I must admit to having doubts when it was first suggested that we audition Michael Bonacini for the show. Here was this tall, suave überchef who owns and runs some of the best restaurants in Toronto. I figured he had some serious Torontosaurus rex 'tude going on and hadn't seen the honest end of a skillet in years. Man, was I wrong. A nicer, sweeter guy you've never met.

Welsh by birthright (can't you tell with a name like Bonacini?), Michael is poised, articulate, insanely knowledgeable about les choses gastronomes, disarmingly friendly and down to earth. Hell, I'd date him if I wasn't married!

Caroline McCann-Bizjak

Caroline is francophone and a woman and a killer chef, which makes her a godsend to a TV producer, as professional cookery is a very chauvinistic, male-dominated business. With a strong grounding in French Canadian cuisine and a disarming ear-to-ear smile, Caroline has long been one of our favourite chefs.

She and her husband have a fruit farm in Beamsville, Niagara, Ontario smack dab in the middle of wine country. She also runs a high-end catering business out of the farm.

Tim McRoberts

Chef McRoberts is our east coast guy. Based in Charlottetown, Prince Edward Island, Tim is Chief Instructor at the Culinary Institute of Canada. Enthusiastic and sharing are two words that apply to Tim, a man who has nurtured and encouraged many generations of young chefs toiling under his aegis. You wouldn't know it to see his easygoing TV way, but he's also probably the most competitive of all our Chefs.

Liz Manville

I first met Liz in New York City where she was big cheese Chef to the Canadian Consul General. Some of that Brooklyn attitude has stuck with our Liz. She's smart, sharp, witty and a total babe in starched Chef's whites, which is not always a good thing when you're trying to hold your own in a professional kitchen full of guys. Sometimes it means you have to work twice as hard. Chef Manville and her husband have recently returned to Vancouver after a tour of culinary duty at the Canadian Embassy in Rome, Italy.

Georges Laurier

When we decided to add a Quebec chef (Quebec being easily the most food-sophisticated province in the country) our thoughts immediately turned to Chef Georges Laurier, then running his own boîte in Gatineau.

Georges is passionate about his cooking and insane about detail. English is not his first language, but he jumped in the deep end with gusto, and acquitted himself well. Today, Georges Laurier is Executive Chef at Gatineau's venerable Café Henri Burger.

René Rodriguez

El Latino. Man, did this guy get mail. I first met him in Ottawa, where he was cooking at the trendy Arc hotel and pulling down some great reviews. Being Cordon Bleu-trained with a Mexican upbringing means René would put fois gras and chipotles in everything if he could. He's the sort of young chef who reads all the time and is constantly looking to push the envelope. He is now Executive Chef at Social on Sussex Drive in Ottawa.

1 The Basics

This section contains the recipes for some of the basics referred to throughout the book.

Bouquet Garni

Preparation: easy

The ingredients in a bouquet garni vary according to which chef is assembling it, but basically it's a bunch of fresh herbs tied together to flavour a liquid.

- These days, most chefs take a green leek leaf and flatten it out. In the middle of the leaf is then placed thyme, a bay leaf and some peppercorns. The leek is folded over to make a little pouch and is tied off with butcher's twine to stop the goodies from slipping out.

Sachet

Preparation: easy

The exact ingredients of a sachet vary from chef to chef, but the basic idea is to combine a bunch of stuff in a piece of cheesecloth and let it float around in a liquid (soup, stock, stew) and release its flavours. The cheesecloth makes for easy extraction.

- Combine a bay leaf, crushed peppercorns, thyme stems and parsley stems in a piece of cheesecloth and tie off with a small length of butcher's twine.

Clarified Butter

Preparation: easy • Makes about ¾ pound (375 g)

By gently melting the butter, you remove most of the water from it, and by skimming the foam off the top and leaving the gooky stuff at the bottom of the pot you've made yourself clarified butter, which has a higher smoking point than regular butter. "Smoking point" means the temperature at which a liquid fat begins literally to smoke (burn) and becomes unusable for frying or sautéing. Regular butter has a pretty low smoking point, which is why you sometimes see recipes calling for a combo of butter and olive oil to raise the smoking point.

Indian cuisine takes the whole clarified butter thing one step further by continuing to cook it until (gook removed) it turns a nice nutty brown colour and flavour. They call this *ghee*, which in turn is not to be confused with *beurre noisette* which is clarified butter cooked until nutty brown and served with the foam and gooky stuff included. This in turn is not the same as *black butter*, which is *beurre noisette* with capers, parsley and vinegar. Confused? This is a good time to pour yourself a glass of wine ...

1 pound unsalted butter (500 g)

- Cut the butter up into cubes and add to a sauce pot to melt over medium-low heat. Look for froth on top.
- Remove from the heat and let stand for a couple of minutes.
- Skim the froth off the top with a small spoon.
- Carefully pour the butter into a measuring cup, making sure to leave behind the solids that have collected at the bottom of the sauce pot.
- Voilà. Clarified butter.
- Can keep in the fridge for 5 days.

Oven-Dried Tomatoes

Preparation: easy • Makes 20 roasted tomato halves • Recipe by Chris Knight

There are two problems with store-bought dried tomatoes. The first is you have no idea what quality the tomato was in the first place. The second is that you have no idea how long they've been sitting there. Dried tomatoes are like dried herbs—they lose more flavour the longer they're on the shelf. Besides, I find most store-bought to be too chewy for my liking. So here's a super easy way to do your own oven-dried tomatoes that guarantees sweet, pliant morsels every time.

10 ripe tomatoes, stems and cores removed

1 Tbsp. kosher salt (15 mL)

1 tsp. pepper (5 mL)

¼ cup olive oil (50 mL)

4 cloves garlic, peeled and sliced ¼ inch/5 mm

6 sprigs thyme

- Preheat oven to 350°F (180°C).
- Cut the tomatoes in half and lay them cut side down on a parchment-lined baking sheet.
- Sprinkle with salt and pepper and drizzle the oil over the top of them.
- Add the garlic cloves.
- Divide the thyme between the tomatoes and bake until the skins become loose, about 10–15 minutes.
- Remove the tomato skins and discard them.
- Pour any juices that have accumulated into a bowl and reserve.
- Return the tomatoes to the oven and reduce the temperature to 250°F (120°C). Continue to roast and pour off the juices until the tomatoes are slightly shrunken and appear cooked.
- Set aside to cool. Transfer to a container and store in the fridge for up to a week, or in the freezer for up to 6 months.
- Use in salads, pizza, pasta or tomato tarte tatin.

Chef's Tip: This method intensifies the flavour of the tomatoes. In the height of tomato season dry as many as you can to enjoy the taste of summer all year round.

Crème Fraîche

Preparation: easy • Makes 1 cup (250 mL)

Crème fraîche has a nice tangy oomph to it that makes it perfect to dollop on top of desserts. It's also great in soups, as it doesn't curdle.

1 cup whipping cream (250 mL)

2 Tbsp. buttermilk (or sour cream) (25 mL)

- Combine the whipping cream and buttermilk in a glass container.
- Cover and let stand at room temperature overnight, or until very thick.
- Stir well before covering and refrigerate for up to 10 days.

Tomato Concassé

Preparation: easy • Recipe by Chris Knight

Concasser is a French culinary term that means to chop coarsely. It's most often associated with tomatoes but applies equally to herbs, veggies and meats. Tomato concassé is usually added to a dish as garnish, or at the last minute. It calls for the skin and seeds to be removed (pretty cool technique) from the tomato before chopping.

- To remove peel from a tomato, cut an X in the bottom of the tomato. Place in boiling water for about one minute or until you see the peel coming away from the pulp. Place in iced water to stop the cooking process. Remove the peel and squeeze the tomato gently to remove the core and the seeds. Chop into small pieces.

Beef Stock

Preparation: easy • Makes about 8 cups (2 L) • Recipe by Chris Knight

¼ cup canola or other neutral oil (50 mL)

4 pounds beef stewing bones (meat on)
    (2 kg)

1 Tbsp. tomato paste (15 mL)

10 cups cold water (2.5 L)

2 cups good red wine (500 mL)

1 large onion, coarsely chopped

2 carrots, coarsely chopped

2 celery stalks, coarsely chopped

2 tomatoes, quartered (skin on)

3 or 4 parsley stems, chopped

½ tsp. thyme leaves (2 mL)

1 bay leaf

1 whole clove

½ tsp cracked black peppercorns (2 mL)

1 clove garlic, crushed

- Preheat the oven to 400°F (200°C).

- Lightly oil a sheet pan and place in the oven to heat. Place the bones on the sheet pan and roast for 30 minutes, turning occasionally.

- Brush the bones with a thin layer of the tomato paste, and roast for an additional 30 minutes, turning occasionally, until evenly browned.

- Place the bones in a stockpot and cover with cold water. Bring to a boil over high heat, and then lower to a simmer. Simmer uncovered. Skim any impurities that bubble to the surface.

- Drain and reserve the fat from the pan; deglaze the pan with red wine and add to the stockpot. Continue to simmer the stock, uncovered, for 3 to 4 hours, skimming as needed.

- Toss the *mirepoix* (onions, carrots, celery) with the fat and brown in the oven for about 20 minutes or until nicely browned.

- Add the browned *mirepoix*, tomatoes and sachet (use parsley, thyme, bay, cloves, peppercorns and garlic) to the pot. (See page 22).

- Simmer for another hour.

- Strain the stock through a fine sieve and transfer to the refrigerator to cool.

- Once chilled, skim the hardened fat off the top.

Curry Powder

Preparation: easy

2 tsp. turmeric (10 mL)

1 tsp. cumin (5 mL)

½ tsp. allspice (2 mL)

½ tsp. ground ginger (2 mL)

¼ tsp. ground cardamom (1 mL)

- Combine all the ingredients.

Chicken Stock

Preparation: easy • Makes about 12 cups (3 L) • Recipe by Chris Knight

1 (4-pound) chicken, cut into 8 pieces,
  plus neck and giblets (except liver)
  (2 kg)

16 cups cold water (4 L)

2 onions, left unpeeled, halved

3 whole cloves

5 garlic cloves, left unpeeled

3 celery ribs, halved

3 carrots, halved

1 tsp. salt (5 mL)

8 long fresh flat-leaf parsley sprigs

10 whole black peppercorns

2 thyme sprigs

1 bay leaf

- Add the chicken parts to the cold water and bring to a boil.
- Add the remaining ingredients and simmer the stock, uncovered, for about 3 hours.
- Skim the impurities off the top every now and then to ensure a nice clear stock.
- Pour through a fine mesh sieve into a large bowl, discarding solids.
- Put the stock in the fridge overnight and by the next morning the fat will have congealed on top. Skim it off. Voilà, perfect chicken stock.

Fish Stock (Fumet)

Preparation: easy • Makes about 8 cups (2 L) • Recipe by Chris Knight

Use only lean fish bones and avoid fatties like salmon and trout for this stock, which is also known as fumet.

2 Tbsp. unsalted butter (25 mL)

1 cup sliced onion (250 mL)

3 parsley stems

*3 pounds fish bones (no heads), rinsed
    well under cold water (1.5 kg)*

1 cup dry white wine (250 mL)

2 Tbsp. fresh lemon juice (25 mL)

8 cups cold water (2 L)

½ cup mushroom trimmings (125 mL)

1 Tbsp. roughly chopped garlic (15 mL)

1 tsp. fresh thyme leaves (5 mL)

4 thin slices lemon

salt and freshly ground black pepper

- Set a large stockpot over a medium heat and add the butter to the pan.
- When the butter has melted, add the onion, parsley and fish bones to the pot. Sweat these by covering the pot for 5 to 7 minutes.
- Add the white wine and lemon juice to the pot. Stir gently and cover with the cold water.
- Add all the remaining ingredients and increase the heat to high.
- Bring the contents of the pot to a boil, then reduce to a simmer.
- Cook the stock uncovered for 1 hour.
- Strain through a fine mesh sieve and cool.

Lobster Stock

Preparation: moderate • Makes about 6 cups (1.5 L) • Recipe by Chris Knight

So you indulge yourself with a big lobster feed. Well, don't throw the shells out when you're done. Wrap them up and stick them in the freezer until it's time for your next chi-chi dinner party. The shells and carcasses hold lots more lobster flavour than the meat does and are the basis for this rich layered stock, which in turn makes a decadent Lobster Bisque (see page 46). The recipe calls for fumet (fish stock) but you can use water in a pinch. This stock can be made well in advance of the bisque and kept in the freezer.

4 lobsters, carcasses and shells

olive oil for drizzling, to cover the shells

1 onion, medium dice

1 carrot, medium dice

1 celery stick, medium dice

4 Tbsp. olive oil (60 mL)

2 Tbsp. tomato paste (25 mL)

2 Tbsp. all-purpose flour (25 mL)

¼ cup brandy (50 mL)

7 cups fumet or water (1.75 L)
(see page 28)

handful parsley stalks

6 stalks tarragon

salt and pepper

- Preheat oven to 375°F (190°C).
- Take the lobster carcasses and remove anything inside, as it would lend a bitter taste if roasted. Wrap the shells in a dish towel and whack away with a meat tenderizer or the back of a big chef's knife until the shells are broken into smaller bits.
- Put the shell pieces in a roasting pan and drizzle with olive oil. Cook in the oven until almost caramelized, about 30 minutes or so.
- Remove the carcasses from the oven and from the pan. Place in a pot and add a *mirepoix* of the onion, carrot and celery and more olive oil (approx. 4 Tbsp. /60 mL). Cook on the stovetop over medium-high heat until the veggies are translucent, stirring every now and then.
- Add the tomato paste and the flour and cook for another two minutes or until the flour browns slightly and makes a bit of a paste.
- Use the brandy to deglaze the roasting pan. Scrape the bottom of the pan to gather all the little bits of lobster, and add to the pot.
- Top the carcasses with the fumet or water and bring to a simmer. Add the parsley and tarragon and cook for 1 hour, skimming impurities.
- Sieve the stock, discarding the bones and keeping the liquid. Season with salt and pepper.

Chef's Tip: Lobster butter is great drizzled over beef and fish. Simply take 1 cup (250 mL) of roasted shells, smash up and add to a pot with 1 cup (250 mL) of butter. Simmer until fragrant. Add brandy to taste, and strain.

Vegetable Stock

Preparation: easy • Makes 8 cups (2 L) • Recipe by Chris Knight

3 Tbsp. canola or olive oil (45 mL)

2 small onions, coarsely chopped

2 large leeks, carefully washed and cut
   into large rings, white and pale
   green parts only

3 medium carrots, washed but not
   scraped, cut into large rings/
   thick slices

2 medium turnips, coarsely chopped,
   not peeled

½ large bulb fennel, coarsely chopped

3 large stalks of celery, coarsely chopped,
   with some leaves

2 small tomatoes, coarsely chopped
   (skin on)

10 cups water (2.5 L)

1 sachet (see page 22)

- Place the oil in a deep pot and add the onions, leeks, carrots, turnips and fennel.
- Sweat the veggies over medium-low heat for about 5 minutes, until translucent but not browned.
- Add the celery and tomatoes.
- Cover and continue to cook over low heat for an additional 10 minutes, stirring occasionally.
- Add the water and sachet.
- Bring to a simmer and simmer gently for 30 minutes, skimming as necessary.
- Strain through a fine mesh sieve and cool in the fridge.

Lamb Stock

Preparation: easy • Makes about 10 cups (2.5 L) • Recipe by Chris Knight

3 pounds lamb bones (1.5 kg)

12 cups cold water (3 L)

2 medium-sized onions, peeled and
    each pierced with 1 whole clove

2 carrots, peeled and diced

2 celery stalks, diced

1 cup parsley stems (250 mL)

3 garlic cloves, diced

2 tsp. salt (10 mL)

12 whole black peppercorns

3 fresh thyme sprigs

- Put the lamb bones and the cold water in a stockpot.
- Bring to a boil over a high heat and skim off the froth.
- Add the remaining ingredients and reduce heat to simmer, partially covered, for 3 hours.
- Strain the broth through a fine mesh sieve, discarding the bones and vegetables. Allow the stock to cool.
- Chill the stock in the refrigerator and skim off the fat.

White Veal Stock

Preparation: easy to moderate • Makes about 12 cups (3 L) • Recipe by Chris Knight

4 pounds meaty veal bones (2 kg)

16 cups cold water (4 L) or enough to
    cover bones

1 large onion stuck with 4 cloves

4 medium leeks, halved lengthways and
    washed

3 carrots, diced

3 celery stalks, diced

2 tsp. salt (10 mL)

1 sachet (see page 22)

2 pounds chicken wings (1 kg)

- In a big stockpot cover the veal bones with the cold water.
- Bring the water to a boil over high heat, skimming off the impurities.
- Reduce heat to medium and simmer, continuing to skim.
- Add the onion, leeks, carrots, celery, salt and sachet.
- Simmer, partially covered, for 4 hours, continuing to skim as necessary.
- Add the chicken wings, skimming the froth and adding boiling water if necessary to keep the ingredients barely covered, for 2 hours more.
- Strain through a fine mesh sieve and cool.
- Chill the stock for 3 hours, then remove the fat.

Brown Veal Stock

Preparation: moderate • Makes about 8–10 cups (2–2.5 L) • Recipe by Chris Knight

8 pounds meaty veal bones (3.5 kg)

½ cup canola oil (125 mL)

salt and black pepper

16 cups cold water (4 L)

3 carrots, diced

1 large onion, studded with 2 whole cloves

3 medium leeks, halved and washed

4 fresh thyme sprigs

1 sachet (see page 22)

2 Tbsp. tomato paste (25 mL)

- Preheat oven to 450°F (230°C).
- Add the bones to a large roasting pan and toss with the canola oil.
- Season with salt and pepper and roast in the middle of the oven for about 45 minutes or until the bones are golden brown, turning once.
- Add the bones and then the water to a large stockpot. Bring to a boil over high heat and skim off any impurities.
- Discard fat from roasting pan. Deglaze with water, scraping up the brown bits, and add them to the stockpot.
- Bring the stock to a simmer over medium heat for about 2 hours, skimming often.
- Meanwhile, add the carrots, onion and leeks to an oiled shallow roasting pan and roast in the middle of the oven until golden brown, 20 to 30 minutes. Let veggies cool.
- Add the roasted vegetables and remaining ingredients to the stock and simmer for a further 2 hours.
- Strain with a fine mesh sieve and refrigerate until the fat congeals.
- Skim fat off the top of the cold stock.
- Return the stock to the stovetop and bring to a gentle boil over medium-high heat.
- Reduce heat and continue to reduce the liquid until you have about 8 to 10 cups (2–2.5 L).

Tarragon White Wine Sauce

Preparation: easy • Makes enough for 6 people • Recipe by Chris Knight

This elegant simple sauce is *mondo killer juju* with scallops, fish or chicken. Very versatile.

1 Tbsp. butter (15 mL)

2 shallots, chopped

2 cups white wine (500 mL)

1 large bunch tarragon

½ cup butter, cubed and cold (125 mL)

salt and pepper

- Melt the 1 Tbsp. (15 mL) of butter in a non-stick saucepan over medium heat. Add the shallots to sauté; they should become translucent but not coloured. This will take about 3 minutes.
- Add the white wine and bring the liquid to a simmer. Separate the tarragon into two bunches. Cut off any woody stems and drop one of the bunches into the liquid.
- Once the white wine has reduced to 1 cup (250 mL) and is scented with tarragon, strain the liquid through a fine mesh sieve, removing the shallots and tarragon.
- Return the liquid to the heat and bring it to a simmer once again.
- The reduction should be hot enough so that steam rises from the surface but it should not be boiling.
- Gradually incorporate the cold butter, keeping the pan in motion while whipping the butter in. Remove from heat.
- Strip the remaining tarragon leaves from the stems. Chop them roughly and drop them into the sauce. Pour the sauce immediately over some pan-fried or poached fish.

Chef's Tip: If the sauce appears to be breaking, it is an indication that it has become too hot. Remove from the heat and continue to add the cool butter, keeping the pan and the sauce in motion. When the sauce loses its oily appearance and dulls slightly, place the pan over low heat and continue to add the rest of the butter.

Pasta Dough

Preparation: moderate to difficult • Makes ½ pound fresh pasta (250 g) • Recipe by Chef Michael Bonacini

2 cups all-purpose flour (500 mL)

1 Tbsp. salt (15 mL)

4 extra large egg yolks

1 egg

2 Tbsp. olive oil (25 mL)

¼ cup cold water (50 mL)

- Make a mound with the flour and salt on your work surface and create a well in the centre of the flour.
- Put the egg yolks and egg in a bowl and lightly mix together with the olive oil and water. Pour the mixture into the well.
- Slowly incorporate the eggs into the flour. Working your fingers in a circular motion, form into a ball and knead for 10–20 minutes—the more the better—until the dough is silky smooth.
- Wrap dough in plastic wrap and let rest in refrigerator for at least 30 minutes.

Savoury Pastry Dough

Preparation: easy • Makes two 9-inch pie shells (23-cm) • Recipe by Chris Knight

2½ cups all-purpose flour (625 mL)

½ tsp. salt (2. mL)

15 Tbsp. unsalted butter, chilled and
   cut into pieces (225 mL)

5 Tbsp. ice water (75 mL)

- Stir the flour and salt together in a clean bowl.
- Add the butter pieces and, using a pastry blender or a fork, cut in the butter until the mixture looks crumbly and the butter is in small pea-sized pieces.
- Add the ice water and, using a wooden spoon, work in very briefly to form a rough dough. Do not make the dough a smooth, homogeneous ball. (Work any unincorporated flour into the dough when rolling out.)
- Wrap the dough and loose flour particles in plastic wrap and refrigerate for at least 1 hour or for up to 1 week before use.
- Extras can be frozen.

Sweet Pastry Dough

Preparation: easy • Makes one 9-inch (23-cm) tart shell • Recipe by Chris Knight

The addition of sugar and egg makes this the richer cousin of a standard pie pastry dough. It bakes to a crisp, more cookie-like texture than the savoury pastry.

1½ cups all-purpose flour (375 mL)

5 Tbsp. sugar (75 mL)

⅛ tsp. salt (.5 mL)

10 Tbsp. unsalted butter, at room temperature (150 mL)

1 whole egg, plus 2 egg yolks

- Combine the flour, sugar, salt and butter in a clean bowl.
- Using a heavy-duty stand mixer fitted with the paddle attachment, mix at a medium speed until the butter is well coated with the flour and is broken into small pea-sized pieces.
- Add the egg and egg yolks and mix until the pastry comes together.
- Remove from the bowl, gather into a ball, wrap in plastic wrap and refrigerate for at least 1 hour or for up to 1 week before use. This keeps frozen for a month.

2 Soups

Chilled Pea and Mint Soup with Lobster

Preparation: easy • Makes 6 servings • Recipe by Chris Knight

If you don't want to pop for the lobster then pan-fried bacon and leeks are also good mounded in the middle of a bowl of this soup just before serving. This is not one you really want to try with frozen peas. If you're not up to steaming the lobsters yourself then have your fishmonger do it for you while you wait. Never ever buy a pre-steamed lobster, as you have no idea how long it has been sitting there.

5 to 6 pounds unshelled fresh peas (2.2 to 2.7 kg)

3 Tbsp. peanut oil (45 mL)

2 shallots, peeled and minced

1 small leek, white part only, minced

3 cups heavy cream (750 mL)

freshly ground black pepper

kosher salt

3 Tbsp. mint, roughly chopped (45 mL)

2 lobsters (1¼–1½ pounds) steamed and meat reserved (625–750 g)

mint sprigs for garnish

- Bring a large saucepan of salted water to a boil. Shell the peas and add them to the water. Cook until tender, approximately 3 to 5 minutes.
- Refresh in an ice bath. Dry and set aside.
- Heat the oil in a saucepan over a medium heat.
- Add the shallots and leek and cook, stirring occasionally, until they begin to soften, approximately 5 minutes.
- Add the peas and cook until they are soft but still bright green. Add the cream, a pinch of pepper and salt and simmer for 5 minutes, stirring occasionally. Allow to cool slightly for a few minutes.
- Stir in the chopped mint. When seasoning, remember that you want to have a pure, fresh spring pea flavour.
- Transfer the soup in batches to a blender while it is still warm and purée. Press the pea soup liquid through a fine strainer and purée again if necessary. Adjust consistency with water.
- Serve with chunks of cold, plain steamed lobster floating in the middle with chopped mint.

Chef's Tip: To keep the green vegetables bright and green, the key is to use a very large pot of boiling water—when you add the vegetables, they will not lower the temperature of the water. Cook the vegetables as fast as possible. Add ¾ cup (175 mL) salt per gallon (4 L) of water. The salt will help to prevent the colour from leaching out of the vegetables. When the vegetables are bright green and cooked, they must be chilled as quickly as possible. Have a big bowl with lots of ice and water ready to plunge the cooked vegetables in.

Chilled Lemon Grass and Coriander Vichyssoise

Preparation: moderate • Makes 6 servings • Recipe by Chef Ned Bell

Say "vichyssoise" and everyone thinks of the classic velvety cold leek and potato soup. Despite its very French name, the soup was actually created in the USA. This version uses a potato base and is infused with the decidedly Asian flavours of lemon grass and coriander. For those watching the old belt holes, this version is made with milk instead of 35% cream. Relax, have a second bowl.

1 large bunch coriander

6 stalks lemon grass

6 green onions

5 cups water (1.25 L)

½ cup unsalted butter (125 mL)

3 medium onions, chopped

2 pounds new potatoes, peeled and diced (1 kg)

1½ cups whole milk (375 mL)

salt and pepper

3 lemons, sliced thinly

- Remove the coriander leaves from the stalks and set the stalks aside.
- Trim the lemon grass by taking off all the tough outer leaves and top. Reserve trimmings. Smash the stalk to release the flavour. Chop finely.
- Chop the green onions finely. Gather up all the trimmings from the lemon grass, green onions and coriander stalks and put them into a large pot with the water. Let simmer for 30 minutes and strain.
- In a large pot, melt the butter and add the chopped onions, lemon grass and potatoes.
- Keep the heat low to allow the vegetables to sweat gently. Keep them covered for approximately 10 minutes.
- Add the strained cooking liquid to the onions and potatoes. Add the milk and the majority of the coriander leaves (keep some aside for the garnish). Season to taste with salt and pepper. Simmer for 20 minutes or until the soup is fragrant and the potatoes are soft.
- Let cool slightly.
- Purée the soup in a food processor and then strain. Taste and season if necessary. Put aside to cool and refrigerate to chill thoroughly.
- Serve with a cube of ice in the centre of each bowl and the remainder of the coriander leaves on top.

Chef's Tip: Vichyssoise should have a very smooth consistency. If necessary, strain twice. It should not have a gritty potato texture.

Lentil and Ham Hock Soup

Preparation: easy • Makes 6 servings • Recipe by Chef Michael Allemeier

I love this soup. I love this soup after skating or skiing or tobogganing. I love this soup for lunch or for dinner. I love this soup in the summer or winter. Man, I love this soup!

If your butcher doesn't sell smoked ham hocks, then it's definitely time for a new butcher.

10 cups water (2.5 L)

¾ pound green lentils, rinsed and picked
    over (375 g)

1 large smoked ham hock
    (1–1½ pounds/500g– 750 g)

1 onion, diced

2 carrots, diced

1 tsp. freshly ground coriander seeds
    (5 mL)

4 cloves garlic, minced

2 Tbsp. canola oil (25 mL)

salt and pepper

- In a large pressure cooker, heat the water, lentils and ham hock. Bring the mixture to a simmer and skim off any impurities.
- Add the diced onion and carrots, coriander, garlic and canola oil.
- Put the top on the pressure cooker and cook for 40 minutes. Follow the manufacturer's instructions regarding pressure per pound.
- Turn off the heat, allow the pressure to reduce and check the contents.
- The lentils should be tender and the meat falling off the hock.
- Remove the hock and let cool.
- Strain the lentils and reserve the broth.
- Purée the lentils until smooth with a bit of texture. Place in a large pot and adjust consistency with reserved broth.
- Peel the skin off the hocks and discard. Dice the meat and add to the soup.
- Simmer the soup for 10 minutes. Season to taste with salt and pepper.

Chef's Tip: A pressure cooker is a special pot with a locking airtight lid. It is ideal for soups, stews and cooking tough cuts of meat. It allows you to cook the food faster without destroying the nutritional value of the food. Each pressure cooker is different, so follow the manufacture's instructions regarding the operating pressure.

Fish Soup

Preparation: moderate • Makes 6 servings • Recipe by Chris Knight

The variations and permutations on the theme of fish soup are endless. This recipe calls for both meaty white fish (that won't fall apart when added to the soup) and lots of different shellfish.

12 large shrimp, peeled and deveined

8 large sea scallops, debearded

12 small hard-shelled clams, cleaned and
    scrubbed

12 mussels, cleaned and scrubbed

¾-pound halibut fillet, cut into 1-inch
    (2.5-cm) pieces (375-g)

2 Tbsp. olive oil (25 mL)

2 Tbsp. garlic, chopped (25 mL)

1½ cups dry white wine (375 mL)

1 tsp. dried hot red pepper flakes (5 mL)

1 tsp. dried oregano (5 mL)

5 cups clam juice (1.25 L)

4 large vine-ripened tomatoes, seeded
    and diced

1 Tbsp. extra virgin olive oil (15 mL)

3 Tbsp. fresh basil leaves, chopped
    (45 mL)

3 Tbsp. fresh flat leafed parsley, chopped
    (45 mL)

- Clean and pat dry shrimp and scallops. Season all the seafood with salt and pepper.
- Heat 1 Tbsp. (15 mL) olive oil in a large skillet. Ensure the pan is hot but not smoking. Add the shrimp and scallops. Cook, turning only once, so that they are crispy on the exterior. They will continue to cook when returned to the skillet later. Drain on paper towel.
- Add the clams, 1 Tbsp. (15 mL) olive oil and garlic to the emptied shrimp/scallop skillet. Sauté for 1 minute.
- Add the wine, red pepper flakes and oregano and cover. Cook for 2 to 3 minutes, stirring occasionally.
- Add the mussels to the skillet and cover again. Cook for another 2 to 3 minutes or until the mussels and clams just begin to open.
- Add the clam juice and diced tomatoes and bring to a simmer.
- Add the halibut, seared shrimp and scallops to the skillet. Simmer until cooked through.
- Taste and adjust seasoning if necessary.
- Ladle into bowls and discard any unopened clams or mussels.
- Drizzle with olive oil and top with basil and parsley.

Asparagus and Morel Soup

Preparation: moderate • Makes 6 servings • Recipe by Chef René Rodriguez

Most chefs go gaga for the morel mushroom. Me, I'm a shiitake man myself. But morel is definitely the 'shroom of choice for this earthy-flavoured soup.

4 artichoke hearts

acidulated water

1 pound fresh asparagus, trimmed and cut into ¼-inch (5-mm) pieces (500 g)

½ shallot, finely chopped

1½ Tbsp. melted butter (20 mL)

4 cups chicken stock, fresh or low-sodium canned (1 L)

4 cloves garlic, peeled

½ pound spinach leaves (250 g)

1 Tbsp. fresh tarragon (15 mL)

pinch of grated nutmeg

salt and pepper

⅛ cup of dried morel mushrooms (25 mL)

2 cloves garlic, minced

3 Tbsp. butter (45 mL)

2 Tbsp. fresh chives, chopped (25 mL)

16 asparagus tips, boiled and refreshed in ice water

- Strip and clean artichokes and add to acidulated water and set aside.
- Place tips of asparagus in boiling water for 30 seconds. Using a slotted spoon, transfer to ice bath, refresh and remove, pat dry with paper towels. Reserve for garnishing the soup.
- Add the shallot to a soup pot with 1½ Tbsp. (20 mL) of melted butter.
- Sauté until translucent.
- Add the stock, artichokes, asparagus and whole garlic and simmer until soft.
- Add the spinach, tarragon and nutmeg and purée with a hand-held blender.
- Strain the purée into a large saucepan. Adjust consistency by adding more stock if necessary.
- Season to taste with salt and pepper.
- Place the mushrooms in a bowl and add boiling water to reconstitute.
- Drain and place on a towel. Once dried, cut in half lengthways and reserve. The soaking liquid can be drained into the soup if preferred.
- Heat a skillet to medium high and add 3 Tbsp. (45 mL) butter, minced garlic and chives. Sauté for one minute.
- Add the morels and cook until they are heated through.
- Place asparagus tips and morels in the bottom of six soup bowls and ladle broth on top.

Chef's Tip: Morels are favoured for their smoked, earthy taste. From April to June they can be purchased fresh. The dried version tends to have a more intense flavour.

Saffron Mussel Bisque

Preparation: moderate • Serves 6 • Recipe by Chris Knight

Saffron gives this rich bisque its deep rusty red colour. What's the difference between a bisque and a soup? About 2 bucks a bowl! Har har. Actually, a bisque tends to be seafood based and thicker than a regular soup. There's a complex rich flavour in this soup pot that's achieved by poaching the mussels in white wine. Be sure to have lots of very hot baguette and very cold butter to go along with this one.

12 saffron threads

1 cup water (250 mL)

1½ cups white wine (375 mL)

2 pounds mussels, cleaned and debearded (1 kg)

3 Tbsp. butter (45 mL)

1 Tbsp. olive oil (15 mL)

1 onion, chopped, medium dice

2 cloves garlic, crushed

1 leek (bulb only), chopped, medium dice

½ tsp. finely crushed fenugreek seeds (2 mL)

1½ Tbsp. all-purpose flour (20 mL)

1¼ cups chicken broth (300 mL)

2 Tbsp. whipping cream (25 mL)

salt and pepper to taste

pinch cayenne

1 Tbsp. chopped fresh parsley (15 mL)

- Place the saffron threads in a small bowl and add a Tbsp. (15 mL) of boiling water to make a saffron tea. Set aside to steep.
- In a saucepan, bring the water and wine to a boil. Add the mussels.
- Cover and cook over high heat, shaking the pan frequently, until the shells are open (approximately 4–5 minutes).
- Strain the mussels over a large pot to reserve the cooking liquid.
- Discard any mussels that remain closed.
- In a large saucepan, heat the butter and oil over medium-high heat.
- Add the onion, garlic, leek and fenugreek seeds and cook for approximately 5 minutes.
- Stir in the flour and continue cooking for 1 minute.
- Add the saffron tea, 2½ cups (625 mL) of the reserved mussel cooking liquid and the chicken broth. Bring to a boil, cover and simmer for about 15 minutes.
- Meanwhile, remove all but 12 of the mussels from their shells. Add all the mussels to the soup and heat through (2 minutes). Add the whipping cream and mix. Season with salt, pepper, cayenne and parsley. Ladle the soup into bowls and garnish with parsley sprigs.
- Try to leave two whole mussels in each bowl.

Chef's Tip: *Why did you pay so much for so little saffron? Saffron is the stigma of a small purple crocus flower. Each flower gives only 3 stigmas, which have to be hand picked! It takes over 14,000 stigmas to make 1 ounce (25 g) of saffron.*

Lobster Bisque

Preparation: difficult • Serves 6 • Recipe by Chris Knight

I'm a bit of a soup nut. I love this bisque. With its deep, rich, lingering flavour, it's the kind of soup that makes you sit back and say wow! I would suggest a small serving at a dinner party as it is so rich and filling.

two 1-pound cooked lobsters
   (two × 500-g)

4 Tbsp. clarified butter (60 mL)
   (see page 23)

1 medium onion, small dice

1 celery stalk, small dice

1 large carrot, small dice

1 tsp. chopped garlic

2 Tbsp. all-purpose flour (25 mL)

½ cup dry sherry (125 mL)

1 Tbsp. tomato paste (15 mL)

4 cups lobster stock (1 L) (see page 29)

2 bay leaves

3 sprigs fresh thyme

¼ tsp. smoked paprika (1 mL)

2 cups heavy cream (500 mL)

salt and pepper

- Remove all the meat and any tamale from the lobsters. Cut the meat up into bite size pieces, place in a bowl and chill.
- Whack away at the shells to make smaller bits.
- Add the clarified butter to a medium-sized sauté pan over medium-high heat. When the butter has melted add the shells, reduce the heat to medium and cook for 5 minutes, stirring.
- Add the diced vegetables and garlic and sprinkle in the flour. Cook for 3 minutes.
- Transfer everything into a large saucepan and deglaze the sauté pan with the sherry. Add the sherry and any pan scrapings to the large pot.
- Reheat the mixture over medium heat and add the tomato paste.
- Slowly add the lobster stock until the bisque thickens. Add the bay leaf, thyme, paprika and cream. Simmer for 5 minutes. Pass the soup through a fine mesh sieve to remove the shell pieces.
- Return the liquid to a pot and warm over a gentle heat for a couple of minutes.
- Add the lobster pieces to the bisque. Remember, the lobster is already cooked so you just want to gently warm it through.
- Serve with a piece of lobster floating in each bowl.

Chef's Tip: Lobster is much easier to take out of the shell before it is fully cooked. When plunged into boiling water it tends to become quite tough. Pour boiling water (with lemon in it) over the lobster to completely submerge it. Let steep 2–3 minutes, remove the lobster and reserve the liquid. Take the lobster meat out of the shell and gently poach the pieces until almost cooked. This gives you more control over the lobster and a more delicate result.

Wild Rice and Wild Mushroom Soup

Preparation: easy • Makes 6 servings • Recipe by Chris Knight

Wild rice is not, of course, actually a rice—it's a grain. And wild mushrooms like shiitakes are now cultivated most of the time. Talk about a misleading headline. DO NOT under any circumstance go and pick your own mushrooms. It is VERY dangerous unless you know what you're doing, and I'd have to come down there and kick your butt all over the forest. This soup, however, is delicious. Wild rice has a real nuttiness to it, and when you steep the dried porcinis in the chicken broth, oizaboiz! The deep, layered, woodsy taste of the broth is to weep.

4 cups chicken broth (1 L)

¼ cup dried porcini mushrooms (50 mL)

2 Tbsp. butter (25 mL)

½ cup finely chopped onion (125 mL)

⅓ cup wild rice (75 mL)

3 large cloves garlic, thinly sliced

¾ cup fresh shiitake mushrooms, stems removed, caps sliced (175 mL)

½ cup enoki mushrooms (125 mL)

salt and pepper

½ bunch fresh chives cut into 1-inch (2.5-cm) lengths

- Pour the chicken broth into a pot and simmer. Crumble in the dried porcini mushrooms. Remove from heat and let steep for 5 minutes.

- Melt the butter in a large pot, add the onion and rice and sauté for 2 minutes.

- Add the chicken broth and porcini mixture. Cover and simmer for 10 to 15 minutes.

- Add the thinly sliced garlic and continue to simmer, covered, for another 10 minutes.

- Add the sliced shiitake mushroom caps. Cover and cook until rice is tender, approximately 10 minutes. Rice should not have split. Adjust consistency if necessary by adding more stock. Season to taste with salt and pepper.

- Ladle into bowls and garnish with enoki mushroom caps and chives.

3 Salads

Fennel, Cucumber, Tomato, Almond and Orange Salad

Preparation: easy • Makes 6 servings • Recipe by Chef Elizabeth Manville

This summer-on-a-plate salad requires the use of a mandolin to shred the fennel nice and thin. Chefs use big metal mandolins but you can buy one pretty cheap, around fifteen bucks or so. The recipe recommends Roma tomatoes, as they have a firmer flesh and fewer seeds than your beefsteak variety, but if that's what's growing in your backyard then by all means go ahead and use beefsteak.

1 cup sliced almonds (250 mL)

2 fennel bulbs

⅓ cup orange juice (75 mL)

4 Roma tomatoes

1 cucumber

2 oranges

½ cup olive oil (125 mL)

salt and pepper

- Preheat the oven to 350°F (180°C).
- Place the almonds on a baking tray and put in oven to toast until golden brown, approximately 5 minutes. Watch carefully, as they can brown and burn easily.
- Use a melon baller to remove the core of the fennel. Shred the fennel head on a mandolin. Place in a bowl and add the orange juice (so that the fennel doesn't turn brown).
- Halve the Roma tomatoes and remove the seeds. Cut the tomato into julienne strips and add to the fennel. Peel and slice the cucumber lengthways into two. Remove the cucumber seeds in the middle with a melon baller. Slice the cucumber thinly so it looks like little half moons. Add to the tomatoes and fennel.
- Peel and cut the oranges into sections, leaving the pith behind. Add the orange segments to the other ingredients. Add the olive oil and season to taste. Remove the toasted almonds from the oven and add directly to the room-temperature salad.

Chef's Tip: Take the green tops from the fennel and place in a pot of boiling salted water. Refresh in a bowl of ice water. Drain and place in a blender and slowly add olive oil. Strain out the fennel and season the oil with salt and pepper. This makes a wonderful bright green licorice-flavoured oil to use on grilled meats, salads and soups. It can be stored in the refrigerator for up to 5 days.

Poached Pear and Gorgonzola Salad

Preparation: easy • Makes 6 servings • Recipe by Chef Elizabeth Manville

Poaching the pears softens and flavours the flesh. Peppery arugula and good stinky cheese make for a taste bud-buzzing combination. I've also poached the pears in late harvest Riesling and then reduced the wine down to make the sweet component of a simple dressing for the arugula. There are some 4000-plus types of pears worldwide, so don't be afraid to ask your greengrocer for help in picking nice small sweet ones.

1 cup light walnuts, halved (250 mL)

3 pears

1 cup red wine (250 mL)

2 cinnamon sticks

½ cup sugar (125 mL)

6 cloves

4 cardamom pods, bruised

arugula leaves to lightly cover 6 plates, stems trimmed, approximately 3 cups (750 mL)

3 ounces Gorgonzola cheese (75 g)

- Preheat oven to 325°F (160°C).
- Place the walnuts on a baking tray. Roast in oven until fragrant and golden brown.
- Remove and let cool.
- Peel and halve the pears and try to leave the stems on. Remove the core with a melon baller. Place in a saucepan.
- Add the red wine, cinnamon sticks, sugar, cloves and cardamom seeds. Poach over low heat for approximately 30 minutes. Turn the pears regularly so that each side gets a chance to rest in the liquid. Remove from heat and let rest in the wine until cool. The pears should be a dark ruby red colour.
- Remove the pears from the wine. Fan each pear half by cutting the pear in thin slices lengthways, almost to the end of the pear but not quite through the stem.
- Arrange the arugula on a plate, with the fanned pear on top.
- Crumble the Gorgonzola overtop and sprinkle with walnuts.
- Dress with something like a honey and black pepper vinaigrette or leftover poaching liquid.

Lobster Salad Napoleon with Pappadums

Preparation: moderate • Makes 6 servings • Recipe by Chris Knight

Lobster Salad Napoleon is so named because one taste makes you want to invade Russia. Um, that makes no sense, does it? Okay, how about this ... one taste and you want to fondle your left nipple in public? Actually, *Napoleon* refers to the plating technique of stacking things on top of the other. Why Napoleon? Beats me. The pappadums act as crispy contretemps separating each layer of yummy lobster mixture when stacked in layers. Don't sub dried tarragon, pop for the fresh as it really will make an amazing difference.

½ cup vegetable oil for frying (125 mL)

6 pappadums (6)

1 tsp. sea salt (5 mL)

2 Tbsp. olive oil (25 mL)

1 cup red bell peppers, finely chopped
    (250 mL)

¾ cup onion, finely chopped (175 mL)

¾ cup mayonnaise (175 mL)

3 Tbsp. fresh tarragon, chopped (45 mL)

1 lemon, juice of

¾ cup English cucumber, seeded and
    finely diced (175 mL)

3½ cups fresh lobster meat—including
    6 whole claws—(875 mL) (approx.
    3 lobsters)

Garnish:

½ cup fresh chives, finely chopped
    (125 mL)

- Heat the vegetable oil in a heavy-bottomed skillet to 365°F (185°C).
- Fry the pappadums, turning them carefully with tongs until they are golden brown and crispy. This happens very quickly (2–3 seconds).
- Remove them from the oil, season with sea salt and drain on a paper towel.
- In a clean skillet, heat the olive oil over moderate heat. Add the bell pepper and chopped onion.
- Cook until the onions and pepper are softened and set aside to cool in a bowl.
- Add the mayonnaise, tarragon, lemon juice and diced cucumber to the cooled pepper and onion mixture.
- Carefully remove the fresh lobster meat from the claws and tail without tearing the meat. Slice the lobster meat into 6 medallions.
- Break each pappadum into four pieces. Place one piece on a serving plate. Top with some of the mix and a lobster medallion. Repeat this process until there are 3 layers ending with a lobster claw.
- Garnish with chives.

Chef's Tip: *A pappadum is an Indian bread made from lentil flour. You can buy them in any Indian grocery store.*

Tangerine and Olive Salad

Preparation: easy • Makes 6 servings • Recipe by Chris Knight

Any orange will do in a pinch, but the tangerine plays nicely against the salty olives. Bib lettuce might be known as "Butterhead" in your part of the world.

6 tangerines peeled and sectioned

½ cup pitted and halved kalamata olives (125 mL)

½ cup pitted and halved green brined olives (125 mL)

6 cups Bib lettuce (1.5 L)

2 Tbsp. white wine vinegar (25 mL)

½ cup olive oil (125 mL)

½ tsp. cumin (2.5 mL)

½ tsp. paprika (2.5 mL)

cayenne (pinch)

3 tsp. freshly chopped mint (45 mL)

- Put the tangerine segments and the black and green olives in a bowl and toss together.
- Add the lettuce and toss.
- Whisk together the white wine vinegar, olive oil, cumin, paprika and cayenne.
- Drizzle over salad just to coat and toss.
- Serve on individual plates and garnish with freshly chopped mint.

Asian Beef Salad in an Umbrella

Preparation: easy • Makes 6 servings • Recipe by Chef Georges Laurier

This salad will surely take care of the carnivore in the family. If you're not familiar with the joys of fish sauce, might I suggest one of the many great Thai cookbooks out there. If you want to talk hurry-up dinner on a Tuesday night, then you have to try cooking Thai; fresh ingredients prepared simply and *à la minute*.

2 Tbsp. butter (25 mL)

6 tortilla shells

7 Tbsp. fresh lime juice (105 mL) (approx. 3 limes)

7 Tbsp. fish sauce (105 mL)

3 Tbsp. sugar (45 mL)

3 shallots, thinly sliced

1½ tsp. crushed dried chili pepper (7.5 mL)

1 pound sirloin steak (500 g)

salt and pepper

1 Tbsp. butter, softened (15 mL)

⅔ cup packed mint leaves, chopped (150 mL)

½ cup coriander, chopped (125 mL)

1 red bell pepper, julienned (sliced ⅛ inch/3 mm)

1½ cups cooked corn (375 mL)

- Preheat oven to 400°F (200°C).

- Preheat grill to medium-high heat, 375°F (190°C)

- In a small saucepan melt the two Tbsp. (25 mL) butter. Place 6 tortillas on a baking sheet and brush both sides of the shells with melted butter. Bake for one minute.

- Remove the warmed tortillas from oven and place them on top of 6 flipped custard cups. Pinch in the sides to form a bowl shape and brush again with the remaining melted butter.

- Bake for another 7 to 8 minutes or until crisp. Remove the tortilla cups from the custard cups and set them aside to cool.

- For the dressing, place the lime juice in a bowl and add the fish sauce and sugar to dissolve. Add the shallots, crushed chili pepper and salt.

- Mix well.

- Season both sides of the sirloin with salt and pepper.

- Smear the 1 Tbsp. (15 mL) softened butter on the sirloin and set it down on the grill, flipping only once.

- For medium-rare, grill beef to rare then rest in a warm place for 10 minutes.

- Slice the meat in long thin strips against the grain.

- Combine the sliced sirloin with the mint, coriander, red pepper and corn. Pour the dressing overtop and toss.

- Scoop the salad into the baked tortilla umbrellas and serve.

Chef's Tip: Fish sauce is made from fermented fish (usually anchovies). It is quite salty and has a strong taste. The different brands vary in taste and flavour. Taste your dressing carefully. You may need to add more sugar or lime juice.

Grilled Pear Salad with Port Vinaigrette

Preparation: easy • Makes 6 servings • Recipe by Chris Knight

This recipe is another good example of what happens when a few good ingredients are prepared simply. Pancetta is a cured cousin of the better known prosciutto ham and it brings a nice saltiness to the dish. The port is reduced by half and plays off the balsamic, which in turn is balanced by the Roquefort (or any good-quality stinky blue cheese).

12 ounces pancetta, sliced (375 g)

1½ cups walnuts, toasted (375 mL)

2 cups ruby port (500 mL)

3 Bosc pears

5 Tbsp. grapeseed oil (70 mL)

1 cup olive oil (250 mL)

¼ cup balsamic vinegar (50 mL)

salt and pepper

2 cups mixed baby greens (500 mL)

1 cup Roquefort cheese, crumbled
    (250 mL)

½ red onion, thinly sliced

- Preheat oven to 350°F (180°C).
- Preheat grill to 375°F (190°C).
- Place the pancetta slices in a skillet and sauté until crisp, approximately 10 minutes.
- Drain on paper towel.
- Spread the walnuts on a baking sheet and toast in the oven for 5 minutes or until fragrant.
- Place the port in a saucepan and simmer until it reduces by half. This should take approximately 20 minutes. Remove from the heat and cool. Once cool it should coat the back of a spoon.
- Peel and slice the pears into ¼-inch (5-mm) slices. Lightly rub the slices with grapeseed oil. (Other oils may be used as long as they are neutral in flavour.) Place the slices on the hot grill and char for approximately 1 minute per side.
- Add the olive oil and balsamic vinegar to the port. Whisk to combine. Season to taste with salt and pepper.
- Toss the baby greens in this dressing. Add the grilled pears, pancetta, cheese and sliced red onion.

4 · Poultry

Pan-Roasted Broiler Chicken in Crème Fraîche Tarragon Sauce

Preparation: easy • Makes 6 servings • Recipe by Chef Michael Bonacini

Tired of pizza on a Thursday night? Give this puppy a shot. It's easy to make and tastes delicious. The combination of tarragon, lemon juice and crème fraîche gives the bird a deep comfort taste that will make you push back from the table with a satisfied tummy rub. This dish goes equally well with sticky rice cooked in chicken stock or garlic chive mashed spuds. Get your hands on some real French green beans to send this over the top.

2 × 3-pound broiling chickens (cut into eighths) (2 × 1.5 kg)

kosher salt and pepper

6 Tbsp. olive oil (90 mL)

3 cups small-diced mirepoix (equal parts onion, celery and carrots) (750 mL)

6 cloves garlic, peeled

1 cup good Riesling (250 mL)

3 cups chicken stock (750 mL) (see page 27)

⅓ cup crème fraîche (75 mL) (see page 25)

⅓ cup 35% cream (75 mL)

3 Tbsp. chopped fresh tarragon (45 mL)

2 Tbsp. fresh lemon juice (25 mL)

- Preheat oven to 400°F (200°C).
- Season the chicken pieces with salt and pepper and brown lightly in olive oil in an ovenproof hot pan over medium-high heat.

  When all the pieces are browned, add the *mirepoix* and garlic. Place in the oven, uncovered, until cooked thoroughly, about 30 minutes.
- Remove the chicken from the pan, leaving the vegetables in. Place the pan over a medium-high heat and deglaze with the white wine.
- Add the chicken stock and reduce the liquid by half.
- Add the crème fraîche and cream to the reduced chicken stock.
- Adjust seasoning and return the chicken pieces to the pan.
- Add the fresh tarragon and lemon juice and serve immediately.

Southern BBQ Chicken

Preparation: moderate • Makes 6 servings • Recipe by Chef Michael Allemeier

Where there's smoke there's flavour. This recipe uses a smoker. If you don't have one, try using a wok with the lid lined with a double thickness of tinfoil to form a tight seal. We recommend free-range birds because they taste better and you never know what those corporate guys are feeding their glow-in-the-dark chickens.

two 4-pound free-range chickens
(2 × 2 kg)

Rub:

2 tsp. smoked paprika (10 mL)

2 tsp. dried basil (10 mL)

2 tsp. fine sea salt (10 mL)

1 tsp. lemon pepper (5 mL)

2 tsp. dried ground thyme (10 mL)

1 tsp. chili powder (5 mL)

1 tsp. cayenne pepper (5 mL)

Baste:

1½ cups pineapple juice (375 mL)

1½ cups rye whiskey (375 mL)

1 cup brown sugar (250 mL)

¾ cup fresh lemon juice (175 mL)

1 cup ketchup (250 mL)

1 cup melted butter (250 mL)

- Butterfly the chicken and lay it flat. Wash and pat dry.
- Mix all the rub ingredients together and rub well into the chicken. Massage the mix into the meat on the front and back. Wrap the chicken in plastic and leave in the refrigerator for 8 hours to marinate.
- Remove 30 minutes before you start smoking.
- Preheat oven to 400°F (200°C).
- Preheat the BBQ smoker to 210°F (100°C).
- Mix up the baste and set aside.
- Combine 6 cups (1.5 mL) of finely shaved cherry wood chips with 3 cups (750 mL) of chips that have been soaked in water for 1 hour and drained well, and place on a metal tray. Place in oven until the chips begin to smoke. Carefully place in smoker and follow manufacturer's directions.
- Fill the water tray with 4 cups (1 L) honey ale and heat in BBQ smoker to 210°F (100°C).
- Cook the chicken for 3 ½ hours or until an internal temperature of 175°F (80°C) is reached. Baste every 30 minutes. While basting, check to ensure there is an even flow of smoke.
- Remove the chicken from the BBQ. Allow to rest for 10 minutes and serve.

Chef's Tip: *To butterfly chicken, simply take poultry scissors and cut along the backbone on each side. Gently press chicken down until it is flat.*

Poussin Stuffed with Chestnut, Red Cabbage and Bacon

Preparation: moderate • Makes 6 servings • Recipe by Chef Georges Laurier

A *poussin* is a small chicken and has a sweeter taste than a regular bird. It also doesn't take as long to cook. Chestnuts, cabbage and bacon are classic stuffing combos for poultry.

Stuffing:

¼ pound slab bacon, diced (125 g)

2 Tbsp. butter (25 mL)

2 Tbsp. olive oil (25 mL)

1 cup chopped onion, small dice
    (250 mL)

3 Tbsp. garlic, finely chopped (45 mL)

½ cup chopped leeks, small dice (white
    part only) (125 mL)

2 cups sliced red cabbage (500 mL)

1½ cups chestnut pieces (375 mL)

½ cup chestnut purée (125 mL)

2 tsp. fresh marjoram (10 mL)

2 tsp. fresh thyme (10 mL)

salt and pepper

Poussin:

6 grain-fed poussins 1–1½ pounds
    (500–750 g) each

salt and pepper

2 Tbsp. olive oil (25 mL)

2 Tbsp. unsalted butter (25 mL)

12 bacon slices for wrapping the poussin

- In a large skillet on medium heat, cook the bacon until slightly crisp. Drain on paper towels and reserve.
- Melt the 2 Tbsp. (25 mL) butter and 2 Tbsp. (25 mL) olive oil together in a hot sauté pan over medium-high heat.
- Add the onion, garlic and leek. Cook until translucent and aromatic.
- Add the cooked bacon and cook for about 1 minute.
- Slice the cabbage in thin strips and add to the pan with the onions. Cook for an additional 3 minutes.
- In a large bowl, mix together the chestnut pieces, chestnut purée, cabbage and onion mix and bacon. Let cool.
- Once the mixture is cool, add the fresh marjoram and thyme. Season the mixture with salt and pepper.
- Separate this stuffing into 6 equal parts.
- Preheat the oven to 375°F (190°C).
- Take the poussins and season the insides with salt and pepper.
- Stuff the birds with the stuffing mixture. Close the neck openings with toothpicks.
- Melt the oil and butter in a hot roasting pan.
  Sear the poussin on all sides until golden brown.
- Wrap 2 slices of bacon around each of the birds.
- Cook in the oven for 20 to 25 minutes, or until cooked through and juicy.
- Cut the poussin lengthwise in two to show the chestnut stuffing.
- Serve with Brussels sprouts and pan jus poured around.

Deep-Fried Marinated Chicken

Preparation: medium • Makes 6 servings • Recipe by Chris Knight

You are going to die when you taste this dish. It is without question the juiciest, most tender fried chicken I've ever had. The secret is in the marinating. And don't go getting twisted into a knot because it's deep-fried. A little deep-fry every now and then isn't going to kill you.

2–3 pound chicken cut up in pieces (1–1.5 kg)

vegetable oil for frying

Batter:

1 cup all-purpose flour (250 mL)

pinch of salt

4 Tbsp. olive oil (60 mL)

4 eggs

1⅓ cups beer (325 mL)

2 cups all-purpose flour reserved for dredging (500 mL)

Marinade:

2 cups onion, small dice (500 mL)

2 bay leaves

1 cup celery stalk, small dice (250 mL)

4 garlic cloves, crushed

2 Tbsp. parsley, chopped (25 mL)

2 tsp. dried oregano (10 mL)

1 lemon, juice of

½ cup good white wine (125 mL)

- Prepare the batter at least an hour before you want to use it. This allows the batter to relax and coat the chicken better.
- Put the flour, salt and oil into a mixing bowl. Separate the eggs and add the yolks to the bowl. Reserve the whites.
- Pour in the beer and beat the ingredients with a wire whisk.
- Cover the bowl and set aside for an hour.
- Season the chicken pieces.
- Mix together the marinade ingredients and marinate the chicken for at least 30 minutes.
- To make the dipping sauce, combine all the ingredients (see next page) in a bowl and whisk them together. Refrigerate until ready to use.
- Just before using the batter, beat the egg whites until they form soft peaks. Fold them gently into the batter mixture.
- Remove the chicken pieces from the marinade, pat dry with paper towel and dredge them in the 2 cups (500 mL) flour. Shake off any excess.
- Preheat the oil to 350°F (180°C) in a large saucepan.
- Dip the chicken pieces in the batter. Ease them into 1 inch (2.5 cm) of the hot oil, turning them as they brown, and cook for about 15 minutes.
- Drain on paper towel. Season immediately with salt and pepper.

continued on next page

Dipping Sauce:

2 cups buttermilk (500 mL)

⅔ cup sour cream (150 mL)

1 Tbsp. roasted garlic purée (15 mL)

4 Tbsp. honey (60 mL)

4 Tbsp. canned chipotle juice (60 mL)

3 Tbsp. finely minced chives (45 mL)

2 Tbsp. lime juice (25 mL)

few drops Tabasco

salt (pinch)

salt and pepper

Chef's Tip: *Always fry in small batches. The food absorbs some of the heat in the oil, causing the oil temperature to drop. The more items that are placed in the oil, the lower the temperature. This will result in soggy, oily food.*

Boneless Stuffed Chicken

Preparation: difficult but well worth it • Makes 6 servings • Recipe by Chef Michael Bonacini

In this recipe Chef uses pretty much every cooking technique known to mankind. However, the result is a chicken like you've never had before. You have to try this at least once so you can say you did it. It'll make for a great yarn the next time you're swapping kitchen war stories.

one 3–3 ½ pound chicken (1.5–1.75 kg)

salt

Chicken:

- Remove the fat and membranes from the whole chicken. Wash and rinse thoroughly under cold water. Sprinkle the outside with salt. Rinse, drain again and pat dry.

continued on next page

1½ cups uncooked rice (375 mL)

1½ cups cold water (375 mL)

Sauce:

4 tsp. gin (20 mL)

1½ tsp. grated fresh ginger (7.5 mL)

¾ tsp. salt (4 mL)

1 Tbsp. sugar (15 mL)

4 tsp. oyster sauce (20 mL)

2 tsp. sesame oil (10 mL)

2½ tsp. soy sauce (12.5 mL)

2 tsp. cornstarch (10 mL)

½ tsp. freshly ground white pepper
(2 mL)

- To bone the chicken, turn it vertically on its tail and loosen the skin around its neck, making sure not to break the skin. Cut the wing joint on each side of the chicken and keep loosening the skin down the body of the bird. When the skin is halfway down the body, cut along the backbone but do not remove. Cut both breastbone joints and remove the entire breastbone with the meat on it. Cut the backbone and remove it. Remove both thigh joints and the thighs with the meat on them.

- Use kitchen shears to cut the last piece of the backbone off. Make sure you leave the tailbone intact. Cut along the drumsticks crosswise and remove the larger end.

- Using nylon thread, sew up the neck cavity of the bird. If you have accidentally pierced the skin anywhere on the chicken you can sew it up.

- Or you can have your butcher do it for you while you go see a movie.

  The chicken meat removed from the whole bird should be diced into ¼-inch (5-mm) pieces.

Rice:

- Place the rice in a bowl with water and cover. Wash three times.

  Rub the rice gently between your palms under cool water. Rinse and drain.

- Place the rice in a cake pan that will fit over your wok as a steamer.

- Add the 1½ cups (375 mL) of cold water to the wok.

- Place a large cake rack over the boiling water in the wok and set your rice (cake) pan on top. Be sure that it is not touching the water. Cover your steamer and steam for 20 to 25 minutes or until the rice is cooked through and sticky. Replenish steaming water as necessary.

- Transfer the rice to a large bowl.

Sauce:

- Mix together the gin, freshly grated ginger, salt, sugar, oyster sauce, sesame oil, soy sauce, cornstarch and white pepper.

Stuffing:

5 Tbsp. peanut oil for stir-frying (70 mL)

2 tsp. minced garlic (10 mL)

2 tsp. minced fresh ginger (10 mL)

¼ pound boneless lean pork, cut into
    ¼-inch/5-mm dice (125 g)

6 shiitake mushrooms, sliced thinly

¾ pound (1½ cups) shrimp, shelled,
    deveined and diced (375 g or
    375 mL)

4 fresh water chestnuts, peeled and diced
    small

4 green onions, trimmed and sliced finely

5 cups peanut oil for deep-frying
    (1.25 L)

Stuffing:

- Heat a wok. Add the 5 Tbsp. (70 mL) peanut oil and coat the wok using a spatula. When the oil is hot, add the garlic and fresh ginger. Stir until light brown.

- Add the chicken pieces and mix well. Cook for a few minutes. Add the pork and mushrooms. Cook for a few minutes. The meat will be white.

- Add the shrimp and cook until pink.

- Make a well in the centre of the wok. Stir the sauce and pour it into the well. Mix thoroughly until the sauce bubbles. Remove from the heat and place in a shallow dish to cool.

- Once cooled, add to the large bowl of steamed sticky rice. Add the water chestnuts and green onions and mix well.

- Preheat oven to 325°F (160°C)

- Stuff the chicken and the chicken skin with the stuffing, being careful not to rip the skin or over-stuff. Sew the bird back up to look as it did before it was boned.

- Place the chicken in a roasting pan and bake, uncovered, for 45 minutes. Flip the chicken and cook for another 45 minutes or until it is completely browned. Cool in the refrigerator for at least 5 hours. This process is necessary if the skin is to be crispy when it's fried.

- Heat the 5 cups (1.25 L) of peanut oil to 375°F (190°C) in a large sauce pot. Place the cooled chicken in a large strainer and lower into the oil for 7–10 minutes until golden and crisp. If you cannot submerge your chicken, ladle the hot oil over exposed areas until the skin crisps up.

- Drain the chicken for at least 7 minutes, place on a platter, slice it across and serve.

Chef's Tip: Peanut oil has a smoke point of 450°F (230°C) and it is difficult to know if your oil is overheating. Check it regularly to ensure it does not exceed 400°F (200°C).

Baked Chicken Casserole with an Apple-Potato Crust

Preparation: moderate • Makes 6 servings • Recipe by Chef Georges Laurier

Want to try something totally different? Amaze your friends and family with the layers of flavours that come out of this dish. Apple cider, parsnips and apples bring Mr. Chicken to a whole new level of drool factor.

3 cups chicken broth (750 mL)

1 cup apple cider or apple juice (250 mL)

1 cup peeled parsnips, cut into ½-inch (1-cm) cubes (250 mL)

1¾ pounds Yukon Gold potatoes, peeled, cut into ½-inch (1-cm) cubes (875 g)

2 large Golden Delicious apples, peeled, cored, cut into ½-inch (1-cm) cubes

5 Tbsp. butter (70 mL)

1 tsp. cinnamon (5 mL)

1 tsp. freshly grated nutmeg (5 mL)

salt and pepper

2 Tbsp. all-purpose flour (25 mL)

2 Tbsp. of dried rosemary (25 mL)

2 Tbsp. minced fresh thyme (25 mL)

8 skinless boneless chicken thighs cut into 1-inch (2.5-cm) pieces

2 Tbsp. olive oil (25 mL)

1 cup frozen peas, thawed (250 mL)

⅓ cup brandy (75 mL)

⅓ cup whipping cream (75 mL)

- Preheat oven to 350°F (180°C).
- Place the chicken broth, apple cider and parsnips in a large pot. Cover and boil until tender, approximately 5 minutes.
- Transfer the parsnips to a bowl using a slotted spoon.
- Add the potatoes and apples to the remaining cider broth mixture.
- Cook until they are tender, about 20 minutes.
- Remove the potatoes and apples with a slotted spoon and place in a clean large bowl. Add 3 Tbsp. (45 mL) of butter to the cinnamon and fresh nutmeg and mash into the potatoes and apples until almost smooth, season with salt and pepper.
- Place the cider broth in another large bowl and set aside.
- Put the flour into a bowl. Rub the dried rosemary and 1 Tbsp. (15 mL) of thyme over the flour. Dust the chicken with the flavoured flour.
- Heat the remaining butter and oil in a large skillet, add the chicken and sear for 5 minutes, using tongs to flip halfway through.
- Place the chicken in a glass baking dish. Top with the parsnips, season with salt, pepper and thyme and cover with the peas.
- In a saucepan add the brandy, whipping cream, reserved broth and cider stock and bring to a quick boil.
- Reduce the heat to medium and let sauce reduce to 1¼ cups (300 mL).
- Season sauce with salt and pepper and spoon over the chicken.
- Cover the chicken with the mashed potatoes and apples and bake for 35 minutes or until the topping is crusty and the chicken is cooked through.

Roasted Stuffed Chicken with Gravy

Preparation: moderate • Makes 6 servings • Recipe by Chris Knight

Okay, this one looks a little daunting on first read, but it's really not. Sure there are a bunch of steps, but they're all easy. This is a Sunday evening dinner when the in-laws are coming. You can spend the whole day in the kitchen, cooking and drinking wine, and end up with an amazing dinner and a nice Chardonnay buzz to get you through your father-in-law's bowling stories.

2–4-pound chicken with giblets
  (1–2-kg)

4 large cloves garlic, peeled and crushed

2 tsp. kosher or coarse salt (10 mL)

2 Tbsp. paprika (25 mL)

- Remove the giblets from the chicken, wrap loosely in plastic food wrap and set aside in the refrigerator until ready to use.

- Discard any excess fat from the body and neck cavities of the chicken.

- In a bowl combine the garlic, salt, paprika and 1 Tbsp. (15 mL) of olive oil. Mix together until smooth.

4 Tbsp. olive oil (60 mL)

2 cups good dry white wine (500 mL)

Stuffing:

½ cup olive oil (125 mL)

4 large yellow onions, peeled and
    chopped

4 large garlic cloves, peeled and minced

½ cup lard (hog lard, not vegetable
    shortening) (125 mL)

1 pound ground lean pork (500 g)

8 cups soft bread crumbs (2 L)

8 hard-cooked eggs, shelled and chopped

1 cup green and black pitted olives,
    coarsely chopped (250 mL)

2 Tbsp. paprika (25 mL)

2 Tbsp. minced parsley (25 mL)

2 Tbsp. dried sage (25 mL)

1 tsp. freshly ground black pepper
    (5 mL)

- Rub this marinade over the chicken, inside and out.
  Place the chicken in a shallow bowl, cover and refrigerate overnight.

- To make the stuffing, heat the olive oil in a large skillet, add the chopped onions, garlic and hog lard and sauté until the onions are translucent and not browned.

- Mince the chicken giblets and add to the skillet with onions.

- Reduce the heat, add the ground pork and cover to steam for approximately 20 minutes.

- Meanwhile, combine the bread crumbs, eggs, olives, paprika, parsley, sage and pepper in a large bowl and mix well.

- Once the skillet mixture has cooked for 20 minutes, add it to the bread crumb mixture and mix well. Let cool.

- Preheat oven to 425°F (220°C).

- To stuff the chicken, spoon the stuffing into the neck cavity first. Enclose the neck by skewering the neck flap against the back of the bird.

- Spoon stuffing lightly into the body cavity, skewer the opening shut and then truss the bird.

- Rub the chicken with 1 Tbsp. (15 mL) of olive oil and place it breast up on a rack in a large shallow roasting pan.

- Place the roasting pan in the oven to roast, uncovered, for 20 minutes.

- Lower the heat to 350°F (180°C), brush the chicken with 1 Tbsp. (15 mL) of olive oil and roast uncovered for 30 minutes per pound (500 g), brushing with the last Tbsp. (15 mL) of olive oil midway through the roasting time.

- When the stuffed chicken has only 40 minutes remaining to roast, pour the white wine around it.

- Serve the roasted stuffed chicken with stuffing wreathed around the chicken. Garnish with green and black olives. The pan drippings act as perfect gravy.

continued on next page

Gravy:

1 cup good dry white wine (250 mL)

6 Tbsp. cold unsalted butter (90 mL)

To make the gravy:

- Pour off the pan drippings into a see-through measuring cup. Once the liquids have settled you'll see that the fat has risen to the top. Spoon off all but 2 Tbsp. (25 mL).

- Deglaze the pan with some good white wine (about 1 cup/250 mL), scraping up all the delicious brown bits from the bottom. Reduce by two-thirds. Return the pan drippings to the pan. If there aren't enough to make 1 cup (250 mL), add chicken stock.

- Bring to a boil and reduce to ¾ cup (180 mL).

- Remove from the heat and whisk in 6 Tbsp (90 mL) of cold unsalted butter (1 Tbsp./15 mL at a time).

- Taste. If it needs a little oomph try some lemon juice and/or Dijon to taste. Serve immediately.

Chef's Tip: Trussing chicken

1 *Pass the middle of a long piece of butcher's twine underneath the joint at the end of the drumsticks and cross the ends of the string to make an X.*

2 *Pull the ends of the string down toward the tail and begin to pull the string back along the body.*

3 *Pull both ends of the string tightly across the joint that connects the drumstick and the thigh and continue to pull the string along the body toward the bird's back, catching the wings underneath the string.*

4 *Pull one end of the string securely underneath the back bone at the neck opening, and tie the two ends of the string with a knot.*

Chicken and Vegetables Braised in Peanut Sauce

Preparation: moderate • Makes 6 servings • Recipe by Chris Knight

This recipe calls for chicken thighs and drumsticks, which are more flavourful than the ever popular breast (also in the recipe). Sambal oelek is a garlicky Asian hot sauce condiment. If you don't have any, you really should get some. In a pinch substitute your favourite hot sauce.

*2 cups unsalted roasted peanuts
(500 mL)*

3¼ cups water (800 mL)

*4½ –5½ pounds chicken drumsticks,
thighs and breast halves (2–2.5 kg)*

salt and pepper

3 Tbsp. vegetable oil (45 mL)

1 cup onion, medium dice (250 mL)

4 garlic cloves, finely chopped

*2 cups canned tomatoes including juice,
diced (500 mL)*

½–1 tsp. sambal oelek (2–5 mL)

2 tsp. salt (10 mL)

*1 large potato, peeled and diced into
1-inch (2.5-cm) pieces*

*1 small turnip, peeled, halved
horizontally, cut into ¾-inch
(2-cm) wedges*

*1 small yam, peeled and diced into 1-inch
(2.5-cm) pieces*

- Preheat oven to 325°F (160°C).
- Place the peanuts in a food processor and blend until they form a paste. Scoop the paste into a bowl and gradually whisk in the water.
- Pat the chicken dry and season with salt and pepper. Heat the oil in a large ovenproof, heavy-bottomed skillet. Add the chicken and brown on all sides. Transfer the chicken to a bowl and set aside.
- Discard all but 2 Tbsp. (25 mL) of fat from the skillet. Add the onion and sauté until it is soft and beginning to brown.
- Add the garlic and stir. Add the peanut paste mixture and more (approx. 3 Tbsp./45 mL) water.
- Add the tomatoes and juice, sambal oelek, salt and browned chicken, and any juices that have run off into the bowl.
- Cover skillet with a lid and braise in the oven for about 30 minutes.
- Transfer the chicken to a bowl and cover to keep warm.
- Place the potato, turnip and yam in the sauce and simmer on stovetop until they are tender, approximately 15–20 minutes.
- Spoon the vegetables onto a platter and leave the sauce to reduce for another 5–10 minutes.
- Place the chicken on a plate and drizzle reduced sauce on top.

Kholbasa-Stuffed Chicken Legs with Bell Pepper, Honey and Onion Compote

Preparation: moderate • *Makes 6 servings* • *Recipe by Chef Georges Laurier*

This recipe uses the chicken leg, which you don't always think of when contemplating *le stuffing*. The chicken is accompanied by bell pepper and onion compote that also works well with pork, so make a double batch and keep some in the fridge. It keeps for a week to ten days.

Chicken:

6 large chicken legs, skin and bones
    removed

½ pound Kholbasa sausage (250 g), cut
    into ½-inch (1-cm) pieces

2 large eggs

2 Tbsp. whipping cream (25 mL)

salt and pepper

1 cup chopped fresh parsley (250 mL)

2 cups clarified butter (500 mL)
    (see page 23)

Compote:

2 cups Spanish onion, thinly sliced
    (500 mL)

1½ cups red bell pepper, thinly sliced
    lengthways (375 mL)

1½ cups yellow bell pepper, thinly sliced
    lengthways (375 mL)

1½ cups green bell pepper, thinly sliced
    lengthways (375 mL)

2 Tbsp. olive oil (25 mL)

2 Tbsp. dry white wine (25 mL)

2 tsp. corn syrup (10 mL)

2 tsp. honey (10 mL)

2 tsp. maple syrup (10 mL)

2 Tbsp. white wine vinegar (25 mL)

2 cups low-sodium chicken broth
    (500 mL)

salt and pepper to taste

- Pound each boneless chicken leg between two sheets of waxed paper to ⅓ inch (8-mm) thickness and season with salt and pepper.
- For the filling, place the sausage, eggs and whipping cream in a food processor and blend until the sausage is finely chopped. Season with salt and pepper and sprinkle with parsley.
- Preheat oven to 350°F (180°C).
- Spread the sausage filling over the chicken legs. Be sure to leave a ½-inch (1-cm) border on the short sides. Starting at a long side, roll up the chicken as you would a jellyroll.
- Place four 9-x 7-inch (23 × 18-cm) foil squares onto a work surface.
- Coat the foil with the clarified butter.
- Place one chicken roll at the centre of each square. Roll foil up tightly around the chicken.
- Lay the chicken rolls on a baking sheet and bake for about 20 minutes or until chicken is cooked through.
- To make the compote, combine the onion, peppers, olive oil, wine, syrup, honey and vinegar in a heavy saucepan. Cover and cook for approximately five minutes, stirring often.
- Add the chicken broth and simmer for approximately 25–30 minutes until the vegetables are tender.
- Separate one cup of this mixture and blend in a food processor until it forms a smooth purée. Add the purée to the compote and continue to simmer for a few more minutes. Season with salt and pepper. This can be made in advance and chilled for several days. It should be served warm.
- Plate the chicken on top of the compote and garnish with fresh herbs.

Risotto with Chicken Livers, Orange Liqueur and Chocolate

Preparation: moderate • Makes 6 servings • Recipe by Chef Georges Laurier

Ahhh, risotto. Creamy, thick, aromatic risotto is great as a side or on its own, and this recipe is insanely delicious. The Grand Marnier and chocolate work so well together and the chicken livers are a powerful counterpoint. Just don't overcook the livers, please—better a little underdone than shoe leather.

2½ cups chicken broth (625 mL)

2 cups water (500 mL)

2 Tbsp. olive oil (25 mL)

1 cup onion, finely diced (250 mL)

1¼ cups Arborio rice (300 mL)

6 Tbsp. Grand Marnier or other orange-flavoured liqueur (90 mL)

2 Tbsp. shaved semi-sweet chocolate (25 mL)

1 Tbsp. butter (15 mL)

¾ pound chicken livers, trimmed, lobes separated, patted dry (375 g)

salt and pepper

½ cup all-purpose flour (125 mL)

½ cup green onions, sliced thin for garnish (125 mL)

- Combine 2 cups (500 mL) of broth with the water in a heavy medium-sized saucepan and bring to a simmer. Remove from heat and cover to keep warm.
- In another saucepan, heat the olive oil and add the onion to sauté for 1 minute. Add the rice and sauté for 2 minutes.
- Add 2 Tbsp. (30 mL) of Grand Marnier and stir until liquid is absorbed. Turn the heat down to low.
- Add the broth and water mix in ½-cup (125-mL) stages, stirring constantly until rice is cooked *al dente*. Stir in the shaved chocolate, and adjust seasoning. Cover until ready to use.
- For the chicken livers, melt the butter in a large skillet over a medium-high heat. Sprinkle the livers with salt and pepper and dust with flour.
- Sauté the livers until pink in the centre, about 2 minutes, and remove to a plate.
- Add the remaining Grand Marnier and remaining ½ cup (125 mL) of broth to the skillet. Reduce to a glaze, stirring up the tasty bits on the bottom of the skillet for about 4 minutes.
- Place the livers back in the skillet and stir to coat with glaze. Divide the risotto among the plates and spoon livers and pan juices overtop.
- Garnish with green onions.

Chef's Tip: It's impossible to give the exact ratio of liquid to rice. Sometimes you'll need less and sometimes more. As a rule add 1 extra cup (250 mL) of stock to your pot to warm up. You won't have to stop and heat up more liquid if you need it and run the risk of ruining your risotto. Good risotto is creamy and cooked to al dente, which is an Italian phrase meaning "to the tooth." It is used to describe pasta, rice and other foods that are cooked only until they still offer a slight resistance when bitten into.

Turkey Mole

Preparation: difficult • Makes 6 servings • Recipe by Chef René Rodriguez

Mole is a classic Mexican preparation featuring chocolate and lots of different types of chilies to bring a complexity of flavour to the dish. If you can't find all the chili types listed below, no worries. Sub as many types as you can get your hands on. It will still have this mind-blowing contradiction of chocolate and chili heat with poultry as an underlying taste structure.

6 Tbsp. rendered pork fat or bacon fat (90 mL)

12 dried mulatto chilies, seeded and deveined

7 dried ancho chilies, seeded and deveined

8 dried pasilla chilies, seeded and deveined

9 pounds thighs and legs of one turkey (4 kg)

12 cups turkey or chicken stock (3 L)

8 cloves garlic, peeled

15 black peppercorns

2 cinnamon sticks

½ tsp. coriander seeds (2 mL)

½ tsp. fennel seeds (2 mL)

1 cup cooked and drained green tomato (250 mL)

10 Tbsp. sesame seeds (140 mL)

½ cup pumpkin seeds (125 mL)

1 cup blanched almonds (250 mL)

6 slices baguette

4 Tbsp. raisins (60 mL)

- Heat 2 Tbsp. (25 mL) of rendered fat in a frying pan and fry the chilies on both sides for 30 seconds.
- Drain the chilies and reserve the fat (which is now chili infused).
- Transfer the chilies to a bowl and cover them with water. Keep them submerged with a heavy plate until soft and pliable, then drain.
- Preheat oven to 375°F (190°C).
- In a large Dutch oven, fry the turkey pieces on all sides until brown.
- Drain off any excess fat.
- Add the stock, garlic, peppercorns, cinnamon, coriander and fennel seeds and braise the turkey in the oven for 2 hours or until tender and cooked. Reserve the braising broth.
- Put 1 cup (250 mL) of water into a blender and blend the chilies until puréed. Fry the purée in the leftover 2 Tbsp. chili-infused fat until smoky, about 5 minutes.
- Put 1 cup (250 mL) of the braising broth in the blender with the green tomato and start the machine. Gradually add the sesame seeds.
- Transfer the purée to a bowl and reserve.
- Melt 6 Tbsp. (90 mL) of fat in a frying pan and fry the pumpkin seeds, almonds, baguette, raisins and tortillas. Drain the fat and add all the ingredients plus 1 cup (250 mL) of water to the same blender and purée.
- Put the chili paste, almond purée and tomato purée into a large casserole and cook for 5 minutes.

4 stale corn tortillas 8 inches (20 cm)
    each, broken into pieces
½ cup bittersweet dark chocolate
    (125 mL)
salt and pepper
sesame seeds for garnish

- Add the chocolate and cook for another 5 minutes. Add 4 cups (1 L) of the turkey braising broth and the turkey pieces and cook for 30 minutes.
- Taste for seasoning and serve with sesame seeds for garnish.

Chef's Tip: *The best pork lard has a browned pork flavour essential to Mexican cooking. The lard that is commercially available in supermarkets is so over-refined it has very little flavour left. Seek out freshly rendered pork fat at Mexican or Chinese markets.*

Prosciutto-Wrapped Turkey Breast with Tangerine Cranberry Sauce

Preparation: easy • Makes 6 servings • Recipe by Chris Knight

When most of us think turkey, we think the whole bird. Nuh hunh. Turkey is available all cut up just like chicken. This recipe calls for a big, juicy turkey breast, wrapped in salty prosciutto and served with a tangy citrus sauce.

4 small tangerines, segmented

1 cup sugar (250 mL)

2 cups fresh orange juice (500 mL)

1½ cups fresh cranberries (375 mL)

20 thin slices prosciutto with no holes

*2 turkey breasts, medium-sized,
    approx. 1½ pounds (750 g) each*

pepper

2 Tbsp. olive oil (25 mL)

plastic wrap

- To make the sauce, combine the tangerine segments with the sugar and put them on a parchment paper-lined baking sheet to marinate in the refrigerator overnight.
- Add the tangerines and sugar to a saucepan with the orange juice.
- Cook until thick and syrupy.
- Add the cranberries and cook until they are soft. Strain, set the fruit aside and return the liquid to the heat to reduce further. Once reduced, pour over the tangerine-berry mix. This sauce tastes even better if you make it a day or two in advance and let it set up in the fridge.
- Preheat oven to 350°F (180°C).
- Line a sheet of plastic wrap with 10 overlapping slices of prosciutto.
- Place the turkey breast in the centre, season with pepper and roll the prosciutto like a jellyroll. The plastic wrap keeps the prosciutto from sticking to the layering surface and allows easy handling.
- Repeat with the remaining turkey breast.
- Heat the olive oil in a large skillet to medium heat and sear the rolls, turning often until the prosciutto is golden brown.
- Place the seared wrapped turkey breast in the oven and bake until cooked to an internal temperature of 160°F (71°C).
- Let the turkey rest for 15 minutes before carving.
- Slice, plate with chive-mashed potatoes and top with sauce.

Chef's Tip: *After the turkey breast is rolled in the prosciutto, wrap tightly in foil, twisting both ends. Refrigerate for 30 minutes. This ensures a perfectly round beautiful roll.*

Stovetop Coq Au Vin

Preparation: easy-schmeasy • Makes 6 servings • Recipe by Chef Tim McRoberts

There is no one way to cooking heaven. All chefs and all home cooks constantly tinker with recipes to suit their palate and personal preferences. For instance, Chef McRoberts uses celery stalk in his bouquet garni and was quite incredulous that the other chefs didn't. Give two chefs some eggs, butter and chives and ask them to make scrambled eggs. Chances are they'll taste different. Such is the world of cooking.

2 Tbsp. olive oil (25 mL)

6 chicken breasts, boneless skinless (6 pounds/2.7 kg)

24 pearl onions

36 baby button mushrooms

1 bottle really good red wine (750 mL)

1 Bouquet Garni (see page 22)

1 Sachet (see page 22)

2 cups chicken stock (500 mL) (see page 27)

salt and pepper

Bouquet Garni:

3 leek leaves 3 inches/ 8 cm long

1 piece celery 3 inches/ 8 cm long

4 sprigs fresh thyme

5 sprigs fresh parsley

Sachet:

10 black peppercorns

2 bay leaves

1 tsp. oregano (5 mL)

- To make the bouquet garni, lay the leek leaves flat, top with celery and place herbs in centre. Tie securely with butcher's twine.
- To make the sachet, place the herbs in a small piece of cheesecloth, make a little bag and secure with butcher's twine.
- Preheat a large saucepan to medium heat and add the olive oil.
- Season the chicken breasts and sear until golden brown, about 2 minutes each side. Make sure to develop some caramelization.
- Remove the chicken and put aside.
- Add the pearl onions and mushrooms. Turn down the heat to medium and sauté until caramelized, about 10 minutes or so.
- Deglaze the pan with the red wine. Add the sachet and bouquet garni.
- Add the chicken stock, bring to a simmer, then add the chicken breasts. Cover the saucepan, leaving the lid slightly askew to allow the steam to escape and liquids to reduce. Simmer until cooked, about 10 minutes.
- When ready, remove the chicken and season the sauce with salt and pepper. Slice the chicken if desired and serve on buttered tagliatelle.
- Pour sauce overtop.
- Best served in a wide-rimmed soup plate or pasta bowl.

Chef's Tip: When peeling pearl onions, blanch them in boiling water first and refresh in cold water. The skins will peel off quickly and easily.

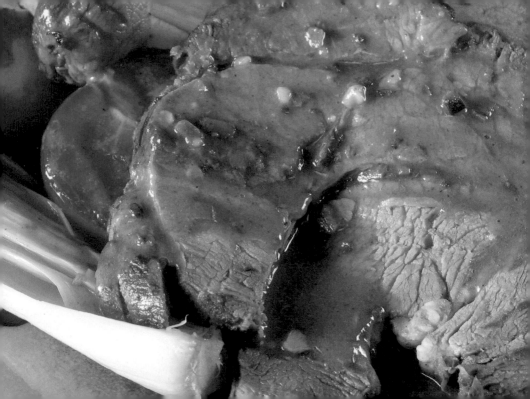

5 Beef & Veal

Prime Rib Roast with Pink and Green Peppercorn Crust and Merlot Gravy

Preparation: moderate • Makes 6 big juicy servings • Recipe by Chef Georges Laurier

Nowadays you rarely see prime rib anywhere except for steak houses, and most of them do a poor job of cooking this wonderful cut of beef.

one 2-rib tied prime beef rib roast, about
    4½ pounds (2 kg)

Crust:

1 tsp. crushed whole allspice berries
    (5 mL)

1½ Tbsp. pink peppercorns, crushed
    lightly (22.5 mL)

1½ Tbsp. green peppercorns, crushed
    lightly (22.5 mL)

1½ Tbsp. of unsalted butter, softened
    (22.5 mL)

1 Tbsp. all-purpose flour (15 mL)

½ Tbsp. firmly packed brown sugar
    (7.5 mL)

½ Tbsp. Dijon mustard (7.5 mL)

¾ tsp. salt (4 mL)

- Preheat the oven to 350°F (180°C).
- Use a mortar and pestle to crush the allspice berries and the pink and green peppercorns.
- Place the mixture into a bowl and mix in the remaining crust ingredients. Stir together to form a paste.
- Pat the beef dry and, using your hands, smear the rub all over the roast.
- Place the roast rib side down in a low-sided roast pan and bake for 1½ hours or until the meat thermometer inserted in the middle fleshy section of the roast registers 125°F (52°C) for medium rare meat.
- When the roast has reached desired doneness, place it on a cutting board and cover loosely with tin foil. Let the meat rest for 15 to 20 minutes while you prepare the gravy. It will continue to cook as it sits. Reserve the juices from the roast.
- Place the roast pan with the reserved juices on the stovetop over medium heat.
- Skim the fat from the top of the liquid.

Gravy:

1½ cups Merlot (375 mL)

1 cup beef demi-glace (store-bought is
    fine) (250 mL)

2 Tbsp. redcurrant jelly (25 mL)

1 tsp. drained bottled horseradish
    (5 mL)

3 Tbsp. chopped fresh flat-leafed parsley
    leaves (45 mL)

salt and pepper

- Add the Merlot and let it reduce to half (about 5 minutes).

- Whisk in the demi-glace, redcurrant jelly, horseradish and parsley and season with salt and pepper to taste.

- Bring to a boil and continue to whisk the flavours together, maybe 5 minutes or so.

- Carve and plate the roast and drizzle with gravy.

Chef's Tip: When cooking any roast, baste every 20 minutes with the pan drippings. This will provide added flavour and moisture. Take your roast out of the oven and baste on the stovetop. This minimizes the loss of heat in your oven. Return to the oven immediately when finished basting.

Braised Short Ribs with Aromatic Vegetable and Rich Beef Sauce

Preparation: moderate • Makes 6 servings • Recipe by Chef Georges Laurier

About ten years ago, chefs all over North America rediscovered the joys of comfort food, including the venerable slow-braised short rib. Braising, of course, is the technique of cooking at low heat for a long period of time to break down connective tissue and chewy fibre in tougher cuts of meat. Typically, that which is braised is first marinated to begin the process and infuse flavour. Braising, unlike roasting say, then involves cooking with liquid (often the very marinade). The result is tender fall-off-the-bone meats that offer up deep rich flavours. My favourite is lamb shanks, which can also be prepared with this recipe.

Might I suggest mashed potatoes infused with tons of butter and freshly grated horseradish on the side.

Bouquet Garni:

3 outer green leek leaves, washed

10 sprigs Italian parsley

2 sprigs thyme

1 bay leaf

- To make the bouquet garni, lay out one green leek leaf and place the herbs on top. Wrap this in the remaining leek leaves to form a circular bundle. Tie with butcher's twine to secure. Set aside.

Red Wine Marinade:

3 cups full-bodied red wine (750 mL)

*½ cup carrots cut into 1-inch (2.5-cm)
    pieces (125 mL)*

*⅔ cup leeks, (white and pale green parts
    only) cut into 1-inch (2.5-cm) pieces
    (150 mL)*

*½ cup onions, cut into 1-inch (2.5-cm)
    pieces (125 mL)*

3 cloves garlic, smashed

*2 pieces prime boneless short ribs about
    1 inch (2.5 cm) thick and 1¾ pounds
    (875 g) each*

OR

*3½ pounds (1.75 kg) boneless short ribs or
    8 pieces bone-in short ribs, about 8
    ounces each (250 g)*

salt and pepper

2–3 Tbsp. canola oil (25–45 mL)

3 Tbsp. all-purpose flour (45 mL)

*2 cups chicken stock (500 mL)
    (see page 27)*

*2 cups white veal stock (500 mL)
    (see page 31)*

- For the marinade, pour the red wine into a large low-sided pot or skillet.
- Add the carrots, leeks, onions, garlic and bouquet garni. Bring to a boil and set aside to cool.
- If using two larger pieces of prime boneless short ribs, trim the excess fat from the meat, leaving the silverskin attached, and cut each piece (across the grain) into two smaller pieces. If using smaller boneless short ribs, there is no need to split them in half.
- Remove the bouquet garni from the cooled marinade. Place the short ribs into a well-sealed plastic bag and pour the marinade in overtop.
- Refrigerate for 24 hours.
- Preheat oven to 275°F (140°C).
- Remove the meat from the marinade and separate the vegetables by straining the liquid into a saucepan. Reserve the vegetables for later.
- Bring the marinade to a simmer and clarify by skimming off any impurities that rise to the top. Remove from heat.
- Season the roast with salt and pepper and dust in flour.
- In a large skillet, heat 2 Tbsp. (25 mL) of oil on high. Sear the meat for 2–3 minutes per side and arrange in one layer in a casserole dish.
- Pour off excess oil from the skillet and return to heat. Sauté the reserved vegetables until they begin to caramelize, maybe 10 minutes or so.
- Spread the caramelized vegetables over the meat in an even layer. Add the clear marinade and the chicken and veal stocks. The liquid should totally cover the meat. If necessary, add more chicken and veal stock.
- Bring the liquid to a simmer, using the casserole dish on the stovetop, and cover.
- Transfer to the oven and braise for 3 to 4 hours.
- Once the meat is very tender, remove and transfer to a large serving dish.
- Strain the cooking liquid into a saucepan and cook until partially reduced, maybe 15 minutes or so. Again skim any impurities off the top of sauce. Season with salt and pepper to taste.
- Pour sauce over ribs and enjoy.

Nut-Crusted Beef Medallions with Beet and Onion Soubise

Preparation: moderate • Makes 6 servings • Recipe by Chef Michael Bonacini

Chefs are always looking for new twists on old chestnuts. How about a nice crunchy nut crust for a butter-smooth tenderloin? Pair that up with a soubise (classic French onion-based dish) that's been jolted with lovely beets and you have made yourself one restaurant-quality entrée.

8 Tbsp. softened butter (120 mL)

6 large shallots (about 1 pound/500g), peeled and thinly sliced

2 pounds beets, trimmed, peeled and thinly sliced (1 kg)

salt and pepper

1 cup red wine (250 mL)

6 large beef medallions (approx. 2 pounds/1 kg)

2 sprigs rosemary, finely diced

½ cup all-purpose flour for dredging (125 mL)

3 eggs, lightly beaten

1½ cups very finely chopped mixed nuts (chestnuts, cashews, almonds) (375 mL)

3 Tbsp. neutral oil such as canola or grapeseed (45 mL)

- Preheat oven to 350°F (180°C).

- Grease the bottom of a shallow casserole or gratin dish with butter.

- Layer the shallots and beets on the bottom of the dish and season with salt and pepper. Repeat until you have 3 or 4 more layers.

- Top with 2 Tbsp. (25 mL) of butter and cover in foil. Bake for 1 hour until tender.

- Transfer the roasted onions and beets into a blender and add the red wine. Blend and season with salt and pepper. Cover to keep warm.

- Season the beef medallions with salt and pepper.

- Add the rosemary to the flour. Dredge the medallions in flour and shake off excess. Dip each medallion in the egg wash, then press into the mixed chopped nuts, making sure to fully cover both sides.

- In a large hot skillet, add the remaining butter, the oil and the beef medallions. Reduce the heat to medium. Cook slowly so the nuts are toasted but not burnt. Turn the meat as often as necessary while cooking for 5–10 minutes for medium-rare fillets.

- To serve, plate some beet and onion purée and top with a beef medallion.

Steak and Kidney Pie with Dark Beer

Preparation: moderate • Makes 6 servings • Recipe by Chef Tim McRoberts

If you've only ever tried steak & kidney pie in a pub after a half dozen pints, then you're in for a treat. This ain't no pre-packaged soggy crust sludge from a microwave. The dark beer brings a real deep layered taste to this dish, and the contrast between the steak and kidney is to die for.

3 pounds chuck steak, trimmed into
  ½-inch (1-cm) pieces (1.5 kg)

1 pound calf kidney, cored and chopped
  (500 g)

1½ cups dark beer (375 mL)

6 Tbsp. lard (90 mL)

3 medium onions, sliced

1 cup all-purpose flour (250 mL)

salt and pepper to taste

1½ cups sliced button mushrooms
  (375 mL)

6 sprigs thyme

2 bay leaves

2 cups beef stock (500 mL) (see page 26)

Pastry:

3 cups all-purpose flour (750 mL)

1 tsp. salt (5 mL)

1½ cups lard (375 mL)

3 Tbsp. ice water (45 mL)

1 egg

1½ Tbsp. apple cider vinegar (22.5 mL)

2 egg yolks, mixed with a splash of milk

- Place the steak pieces and calf kidneys in a large bowl and pour dark beer overtop. Cover and leave for at least 4 hours—preferably overnight—in the refrigerator.
- Separate the meat from the marinade and reserve marinade for later use.
- In a large saucepan, melt 1 Tbsp. (15 mL) of lard and gently fry the sliced onions. Remove the onions from the saucepan and set aside.
- Season the flour with salt and pepper and use to coat the meat. Add another Tbsp. (15 mL) of lard to the saucepan to melt. Add the floured meat in batches and fry until the pieces are browned on all sides. Add more lard as needed.
- Return the onions and any leftover flour to the saucepan. Stir well.
- Add the mushrooms, thyme, bay leaves, reserved marinade and stock.
- Bring slowly to a simmer, stirring as the sauce thickens.
- Cover and cook gently for 1½ hours or until meat is tender and sauce is very thick.
- Remove the herbs from the sauce. Add salt and pepper to taste and leave to cool.
- For the pastry, sift the flour and salt into a bowl.
- Add the lard and, using two knives, cut into the flour mixture until it resembles large peas.
- Whisk the egg, ice water and vinegar together in a small bowl, pour over the flour mixture and gently blend the ingredients with a fork.

continued on next page

- Divide the dough into two disks and chill, covered, for 30 minutes.
- Preheat oven to 400°F (200°C).
- Dust work surface lightly with flour and roll two pastry disks approximately 2 inches (5 cm) larger than your pie plate. Gently roll one disk around a rolling pin and place in the bottom of a 12-inch (30-cm) deep-dish pie plate.
- Dampen the outer rim of the pie plate with egg wash and gently and evenly fold the overhanging pastry up on the edge of the pie plate.
- Brush again with egg wash. This will give you a nice thick crust.
- Fill the pie with the cooled filling. Top with pastry and, with your thumb, crimp the edges of the pastry to seal.
- Make three decorative 1-inch (2.5-cm) cuts in the centre to allow steam to escape and brush evenly with egg wash.
- Bake for 15 minutes. Reduce heat to 350°F (180°C) and continue to bake until crust is golden brown, approximately 35 minutes.
- Let cool for 15 minutes before slicing.

Chef's Tip: When cleaning kidneys, make a cut though the centre of the kidney, dividing it into two equal pieces. Lift away the kidney fat and cut it away with the tip of a sharp knife.

Olive-Stuffed Pot Roast

Preparation: easy • Makes 6 servings • Recipe by Chef Tim McRoberts

That's right ... olive stuffed. Read the recipe—it's very cool. This is a great time for me to plug your friendly neighbourhood butcher. He (I'm such a sexist snob, but all the butchers I've ever known have been guys) knows a good cut of meat from a bad one. He will only sell you the good stuff. If you go to a supermarket, then you 're taking your chances with some pre-wrapped cut. You work hard for your dough and you deserve the best your money can buy. Remember, a butcher is not any more expensive than the big grocery store that sells hygiene products, lawn furniture and canned goods. All it takes is one more stop on the way.

¾ cup black canned pitted olives
    (175 mL)

¾ cup green canned pitted olives
    (175 mL)

⅓ cup chopped parsley *(75 mL)*

¼ cup freshly shredded Parmesan Cheese
    (50 mL)

3 tsp. chili powder *(15 mL)*

1 tsp. pressed garlic *(5 mL)*

salt and pepper

one 5-pound cross rib beef roast
    (2.2 kg)

2 Tbsp. olive oil *(25 mL)*

1 cup chopped onion *(250 mL)*

1 cup tomato sauce *(250 mL)*

2 Tbsp. all-purpose flour *(25 mL)*

- Preheat oven to 350°F (180°C).
- Drain the canned olives, reserve the juice and set aside.
- Chop the olives and combine with the parsley, Parmesan, 2 tsp. (10 mL) chili powder, garlic and salt and pepper to taste.
- Using a long thin blade, slice about 15 slits into the roast. A larding needle may also be used. Stuff the olive mixture into the slits.
- In a large skillet, heat the oil and brown the roast on all sides. Add the onion to the skillet and brown lightly.
- In another bowl mix together the tomato sauce, olive juice and remaining chili powder.
- Pour over the roast and bring to a boil. Reduce heat, cover and simmer for about 2 hours, basting every 30 minutes.
- Remove roast to rest. Mix the flour with cold water and add a little of the hot liquid to it.
- Combine with the pan juices, whisk and bring it to boil to create gravy.
- Season with salt and pepper.
- Carve roast, serve with gravy and enjoy!

Ravioli Stuffed with Ground Veal and Cumin

Preparation: moderate to easy • Makes 6 servings • Recipe by Chris Knight

While our chefs would always make their own dough, we cut that step out here as most people don't have pasta makers. In fact, most foodies who own pasta makers have them stored safely way back in the cupboard.

Filling:

3 Tbsp. butter (45 mL)

3 medium sized shallots, minced

4½ pounds ground veal loin (2 kg)

1 cup dry white wine (250 mL)

9 tsp. hoisin sauce (45 mL)

3 tsp. dried cumin (15 mL)

salt and pepper

72 wonton wrappers

Egg wash:

2 eggs lightly beaten

3 Tbsp. milk (45 mL)

Sauce:

3 Tbsp. butter (45 mL)

2 medium onions, chopped finely

3 garlic cloves, minced

1 bottle good-quality white wine (750 mL)

3 cups 35% cream (750 mL)

salt and pepper

1½ cups fresh torn basil (375 mL)

- Heat a sauté pan, add the butter and sauté the shallots for 1 minute.
- Add the ground veal. Cook for 1 minute (the veal should still be quite pink).
- Deglaze the pan with the wine. Add the hoisin sauce and cumin and season to taste with salt and pepper.
- The filling should be quite moist and the veal still tender pink. Cool.
- Place a large pot of salted water on to boil.
- Place a teaspoon of the filling in the middle of a wonton wrapper.
- Brush the edges with the egg wash.
- Place a second wonton on top and smooth out the air bubbles, pushing from the middle outwards with your fingertips, making sure all the sides are sealed. Repeat with the remaining wrappers.
- Cook the ravioli in boiling water until they float to the surface, about 5 minutes.
- To make the sauce, set a sauté pan over medium-high heat. Melt the butter, add the onions and garlic and sauté until caramelized, maybe 7 minutes or so.
- Add the white wine and let reduce by two-thirds. Add the cream and simmer for 4 minutes. Season with salt and pepper.

Pour over the ravioli, and top with the torn basil.

Veal and Asparagus Stew in Lemon Sauce

Preparation: moderate • Makes 6 servings • Recipe by Chris Knight

This is a classic dish that makes use of one of the fattier veal cuts with all sorts of veggies in a stew that gets its zing from the lemon juice. Guess what? You get to make a roux, which is a combo of flour and fat forming a paste as the base for a lump-free velvety smooth sauce. This is one of those dishes that tastes even better the next day.

Bouquet Garni:

3 leek leaves (green part)

1 bay leaf

3 sprigs fresh tarragon

4 sprigs fresh thyme

2¾ pounds boneless veal shoulder, cut into 1¼-inch (3-cm) cubes (1.375 kg)

2 Tbsp. olive oil (25 mL)

2 tsp. minced garlic (10 mL)

¾ cup finely chopped carrot (175 mL)

½ cup finely chopped celery (125 mL)

1 cup finely chopped onion (250 mL)

1 cup cold water (250 mL)

1¼ cups dry white wine (300 mL)

10–12 black peppercorns

½ cup plus 1 Tbsp. unsalted butter (140 mL)

10–12 small pearl onions, peeled

pinch salt

- To make the bouquet garni, place the leek leaves flat. Place all the herbs on the leaves and tie securely with butcher's twine.
- Remove any excess fat from the veal and cut into 1¼-inch (3-cm) cubes.
- Heat the olive oil in a large heavy-bottomed skillet. Sear and brown veal cubes in the oil.
- Add the garlic, carrot, celery and onion. Cook for 1 to 2 minutes, stirring to mix the flavours together.
- Add the cold water, wine, bouquet garni and peppercorns. Bring to a boil.
- Reduce the heat and simmer for 1½ hours, or until tender.
- Skim off any impurities that may come to the surface. The meat should remain covered with liquid while cooking. You may add hot water during cooking if necessary.
- Pierce the veal with a fork after the allotted time to ensure that it slips easily into the meat. Using a slotted spoon, remove the meat and set aside. Cover to keep warm.
- Strain the veal cooking liquid into a bowl, pressing down on the vegetables to release as much flavour as possible.
- Return the liquid to the same pan and cook over moderately low heat to reduce by half.
- Melt 1 Tbsp. (15 mL) of butter in a skillet. Add the pearl onions and a pinch of salt. Cover and cook for approximately 5 minutes, stirring occasionally to ensure the onions don't stick.

continued on next page

¼ cup chicken stock (50 mL)
    (see page 27)

½ pound button mushrooms, sliced
    (250 g)

1 pound asparagus, woody stems
    removed, cut into 2-inch/5-cm pieces
    (500 g)

½ cup all-purpose flour (125 mL)

1¼ cups whipping cream (300 mL)

2 lemons, juice of

salt and pepper

lemon juice to garnish

½ cup fresh parsley, chopped (125 mL)

- Add the chicken stock and continue to cook for 15 minutes over moderate heat.
- Place the button mushrooms in the warm mixture for 5 minutes.
- Blanch the asparagus in a pot of boiling salted water for 3 minutes. Drain, then cool the asparagus under cold running water or in an ice bath.
- Melt ½ cup (125 mL) of unsalted butter in a skillet.
- Add the flour and mix together well to form a paste, or roux. Cook, stirring constantly, until it becomes a light beige colour. Cool slightly.
- Whisk into the reduced cooking liquid, stirring constantly. This will thicken the sauce.
- Add the cream and mix until smooth. Add the lemon juice and season to taste with salt and pepper.
- Add the veal, asparagus, onions and mushrooms to the cream sauce and cook for 5 minutes until heated through. Serve in a deep serving dish.
- Drizzle with more lemon juice and garnish with fresh parsley.

Porcini-Dusted Veal Chops with Wild Mushrooms and Fava Ragout

Preparation: moderate • Makes 6 servings • Recipe by Chris Knight

Dried porcini mushrooms are the Viagra of cooking. Making a soup or sauce? Drop a handful of dried porcini into your stock, nuke for 5 minutes, then steep for 10 minutes longer. Use as per the recipe. The 'shrooms add a deep woodsy depth to your liquid that will have your guests dancing around the table. In this recipe they are ground up and used much as you would use salt and pepper but with an orgasmic result ... the wild 'shrooms and fava ragout offer a nice texture counter balance to the juicy chop.

2 cups reduced low-sodium chicken broth
(500 mL)

½ cup beef broth (125 mL)

⅓ cup finely chopped shallots
(75 mL)

½ cup dried porcini mushrooms
(125 mL)

6 veal rib chops, 9 ounces each, trimmed
(6 × 275 g)

salt and pepper

7 Tbsp. unsalted butter
(105 mL)

½ cup fresh shiitake mushrooms,
stemmed and sliced (125 mL)

½ cup torn fresh oyster mushrooms
(125 mL)

½ cup torn fresh chanterelle mushrooms
(125 mL)

½ cup sliced white mushrooms
(125 mL)

6 Tbsp. sweet Marsala wine (90 mL)

- Combine the chicken and beef broths and half the shallots in a heavy medium-sized saucepan. Simmer over medium heat until hot. Once hot, remove from the heat and add half the porcini mushrooms. Let stand until mushrooms are soft.

- Using a slotted spoon, transfer the softened porcini mushrooms to a clean work surface. Chop the mushrooms coarsely and set aside.

- Return the broth to a simmer and reduce liquid to ¼ cup (50 mL), maybe 15 minutes or so. Reserve.

- Preheat oven to 400°F (200°C).

- In a spice grinder (or with a mortar and pestle), grind the remaining porcini mushrooms to a fine powder.

- Season both sides of the veal chops with salt and pepper, then dust with the porcini powder.

- Melt 2 Tbsp. (25 mL) of butter in a large preheated skillet and cook the chops for approximately 2 to 3 minutes per side until a nice crust has developed. Place the chops on a baking sheet and cook in the oven to medium rare, approximately 10 minutes. Remove from oven and tent with foil.

- Melt 2 Tbsp. (25 mL) of butter in the skillet used to sear the veal chops. Add the remaining mushrooms except the porcinis. Sauté until tender, around 6 to 8 minutes.

continued on next page

1½ pounds fresh fava beans, shelled,
   blanched and peeled (750g), 1 cup
   frozen baby lima beans, thawed
   (250 mL) or 1 pound dried fava
   beans (500g) (see below)

1½ tsp. minced fresh sage (7.5 mL)

1½ tsp. minced fresh rosemary (7.5 mL)

1½ tsp. minced fresh thyme (7.5 mL)

fresh sage leaves for garnish

- When the mushrooms are tender, add another 2 Tbsp. (25 mL) of butter, the remaining shallots and the chopped porcini mushrooms to the skillet. Sauté until the mixture looks slightly dry.

- Add the Marsala and cook until the liquid is reduced by ⅔, about 3 minutes.

- Add the reserved broth mixture, fava (or lima) beans and chopped herbs.

- Bring to a simmer, add 1 Tbsp. (15 mL) butter and season to taste with salt and pepper. Serve with veal chops.

Chef's Tip: *The best veal to purchase is milk-fed veal, which is no more than 12 weeks old. The flesh is delicate and tender with a creamy white-pink tinge. While the animal's diet is milk, the meat remains quite low in fat. Extra caution should be taken to ensure you don't overcook the tender meat.*

If fresh fava beans are not available, use dried. To cook dried fava beans, soak the beans overnight. Remove any that float to the surface or have blemishes. Place in a pot, cover with chicken stock and bring to a simmer. Add some flavourings, such as leek and thyme. Any beans that have not fully hydrated will float to the top—discard these. Simmer until tender.

Veal Kidneys in Calvados

Preparation: moderate • Makes 6 appetizers • Recipe by Chef Georges Laurier

The best ingredients prepared simply to allow their tastes to shine through are the hallmark of this classic French dish. Overcooked kidneys are a crime, so watch the cooking time carefully. Calvados is a dry apple brandy. Watch you don't flambé when you add it to the saucepan. It isn't all that expensive and is a good addition to your kitchen pantry, for both cooking and the odd nip at the bottle when something goes south on you.

6 veal kidneys

salt and pepper

¼ cup unsalted butter (50 mL)

3 shallots, finely diced

¼ cup calvados (50 mL)

¾ cup 35% cream (175 mL)

1½ Tbsp. Dijon mustard (7.5 mL)

½ cup chervil (125 mL)

- Clean the kidneys, removing all fat and sinews. Slice them through the equator, then into 1-inch (2.5-cm) pieces. Season with salt and pepper.
- Put half the butter into a pan over high heat. As soon as it begins to foam, add the kidneys. Leave them to brown, and turn after approximately 2 minutes.
- Remove the kidneys after another 2 minutes. Put them on a plate and keep them warm.
- Put the shallots into the same pan and cook until tender.
- Add the calvados and scrape any brown pieces from the bottom of the pan. Be careful not to overheat the pan in case the calvados catches fire.
- Add the cream and simmer for a couple of minutes, stirring constantly.
- Pass the sauce through a fine mesh sieve.
- Add the Dijon mustard and stir well.
- Return the sauce to the heat and add the kidneys.
- Season to taste with salt and pepper and add the chervil.
- Serve with wilted arugula and crispy potatoes.

6 Pork

Lavender and Rosemary Pork Tenderloin

Preparation: easy • *Makes 6 servings* • *Recipe by Chris Knight*

Lavender and rosemary are classic flavouring agents for pork. They work very well together. If you can't find fresh lavender in your neighbourhood, then half the amount of dried will do almost as well.

4 sprigs fresh lavender, finely chopped

⅔ cup finely chopped sprigs rosemary (150 mL)

3 Tbsp. finely chopped garlic (45 mL)

3 Tbsp. finely chopped onion (45 mL)

1 bay leaf

2 cups sweet white wine (500 mL)

two 2-lb. pork tenderloins (2 × 1 kg)

salt and pepper

- Preheat the oven to 375°F (190°C).
- Put the lavender, rosemary, garlic, onion and bay leaf in a large bowl and mix.
- In a small saucepan, reduce the white wine by half over a medium-high heat.
- Add the herb mix to the reduced wine and reduce heat to medium.
- Continue to reduce until you get a syrupy consistency.
- Pat the pork tenderloins dry with paper towel. Coat with the reduced mixture.
- Place the tenderloins in a baking dish and cook in the oven for 25 minutes, or until still slightly pink in the middle.

Pork Tenderloin Au Poivre

Preparation: moderate • Makes 6 servings • Recipe by Chris Knight

First you got your tenderloin, the leanest and sweetest cut from the pig. Then you got your spicy pepper crust and some high heat. Hell, you don't even need a recipe for this one. Just remember, pink in the middle is a good thing when it comes to pork tenderloin. Please don't overcook. I've seen too many pork tenderloins end up as shoe leather. Pork is delicate and yummy. Treat it with love and care.

6 Tbsp. whole black peppercorns (90 mL)

2 Tbsp. coriander seeds (25 mL)

3 pounds pork tenderloin (1.5 kg)

2 tsp. coarse salt (10 mL)

canola or peanut oil, for frying

- Preheat the oven to 375°F (190°C).
- Put the peppercorns into a coffee grinder and pulse for a few seconds.
- Add the coriander seeds and pulse them until coarsely ground (you could also use a mortar and pestle).
- Trim the fat and silverskin from the tenderloin.
- Rub the tenderloin with some of the oil.
- Season the pork tenderloin with salt and roll it in the peppercorn mixture, making sure it is well covered.
- In a medium-sized frying pan bring 2 Tbsp. (25 mL) of oil to a sizzle over a high heat and sear the pork tenderloin on all sides, about 2 minutes each side. Open a window or turn on the fan, as the pepper will create a lot of smoke as it sears.
- Transfer the pork tenderloin to the oven to cook for 25 to 30 minutes or until medium-well done.
- Let the meat rest for 5 minutes and slice.

Pork Braised in Milk

Preparation: easy • *Makes 6 nice servings* • *Recipe by Chris Knight*

Braising is the art of slow cooking over low heat, turning otherwise tough and fatty cuts of meat into rich, tender meals. Now, braising in milk might sound odd, but it is so good. As the pork cooks, the lovely piggy juices insinuate themselves into the milk which gets thicker and thicker and richer and richer. Yum.

For the pork rib roast, have your butcher detach the meat in one piece from the ribs and split the ribs into two or three parts. By splitting it into parts it will brown more thoroughly and the roast will benefit from the flavour the bones give.

The other recommended cut of pork for this dish is the Boston Butt. This is the boneless roll of muscle at the base of the neck. There is a layer of fat in the centre of the Boston Butt that runs the length of the muscle, making the cut very juicy and tasty.

Do not remove any fat from either cut of meat. Most of it will melt in the cooking and will also baste the meat and keep it from drying out. When the roast is done, you will be able to draw the remainder of the fat out and discard it.

2½ pounds pork rib roast or 2 pounds Boston Butt (1.25 kg or 1 kg)

2 Tbsp. butter (25 mL)

2 Tbsp. vegetable oil (25 mL)

salt and pepper

3 cups whole milk (750 mL)

- Set a heavy-bottomed pot (making sure it will snugly accommodate your cut of pork) on medium-high heat, and melt the butter and heat the oil.

- Fat side down, brown the pork. Turn the meat and brown evenly on all sides. If the butter turns a dark brown, lower the heat.

- Add salt, pepper and 1 cup (250 mL) of whole milk. Add the milk gently, and ensure that it does not boil over.

- Allow the milk to simmer, turn the heat down and cover the pot with the lid askew.

- Cook the pork for approximately 1 hour, turning the meat from time to time, until the milk has thickened into a brown sauce.

- Once the milk has thickened, add one more cup (250 mL) of milk, let it simmer for about 15 minutes, then cover the pot with the lid. Place lid on tightly, turning the pork from time to time.

continued on page 104

- After 30 minutes, set lid slightly askew. When there is no milk left in the pot, add another ½ cup (125 mL) of milk. Continue cooking until the pork feels tender when prodded with a fork. The milk will coagulate into small nut-brown clusters.

- Altogether the cooking process will take approximately 2½ to 3 hours. If the milk should totally evaporate before the pork is fully cooked, add ½ cup (125 mL) more and repeat the process if necessary.

- When the pork is tender and all the milk has thickened into nut-brown clusters, transfer it to a cutting board and let settle for 15 minutes. Then cut into ⅜-inch (9-mm) thick pieces and place on a serving platter.

- Spoon out fat from pot and leave behind the milk clusters. Add 2 to 3 Tbsp. (25 to 45 mL) of water. Boil the water away over a high heat while using a wooden spoon to scrape loose cooking residue from bottom and sides of the pot.

- Pour pot juices over the pork and serve immediately.

Braised Pork Shoulder

Preparation: moderate • Makes at least 6 servings • Recipe by Chef René Rodriguez

Food writers sometimes describe a dish as fork tender. I've always wondered about that one. Pork shoulder is an inexpensive cut of meat that is rendered (pardon the pun) tender and juicy through a combination of spicy citrus marinade and slow cooking with liquid (that would be braising, of course).

Chef Rodriguez gives this dish a Mexican twist by using canned chipotles (you can get them pretty much anywhere these days) and a *mojito* paste in which you fry the pork once it's braised. Oh mama, this one's good.

Marinade:

1 bunch fresh cilantro

2 cups orange juice (500 mL)

1 cup freshly squeezed lime juice (250 mL)

1 cup canola oil (250 mL)

½ cup canned chipotle chilies (125 mL)

2 bay leaves, crushed

5 cloves garlic

1 Tbsp. coarse or kosher salt (15 mL)

1 Tbsp. coriander seeds (15 mL)

1 Tbsp. ground toasted cumin seeds (15 mL)

1 Tbsp. crushed black peppercorns (15 mL)

5–6-pound bone-in pork shoulder, skin removed and fat still attached (2.2–2.7-kg)

- Combine all the marinade ingredients in a food processor and mix for two minutes until well combined.
- Place the pork shoulder in a large bag with the marinade and seal with a twist tie. Wrap this in another bag.
- Transfer the pork to a bowl large enough to hold the bag and marinate it in the fridge for two days, turning the bag occasionally to make sure the marinade covers the pork.
- Preheat the oven to 325°F (160°C).
- Remove the pork from the bag. Transfer it to a roasting pan, fat side up.
- Add 3 cups (750 mL) of water to the pan and pour the marinade on top of the pork. Cover with foil and cook for 1½ hours.
- Turn the pork fat side down and cook for another 1½ hours or until the meat is almost falling off the bone.
- Increase the oven temperature to 400°F (200°C) and discard the foil.
- Cook the pork for another ½ hour, fat side up, until brown.
- Remove the pork from the oven and let it sit for a few minutes.
- Test with a meat thermometer in the thickest part of the pork, not touching bone. The temperature should read 140°F (60°C).
- Set the pork aside to cool. Pull the meat from the bone with your fingers.

continued on next page

Mojito:

2 cups orange juice (500 mL)

2 Tbsp. minced garlic (25 mL)

½ cup canola oil (125 mL)

1 cup minced shallot (250 mL)

1 jalapeño, diced and seeded

6 Tbsp. lime juice (90 mL)

½ tsp. coarse salt (2.5 mL)

3 Tbsp. peanut oil for frying (45 mL)

½ cup cilantro, chopped (125 mL)

salt and pepper

- Mix together all the ingredients for the *mojito*.
- Heat 3 Tbsp. (45 mL) of peanut oil in a frying pan. Add the pulled pork pieces and fry for a few minutes until crisp on the edges.
- Add ½ cup (125 mL) of the *mojito* and cook for a few minutes until the liquid has evaporated. Season with chopped cilantro, salt and pepper and serve on a bed of salad with sour cream.

Chef's Tip: *When purchasing pork look for meat that is pale pink. The darker the flesh, the older the animal. Also, look for a shoulder with lots of nice marbling. The fat should be creamy white. Never purchase pork with yellow fat. This means the animal was very old.*

Brined and Fruit-Stuffed Pork Chops

Preparation: moderate • Makes 6 servings • Recipe by Chef Ned Bell

The biggest complaint most people have about pork chops is how dry they turn out. First of all, it seems to be a North American tradition to overcook pork until it's as tough as shoe leather. The other reason is that there isn't much fat (as in marbling) in a pork chop. The solution is brining, which is just soaking the meat in flavoured water to "juice up."

Give it a shot ... no more dry chops for you! You could skip the stuffing, but it really does make this a moist and flavour-layered entrée.

Brine:

6 cups apple cider (1.5 L)

2 cups water (500 mL)

¾ cup salt (175 mL)

⅓ cup (packed) golden brown sugar (75 mL)

¼ cup coarsely ground black pepper (50 mL)

2 Tbsp. dried rubbed sage (25 mL)

3 tsp. ground cinnamon (15 mL)

six 1½-inch (4-cm) thick centre-cut pork loin chops, excess fat trimmed

Stuffing:

2 cups garlic croutons (store-bought are fine) (500 mL)

1 cup chopped apple (250 mL)

1 cup shredded cheddar cheese (250 mL)

3 Tbsp. raisins (45 mL)

- Combine all the brine ingredients in a large bowl. Stir until the sugar is completely dissolved and then add the pork chops. Cover and refrigerate for at least 4 hours and up to 2 days.
- Remove the chops and pat dry with a clean towel. Discard the brine.
- Cut a deep stuffing slice at the centre of each chop, but don't go all the way through the meat.
- For the stuffing, combine the garlic croutons, chopped apple, shredded cheese and raisins in a large bowl and toss.
- In a second bowl, combine the melted unsalted butter, orange juice, orange zest, apple cider, salt, cinnamon and fresh nutmeg.
- Pour this liquid mix over the dry mix containing the croutons and toss until generously coated.
- Using a spoon or piping bag without a tip, gently stuff the pork chops with the mix. Close the opening with a wooden toothpick.
- To cook the pork, heat a Tbsp. (15 mL) of olive oil in a large frying pan over high heat. Add the pork chops and brown on each side for no longer than 3 minutes.
- Plate the pork chops and cover to keep warm.
- In the same skillet your chops just came from, sauté the onion over medium heat until soft.

continued on next page

3 Tbsp. unsalted butter, melted
  (45 mL)

2 Tbsp. orange juice (25 mL)

2 tsp. orange zest (10 mL)

2 Tbsp. apple cider (25 mL)

½ tsp. salt (2.5 mL)

pinch cinnamon

pinch fresh nutmeg

Cooking the Pork:

2 Tbsp. olive oil (30 mL)

1½ cups onion, thinly sliced (375 mL)

3 (about 2 cups) Granny Smith apples,
  peeled, cored and thinly sliced
  (500 mL)

1 cup chicken broth (250 mL)

⅔ cup apple cider (150 mL)

½ cup Calvados (125 mL)

3 Tbsp. raisins (45 mL)

½ tsp. ground ginger (2.5 mL)

⅔ cup whipping cream (150 mL)

2 Tbsp. Dijon mustard (25 mL)

salt and pepper

6 wooden toothpicks, soaked in water

- Stir in the apple slices and sauté until they are golden, for another 3 minutes.

- Add the broth, cider, Calvados, raisins and ginger. Stir and incorporate all of the flavours, including the browning bits from the bottom of your pan.

- Add the cream and mustard and bring the sauce to a boil. Reduce heat to medium-low and return the pork to the pan. Cover and cook for 3–5 minutes. Turn over at least once. Internal temperature of the pork should be 150°F (65°C).

- Plate the chops. Let the sauce thicken for another 5 minutes, season with salt and pepper and spoon over the pork.

Chef's Tip: *Thanks to improved feeding techniques, trichinosis in pork is rarely an issue. Cooking to a temperature of 140°F (60°C) will kill any trichinae. However, most experts recommend a temperature of 150–160°F (65–70°C). In general there is no need to overcook your pork.*

Maple Syrup-Glazed Pistachio Pork Roast

Preparation: moderate • Makes 6 servings • Recipe by Chef Michael Bonacini

There's nothing more Canuck than a nice bit of pig, glazed in maple syrup. Chef Bonacini goes one step further with sherry-marinated apricots and buttery soft pistachios. That crazy Welshman!

5 dried apricots, diced

⅓ cup sherry (75 mL)

40 whole, natural pistachios, shelled but not skinned

- Soak the diced apricots in the sherry for about 30 minutes.
- Preheat oven to 325°F (160°C).
- Spread 24 of the shelled pistachios in one layer on a baking sheet.

continued on next page

Maple Syrup Glaze

2½ pounds boned and rolled pork loin
(1.25 kg)

salt and pepper

2 Tbsp. olive oil (25 mL)

2 Tbsp. fresh thyme, chopped (25 mL)

1 Tbsp. fresh rosemary, chopped (15 mL)

Pistachio Sauce

Maple Syrup Glaze:

2 Tbsp. maple syrup (25 mL)

2 Tbsp. dry sherry (25 mL)

dash of ground cinnamon and pepper

Pistachio Sauce:

3 Tbsp. maple syrup (45 mL)

2 Tbsp. dry sherry (25 mL)

1 Tbsp. soy sauce (15 mL)

2 tsp. cornstarch (10 mL)

¼ cup pistachios, shelled and skinned
(50 mL)

- Bake in the oven for 4 to 5 minutes or until fragrant.
- Place nuts on clean towel and let cool. Remove the skins by rubbing the nuts between two clean towels. Set aside.
- Roughly chop the remaining pistachios.
- Prepare the glaze by combining the maple syrup, sherry, cinnamon and pepper in a small bowl. Reserve.
- Open out the pork roast. Season the inside with salt and pepper and sprinkle with the sherry-soaked apricots and the chopped nuts. Tie off the roast using butcher's twine.
- With a sharp knife, make 24 slits, 1 inch (2.5 cm) deep all over the roast.
- Insert a whole pistachio nut into each slit. Rub the roast with oil, thyme, rosemary, salt and pepper.
- Sear the roast in a skillet, then place on a rack in a roasting pan and transfer to the oven. Insert a meat thermometer and roast to an internal temperature of 150°F (65°C), approximately 1¾ to 2 hours.
- Baste with a pastry brush several times with the maple syrup glaze during the last half hour.
- When cooked, transfer to a serving platter and tent with foil. Reserve the pan drippings for the pistachio sauce.
- Heat the roasting pan, with drippings, on the stove and add some boiling water to make approximately ½ cup (125 mL) liquid. Scrape up the tidbits on the bottom.
- In a small bowl mix together the maple syrup, sherry, soy sauce and cornstarch and add to the drippings. Cook and stir until thickened.
- Add the pistachios and stir.
- Serve over the pork roast.

Chef's Tip: *When purchasing maple syrup buy a high-quality pure maple syrup. Maple syrup is graded according to colour and flavour, starting from light amber (grade A) moving down the scale as the colour deepens. For cooking purposes look for a grade B. It is dark amber in colour and robust in flavour. Save the light amber syrup for pancakes.*

Szechuan Pork Ribs

Preparation: moderate • Makes 6 servings • Recipe by Chef Tim McRoberts.

There are three ingredients that you might have trouble finding: szechuan peppercorns, star anise and five-spice powder. If you can't readily find them, then you have two choices: go to your local grocer and explain what century this is and that you need more condiments and spices than ketchup and pepper OR move to a place where your culinary yearnings are appreciated. Okay, so maybe you're not going to move over five-spice powder, but any retailer worth his kumquat will stock the ingredients you ask for.

5 cloves garlic, crushed

3-inch piece fresh root ginger, finely grated (8-cm piece)

3 tsp. Szechuan peppercorns, finely crushed (15 mL)

1 tsp. ground black pepper (5 mL)

2 tsp. finely ground star anise (10 mL)

2 tsp. Chinese five-spice powder (10 mL)

9 Tbsp. dark soy sauce (135 mL)

4 Tbsp. sunflower oil (60 mL)

2 Tbsp. sesame oil (25 mL)

3 baby back pork ribs slabs, 14 inches (35 cm) each

- In a bowl mix together the garlic, ginger, szechuan peppercorns, black pepper, star anise, Chinese five-spice powder, soy sauce, sunflower oil and sesame oil.
- Lay the baby back ribs in a large shallow dish, pour the marinade evenly over them, cover and chill overnight.
- Remove the ribs from refrigerator 1 hour before cooking.
- Prepare BBQ to medium heat, 375°F (190°C).
- Once the ribs are at room temperature, remove from the marinade and pat dry. Pour the remaining marinade into a pan and bring to a boil. Lower the heat and simmer for 3 minutes.
- Lay the ribs on the grill and sear for 3 minutes on each side. Tent with heavy-duty tinfoil and cook for 30 to 35 minutes.
- Baste occasionally with the heated marinade, until meat is tender and golden brown. Stop basting after 25 to 30 minutes.
- Cut into single ribs to serve and enjoy!

Chef's Tips: Make your own Chinese five-spice powder by grinding equal parts cinnamon, cloves, fennel seed, star anise and Szechuan peppercorns.

For more control over heat when grilling, place the ribs bone side up on the grill, cook for 7 minutes, then turn over (bone side down). Turn off the side of your BBQ that the ribs are on and continue to cook until done.

Prosciutto-Wrapped Breadsticks with Fig Dip

Preparation: easy • Makes 18 breadsticks • Recipe by Chef Michael Bonacini

This is a killer hors d'œuvres for a dinner party. You're all sitting around drinking prosecco with a splash of strawberry liqueur or vanilla-infused cognac, listening to Miles Davis or De Phazz and these guys hit the table with some olives and cheese. Perfect. You are the ultimate in cool. You are together. They ask for the recipe. You shake your head with modesty and tell them it's just something you whipped up. Spousal unit looks at you with affection. The meal that follows is flawless, the wine flows, the conversation is sterling. Later, when everyone has gone home, you play Escaped Convict And The Warden's Wife. Word of your dinner party spreads and you get invited to the best exclusive parties. You meet a Dot Com Bazillionaire who finances your idea for a cooking show based on HOW to cook instead of WHAT to cook. You retire and buy an island off the coast of Sardinia. All this because of a breadstick.

½ cup finely chopped stemmed dried black figs (125 mL)

½ cup balsamic vinegar (125 mL)

½ cup water (125 mL)

1 Tbsp. sugar (15 mL)

1 Tbsp. Dijon mustard (15 mL)

1 Tbsp. fresh lemon juice (15 mL)

3 Tbsp. fresh chives, chopped (45 mL)

salt and pepper

18 thin slices prosciutto

18 breadsticks

- Place the dried black figs in a saucepan.
- Add in the balsamic vinegar, water and sugar and bring to a boil.
- Reduce heat and simmer until slightly thick, about 5 minutes.
- Pour the fig mix into a blender and add the Dijon, lemon juice and chives and pulse until coarsely mixed together. Season with salt and pepper to taste.
- Spread one side of a prosciutto slice with fig spread, fold lengthways and wrap around a breadstick. Repeat until all the breadsticks have been wrapped.

Chef's Tip: *Prosciutto is an Italian ham that has been air dried. Italian prosciutti are designated* prosciutto cotto, *which is cooked, and* prosciutto crudo, *which is raw (because of curing it's ready to eat). For this recipe use the* crudo *as its soft texture will roll nicely.*

7 Game Meat

Confit of Duck

Preparation: moderate • Makes 6 servings • Recipe by Chef Caroline McCann-Bizjak

This *confit* recipe doesn't call for storing the cooked duck legs in their own fat for a couple of weeks. It does, however, call for 2½ pounds (1.25 kg) of rendered duck fat. The secret to turning the legs from chewy and border-line inedible into sweet falling-off-the-bone is the long slow cooking process, submerged in fat over low heat.

6 duck legs

¼ cup coarse or kosher salt (50 mL)

1 Tbsp. sugar (15 mL)

2½ pounds goose or duck fat (1.25 kg)

4 garlic cloves, whole

1 tsp. black peppercorns (5 mL)

½ tsp. whole cloves (2 mL)

½ cup raspberry vinegar (125 mL)

salt and pepper

¼ cup chives, chopped (50 mL)

- Sprinkle the duck with the salt and sugar. Place in a non-reactive dish, cover and refrigerate for 24 hours.
- Brush all the salt from the duck.
- Put the duck fat in a heavy pan over a medium heat to melt.
- Add the duck legs, garlic, peppercorns and cloves. Make sure the legs are covered with fat.
- Cook slowly for 2 hours, over a medium-low heat (approx. 250°F/ 120°C). Take the legs out of the fat to cool.
- Strain the fat through a colander lined with cheesecloth.
- Heat approximately 3 Tbsp. (45 mL) of the strained fat in a non-stick skillet over a high heat. Add the duck legs and cook until crispy on one side. Remove from heat.
- Add the raspberry vinegar to the pan. Be careful, it will crackle and spit. Stir to release the brown bits on the bottom of pan.
- Season the vinegar with salt and pepper. Just before serving, add the chopped chives.

Chef's Tip: For extra crispy duck skin, don't overcrowd your pan when you are in the final stage. Your pan will stay hot, and the duck will be crispy.

Cinnamon-Scented Duck Breast with a Balsamic Reduction

Preparation: moderate • Makes 6 servings • Recipe by Chris Knight

I think cinnamon is the most underrated of all the spices. It is a sweet perfume that insinuates itself into the very fibre of what you partner it with. It is particularly yummy with duck. You can get duck breasts at any decent butcher store. Pleeeaaaassseee ... don't overcook the duck! It's a bird, yes, but it's not chicken. It has to be served medium to medium rare. Trust me on this. Overcooked duck is soooo horrible. Duck is a dark meat. Think of it as beef when you're cooking it. Okay? Promise? The balsamic vinaigrette at the end is an amazing tart counterpoint to the duck.

Duck:

1½ Tbsp. ground cinnamon (22 mL)

5 Tbsp. fine sugar (60 mL)

6 large duck breasts

salt and pepper

Sauce:

1½ cups balsamic vinegar (375 mL)

3 tsp. ground cinnamon (15 mL)

3 cloves, whole

1 Tbsp. honey (15 mL)

- In a small bowl mix together the cinnamon and sugar.
- Score the fat of the duck breast and season with salt and pepper.
- Spread the cinnamon sugar over the duck and press into the fat.
- Set aside in the refrigerator to marinate for 4 to 12 hours.
- Preheat the oven to 375°F (190°C).
- Place the balsamic vinegar, cinnamon, cloves and honey in a saucepan set over medium heat. Let the sauce reduce to ¾ cup (175 mL), maybe 20 minutes or so.
- Meanwhile, heat an ovenproof skillet over medium heat.
- Sear the duck breast until the fat has rendered and the skin is crispy.
- Transfer the duck to the oven to finish cooking for approximately 5 minutes. Keep in mind duck is best served medium rare.
- Strain the balsamic reduction and season to taste with salt and pepper.
- Remove the duck from the oven and set aside to rest in a warm place for a couple of minutes.
- To serve, slice the duck very thin and drizzle with the balsamic reduction.

Chef's Tip: When scoring a duck breast, take a sharp knife and make a criss-cross pattern over the fat side of the duck. This will allow the fat to dissolve much more quickly, without overcooking the duck.

Tea-Smoked Duck

Preparation: difficult • Makes 6 servings • Recipe by Chef Michael Bonacini

I remember the day Chef Bonacini first suggested this recipe. First of all it's about cooking a whole duck, something most people have never done before. Then, for one recipe mind you, the duck is steamed, smoked AND roasted! Guess what? It's possibly the best whole duck recipe I've ever had. Sure you need time for this one, but not all recipes have to be half-hour jobs, right?

one 7-pound fresh duck (3.15 kg)
¼ cup coarse salt (50 mL)

- Have the butcher clean the duck well, removing membranes, fat and head, but leaving the wings attached.
- Wash under cold water and pat dry.
- Sprinkle with ¼ cup (50 mL) of salt on the outside of the duck and rub it thoroughly.

two 2-inch cinnamon sticks

    (two × 5-cm sticks)

3 pieces star anise

1-inch piece ginger, sliced (2.5-cm piece)

1 Tbsp. maple syrup (15 mL)

2 Tbsp. sugar (25 mL)

1 Tbsp. salt (15 mL)

⅓ cup dry sherry (75 mL)

1 cup green tea leaves (250 mL)

- Place in the refrigerator and marinate for 6 hours.
- Rinse well and pat dry with a clean towel.
- Place the duck in the steamproof rack of a large wok. Place cinnamon sticks, star anise and ginger into the cavity.
- Using a pastry brush, coat the duck with the maple syrup.
- Combine the sugar and 1 Tbsp. (15 mL) salt in a small bowl. Sprinkle the duck, inside and out, with this mixture.
- Pour sherry inside the cavity of the duck.
- Bring 4 cups (1 L) water to boil in the bottom of the wok. Place the steam rack with the duck over the water. The water should not touch the duck. Reduce the heat and cover. Allow the duck to steam for 1 hour.
- Replenish the water in the steamer when necessary, checking every 20 minutes.
- Remove the duck and let it sit at room temperature until cool.
- Clean and dry the wok.
- Place the tea leaves in the clean dry wok over high heat until the leaves begin to smoke. Reduce the heat slightly and place the steamed duck on a rack over the leaves.
- Place a wet cloth around the rim of the wok and use it to seal the lid on top. Smoke for 10–15 minutes
- Heat the oven to 400°F (200°C).
- Transfer the smoked duck to a roasting pan.
- Roast in the oven for 30 minutes. Flip the duck and continue to roast, uncovered, for another 30 minutes.
- Remove the duck and let it cool until it reaches room temperature.
- Carve and serve.

Chef's Tip: Steaming the duck before it's roasted gives the skin an opportunity to be crispy. Sencha green Japanese tea has a strong flavour and is perfect for smoking. Kombuca lime is a Japanese green tea infused with lime and would also work nicely.

Roasted Pheasant in Creamed Port Gravy

Preparation: moderate • Makes 6 servings • Recipe by Chef Michael Bonacini

If possible, get your hands on female pheasants. They tend to be smaller (3 pounds/1.5 kg) and have more tender meat. I guess it's because the guy pheasants spend all their time running around trying to be the alpha pheasant.

3 medium pheasants

salt and pepper

1 bay leaf

4 whole cloves

3 Tbsp. finely chopped fresh parsley (45 mL)

6 Tbsp. finely chopped celery leaves (90 mL)

12 black peppercorns, crushed

1 lemon, sliced

20 juniper berries

3 whole tangerines

3 cloves garlic

¾ pound larding pork or bacon (375 g)

3 medium onions, sliced thinly

½ cup finely chopped wild mushrooms (125 mL)

3 cups chicken stock (750 mL) (see page 27)

5 cups port (1.25 L)

¾ cup tangerine liqueur or orange juice (175 mL)

12 fresh figs

1½ cups sour cream (375 mL)

- Rub the pheasants with salt and pepper.
- Stuff the birds with the bay leaf, cloves, parsley, celery leaves, peppercorns, lemon and juniper berries.
- Peel the tangerines and insert the garlic cloves. Place one tangerine inside each pheasant.
- Close the body cavities of the pheasants and secure them with toothpicks or needles.
- Place the larding pork or bacon on the breast sides of the pheasants. This will add more fat to aid in keeping the pheasants moist.
- Add the onion slices and mushrooms to the bottom of a roasting pan.
- Place the pheasants on top.
- Pour the chicken stock, port and tangerine liqueur or orange juice into the roasting pan. Roast for 40–45 minutes (at 350°F/180°C) basting every 10 minutes. Remove from the roasting pan and cover with foil.
- Strain the liquid in the roasting pan. Press the vegetables to release all of their flavour. Let stand for 10 minutes.
- Skim any fat that rises to the top.
- Strain again if necessary. Season to taste with salt and pepper. Cook to reduce the liquid by half.
- Slice the figs in half, and remove any tough stems.
- Heat a separate pan over medium-high heat. Add the olive oil and the figs. Cook the figs until slightly caramelized, maybe 5 minutes or so.
- Add ¼ cup (50 mL) of the reduced port gravy. Remove from heat.
- Just before serving, add the sour cream to the port gravy. Whisk to produce a smooth sauce.
- Carve the pheasants and serve with the port gravy.

Drambuie Duck

Preparation: moderate • Makes 6 servings • Recipe by Chef Michael Bonacini

Sounds like a bad superhero cartoon ... LOOK, UP IN THE SKY! IT'S DRAMBUIE DUCK! Yup, rich juicy duck breasts cooked medium rare with a bracing of the honey liqueur, Drambuie—sounds lovely with parsley roast spuds and shallots and a nice glass of red with legs up to here.

½ cup all-purpose flour (125 mL)

½ tsp. salt (2 mL)

½ tsp. pepper (2 mL)

1 tsp. freshly chopped thyme (5 mL)

*6 medium duck breasts, skinned,
    boneless (chicken can be substituted)*

*½ cup + 2 Tbsp unsalted butter
    (150 mL)*

3 cloves garlic, crushed

6 shallots, chopped

*2 cups chicken stock (500 mL)
    (see page 27)*

1½ cups 35% cream (375 mL)

2 Tbsp. Drambuie (25 mL)

¼ cup chopped parsley (50 mL)

salt and pepper

- Place the flour in a shallow dish and season with salt, pepper and chopped thyme.
- Dredge the breasts through the flour. Shake off the excess flour.
- Heat a skillet and add the ½ cup (125 mL) of butter. Sauté the duck breasts until browned. This may have to be done 1 or 2 at a time, depending on the size of the skillet.
- When they are browned, set them on a plate until later.
- In the same skillet melt 2 Tbsp. (25 mL) butter. Add the garlic and shallots to the pan and sauté for 2 minutes.
- Add the chicken stock. Bring to a boil, return the breasts to the skillet and cover. Simmer over low heat, for 10 minutes.
- The breasts should become soft to the touch. Transfer the duck from the pan and cover with foil.
- Add the cream and Drambuie to the now empty duck pan. Simmer for 5 minutes. The mixture should reduce and thicken. Season to taste with salt and pepper.
- Return the duck breasts to the pan and coat them in sauce by stirring.
- Add the fresh parsley.
- Carve breast at a 45° angle and drizzle sauce overtop.

Tempura Foie Gras with Truffled Ponzu

Preparation: difficult • Serves 6 appetizers • Recipe by Chef René Rodriguez

FRIGGIN' DEEP-FRIED FOIS GRAS??? ARE YA NUTS? That's exactly what I said when Chef Rodriguez first suggested the recipe. After all, fois gras is pretty much nothing but a big slab of duck-flavoured fat that he wants to deep-fry in, well, more fat! Plus, tempura is tricky and it's okay if you gotta do a carrot slice over again but fois gras costs a car payment. But, it is a pretty cool idea, you have to admit ...

Ponzu:

¾ cup orange juice (175 mL)

2 Tbsp. mirin (25 mL)

¼ cup fresh lime juice (50 mL)

¼ cup soy sauce (50 mL)

2 Tbsp. minced green onions (25 mL)

1 Tbsp. truffle oil (15 mL)

½ tsp. Tabasco (2 mL)

2 cups rice flour (500 mL)

1 can cold club soda (200 mL)

six 1-ounce cubes foie gras (6 × 25-g)

salt and pepper

6 small strips nori sheets

2 Tbsp. all-purpose flour for dusting
    (25 mL)

1 egg white, lightly beaten

peanut oil for frying

pickled ginger

- For the ponzu, combine all the ponzu ingredients in a bowl and mix well. Refrigerate until ready to use.
- To make the foie gras, put the rice flour in a bowl and make a well in the middle.
- Add the cold club soda and mix well until batter forms. Set aside.
- Season the foie gras with salt and pepper.
- Wrap each piece like a present in the nori strips. Ensure all the foie gras is covered with nori.
- Secure each one with a wooden skewer. Dust the pieces with a little flour.
- In a separate bowl beat the egg white with a fork until frothy.
- Preheat the oil to 375°F (190°C).
- Dip the foie gras packages into the egg white and then the batter.
- Fry them in the hot oil until crisp, about 1 minute. DO NOT LEAVE UNATTENDED.
- Drain on paper towel.
- Serve the hot foie gras with ponzu sauce on the side and garnish with pickled ginger.

Chef's Tip: *Ponzu is a Japanese sauce traditionally made with seaweed, bonito fish, soy sauce, sake and rice wine vinegar. It is tart and sweet and pairs well with the richness of the foie gras.*

Tian of Stone Fruits with Quail and a Warm Chardonnay Vinaigrette

Preparation: moderate • Makes 6 servings • Recipe by Chef Michael Bonacini

Mmmmm ... quail! Of course, you really should try to get your birds fresh, but frozen will do. If you're not up to "flattening" the little guys (see recipe below), then have your butcher do it for you.

Tian, by the way, simply refers to a shallow casserole but sounds better on a menu, don't you think?

6 quail

salt and pepper

3 Tbsp. olive oil (45 mL)

6 plums

6 small peaches

3 Tbsp. unsalted butter (45 mL)

2 shallots, diced

2 cups chardonnay (500 mL)

½ cup sherry wine vinegar (125 mL)

½ lemon, juice of

- Preheat the oven to 350°F (180°C).

- Wash and trim the wing tips from the quail. Turn them backbone up and cut the bone out with a sharp French knife or poultry shears.

- Flatten the quail out on the work surface by pressing them flat on their breasts. They should look like squashed toads. Season with salt and pepper.

- Heat 2 Tbsp. (25 mL) of olive oil in a large pan. Once the pan is hot, add the quail and cook until they begin to turn golden brown.

- Place in the oven to continue to cook for 10 minutes. Remove the quail from the pan and let rest for 10 minutes.

- Meanwhile, prepare the fruit. Halve the plums and peaches and remove the stones.

- Add 1 Tbsp. (15 mL) butter and 1 Tbsp. (15 mL) olive oil to a skillet, over a medium-high heat.

- Add the plums and peaches, cut side down, to release the sugars. Sauté until they begin to soften and release their juices and caramelize around the edges (approximately 3 minutes). Remove the fruit and set aside in a warm place.

- Add the remainder of the butter to the pan that the quail was cooked in and scrape it well to remove the caramelized dark bits.

- Add the diced shallots and sauté until golden for approximately 2 minutes. Deglaze the pan with the chardonnay and allow the liquid to reduce by approximately one-third.

- Add the vinegar and a squeeze of lemon juice. Bring the liquid to a simmer for a couple of minutes.
- Serve the oven-roasted quail with the tian of fruits, salad and the warrn chardonnay vinaigrette.

Chef's Tip: *Quail, like most game birds, have little fat and should be served medium or medium rare.*

8 Lamb

Roasted Lamb Rack with a White Port Sauce

Preparation: moderate • Makes 6 servings • Recipe by Chris Knight

Here's the first of four lamb rack recipes. The meat is tender and sweet and doesn't take a long time to cook. It's the sort of cut that takes on quite different and subtle flavour changes depending on the sauce that goes with it. In this first recipe the influences are earthy and woodsy (garlic, mushrooms and port).

3 lamb racks (6 ribs each), bones cleaned

rock salt for seasoning

1 Tbsp. crushed mixed peppercorns (pink, green and black) (15 mL)

2 Tbsp. unsalted butter (25 mL)

1 Tbsp. olive oil (15 mL)

8 fresh large shiitake mushrooms

1 Tbsp. minced garlic (15 mL)

2 cups chicken stock (500 mL) (see page 27)

1 cup white port (250 mL)

1 Tbsp. sherry vinegar (15 mL)

- Preheat oven to 400°F (200°C).
- Season the lamb racks with the salt and crushed peppercorns.
- In a large ovenproof skillet, heat the butter and olive oil over a medium-high heat.
- Sear racks until nicely browned on each side.
- Cover the bone tips with foil to prevent burning.
- Place in oven and roast for approximately 11 minutes for medium rare.
- Remove the cooked lamb from the skillet and tent with foil.
- To the same skillet add the mushrooms and garlic. Sauté. Stir to scrape up the juicy brown bits from the bottom of the skillet.
- Add the chicken stock and white port.
- Reduce by half over medium heat.
- Add the sherry vinegar to tart up the sauce.
- Carve the lamb between each bone and drizzle with the sauce.

Chef's Tip: *White port is the same as regular port, only made with ... you guessed it ... white grapes. If you can't find any then go ahead and use the tawny variety.*

Filet of Lamb with Pan Reduction, Lavender and Rosemary Jus

Preparation: easy to moderate • Makes 6 servings • Recipe by Chris Knight

There are two things the French do better than anyone else in the world: runny cheese and lamb (notice wine isn't on the list). Lavender and rosemary are two things a lamb would be inclined to eat in the course of a day's grazing in Provence. And so do they make for a wonderful jus to go along with this recipe. *Goût de terroir* comes full circle. Alas, lavender has been relegated to bathroom potpourri and old lady's perfume on this side of the pond. If you can't get any fresh near you, half as much dried will do. And my wife (she of the green thumb) tells me it grows quite easily in the garden.

¼ cup unsalted butter (50 mL)

2 Tbsp. olive oil (25 mL)

12 lamb filets, approx. 2½ ounces (70 g) each

salt and black pepper

3 shallots, peeled and finely chopped

2 Tbsp. garlic, chopped (30 mL)

1 lime, zest and juice

⅓ cup red wine vinegar (75 mL)

1 cup red wine (250 mL)

4 cups white veal stock (1 L) (see page 31)

2 Tbsp. fresh lavender, chopped (25 mL)

2 Tbsp. rosemary, finely chopped. (25 mL)

- In a large skillet heat 2 Tbsp. (25 mL) of butter and the olive oil over medium-high heat.
- Season the lamb filets with salt and pepper and sear them in the skillet.
- Remove the filets, and add the shallots and garlic. Sauté until translucent. Set aside.
- Add the lime zest and 2 Tbsp. (25 mL) of juice.
- Deglaze with the red wine vinegar and the red wine.
- Add the veal stock, lavender and rosemary.
- Reduce the sauce in the skillet to half.
- Strain the sauce through a fine mesh sieve and keep warm on a low burner.
- Whisk in the remaining butter and season with salt and pepper.
- Serve the filets with the sauce.

Apricot-Glazed Rack of Lamb

Preparation: moderate • Makes 6 servings • Recipe by Chris Knight

The secret to this recipe is in the apricot glaze, which is easily made using apricot preserves. The sweetness of the apricots and the heat from the chilies make this a dish with a complexity of taste that belies its simplicity of preparation.

3 racks lamb (6 ribs each)

2 Tbsp. olive oil (25 mL)

salt and pepper to taste

paprika to taste

1 cup apricot preserves (250 mL)

1 cup water (250 mL)

4 cloves of garlic, minced

2 lemons, juice of

1 Tbsp. butter (15 mL)

2 Thai chilies, stemmed, seeds removed, then minced

- Preheat the oven to 400°F (200°C).
- Rub the racks of lamb with 1 Tbsp. (15 mL) of olive oil and season with salt, pepper and paprika.
- Heat the remainder of the oil in an ovenproof skillet.
- Place the rack fat side down and sear until the meat is nicely browned.
- Cover the bones with foil to prevent burning.
- For the apricot glaze, add the apricot preserves to some hot water in a pan, allowing it to dissolve.
- Add the garlic, lemon juice, butter and chilies. Let this reduce to a thick sauce. It should easily coat the back of a spoon.
- Brush the glaze over the seared racks of lamb. Place the rack back in the skillet and roast in the oven for 11 minutes for medium rare. Baste with the glaze once during roasting.
- Remove from the oven and let rest 10 minutes before carving.

Tangy Braised Lamb Shanks

Preparation: moderate • Makes 6 servings • Recipe by Ned Bell

Another outstanding recipe for the shank. It calls for the shanks to be "frenched," which means cutting the meat away from the bone so it doesn't "stretch" as it shrinks during the cooking. Get your butcher to do it for you.

2 chipotle chilies

1 cup boiling water (250 mL)

2 Tbsp. vegetable oil (25 mL)

6 lamb shanks, frenched (1–1½ pounds)
    (500–750 g)

salt and pepper

2 medium white onions, thickly sliced

½ cup raisins (125 mL)

2 Tbsp. minced garlic (25 mL)

1 tsp. dried oregano (5 mL)

1 tsp. sugar (5 mL)

1 tsp. cumin (5 mL)

28 oz peeled canned tomatoes
    (800 mL)

2 cups beef stock (500 mL)
    (see page 26)

4 bay leaves

1 Tbsp. cider vinegar (15 mL)

- Place the chipotle chilies in a bowl with the cup (250 mL) of boiling water. Set aside to soak for 1 hour.

- Heat the oil in a heavy skillet.

- Season the lamb shanks with salt and pepper.

- Place the shanks in the hot oil and brown on all sides (approximately 10 minutes). Remove the meat from the skillet and set it aside.

- Remove all but 2 Tbsp. (25 mL) of the oil from the skillet, being sure not to remove any of the browned bits left behind from browning the lamb shanks—these are flavour! Add the onions and sauté over a medium heat until soft.

- Remove from the water the chilies that have been soaking for an hour and place them in a blender with ⅓ of the soaking liquid. Purée until smooth.

- Reduce the heat on the onions to low. Stir in the raisins, garlic, oregano, sugar and cumin. Pour in the chili purée and cook, stirring constantly for a few minutes. Add the tomatoes, beef stock and bay leaves and bring to a boil.

- Add the browned lamb shanks and simmer over a low heat, covered, turning occasionally until the lamb is very tender, about 2 to 2½ hours.

- Remove the lamb shanks, place them on serving dish and keep warm.

- For the sauce, skim and discard the fat from the cooking sauce.

- Stir in the vinegar and return to a boil, uncovered, over medium-high heat. Stir frequently until the sauce is thickened, approximately 10 minutes. Spoon sauce over lamb shanks and serve.

Lamb Roasted in Oiled Parchment with Pecorino

Preparation: moderate • Makes 6 servings • Recipe by Chris Knight

Parchment paper costs a couple of bucks and is a must-have in your pantry arsenal. In this recipe, the leg of lamb is wrapped in the paper so that it steams in its own juices while cooking. The result is both tender and dramatic. Place the whole thing on the table in front of your guests and peel the paper back ... watch the intensely flavoured steam escape and perfume the room ... allow the oohs and ahhs to subside before you carve.

½ cup olive oil (125 mL)

2 lemons, juice of

1 Tbsp. dried oregano (15 mL)

1 Tbsp. dried thyme (15 mL)

2 bay leaves, crumbled

1 Tbsp. minced garlic (15 mL)

freshly ground black pepper

1 tsp. sugar (5 mL)

3 pounds boneless leg of lamb, cut into
    6 equal portions (1.5 kg)

parchment paper

coarse salt

6 slices pecorino cheese, cut ⅟₁₆ inch
    (2 mm) thick

butcher's twine

- In a large bowl, combine the olive oil, lemon juice, oregano, thyme, bay leaves, garlic, pepper and sugar.
- Place the lamb in the marinade, being sure to coat all sides.
- Cover the bowl with plastic wrap and place in the refrigerator for at least 3 hours.
- Preheat oven to 375°F (190°C).
- Cut the parchment paper into twelve 14-inch (35-cm) square pieces.
- Overlap two pieces on top of a table.
- Place one portion of lamb on the parchment without wiping off the marinade and season sparingly with salt and pepper (remember that pecorino is salty).
- Place a slice of cheese on top of the leg of lamb and spoon an additional helping of the marinade on top.
- Fold the part of the parchment paper nearest you over the lamb and cheese, and cover with the opposite side. Tuck the two sides under the lamb and secure the wrap with butcher's twine. Repeat until all the pieces of lamb are wrapped.
- Using a pastry brush, lightly oil a baking dish. Place the lamb packages in the dish and bake for 20 minutes.
- Lower oven heat to 325°F (160°C) and continue to cook the lamb for another 25–40 minutes, or until tender.
- When the lamb is cooked, cut the butcher's twine and lift the wrapped legs of lamb from the baking dish. Carefully undo the parchment wrapping to reveal the contents. Be careful to avoid the steam and not to spill the sauce. Serve in the peeled back parchment wrapping.

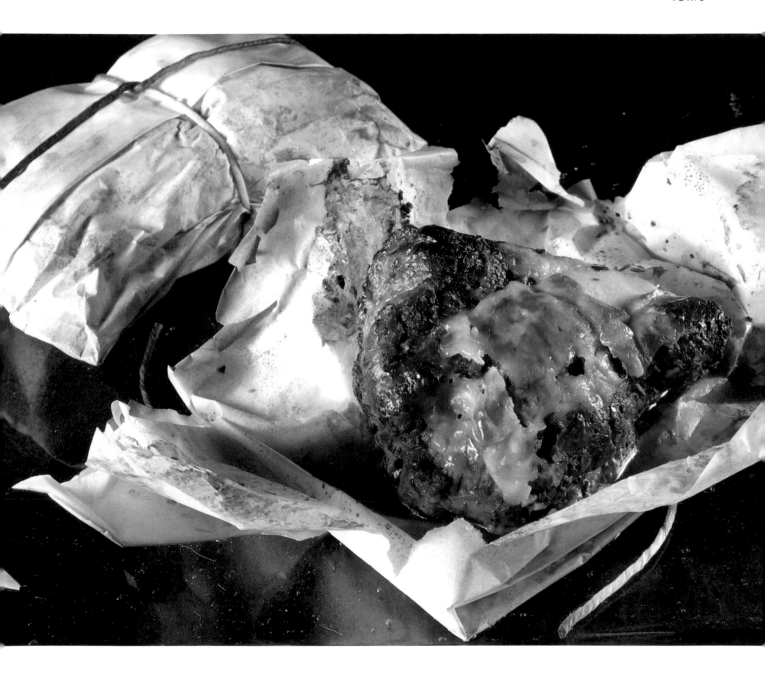

Chef's Tip: *For real fun, serve the dish with the parchment paper intact and have your diners peel back their own (but be careful) and WHOOSH! This heavenly rush of aroma and hot steam will escape, making them heady and woozy and putty in your hands.*

Crown Roast of Lamb with Mustard Rub

Preparation: moderate • Serves 6 very hungry people • Recipe by Chris Knight

This was one of those Sunday night dinner favourites back in the days when families actually sat down and made a big deal out of it. Yes, it was usually post-church and big in the suburbs (I hate the suburbs) and was served with mint sauce (I hate mint sauce more than I hate the suburbs), but it remains a fine meal that should grace our tables more often.

3 Tbsp. unsalted butter at room temperature (45 mL)

2 Tbsp. plus 1 tsp. Dijon mustard (30 mL)

2 Tbsp. chopped fresh rosemary (25 mL)

1 crown of lamb, made from two 8-rib racks (about 4½ pounds/2 kg total)

1 Tbsp. cracked black pepper (15 mL)

salt to taste

2 large shallots, chopped

2 cups dry white wine (500 mL)

1 cup chicken stock (250 mL) (see page 27)

3 Tbsp. chopped fresh mint (45 mL)

salt and pepper to taste

- Preheat oven to 400°F (200°C).
- Mix together 2 Tbsp. (25 mL) butter, 2 Tbsp. (25 mL) Dijon mustard and 1 Tbsp (15 mL) rosemary in a bowl.
- Season the lamb with black pepper and salt.
- Rub the Dijon-butter mixture generously over the lamb racks and place in a roasting pan. Cover the tips of the roast with foil so that they won't burn.
- Place in oven for 12 minutes.
- After 12 minutes, reduce heat to 350°F (180°C).
- Continue to roast until a meat thermometer reaches 130°F (54°C). Insert the thermometer into the thick part of the meat, not touching the bone.
- Transfer the lamb rack to a platter, tent with foil and let stand for 15 minutes.
- Pour off the fat from the roasting pan and discard.
- Add the remaining butter and cook over low heat on the stovetop.
- Add the shallots and remaining rosemary and sauté until the shallots are tender.
- Increase heat to medium-high, add the wine and bring to a boil. Be sure to scrape up any tasty morsels from the bottom of the pan.
- Add the chicken stock and bring to a boil again until slightly thickened.
- Stir in 1 tsp. (5 mL) Dijon and the fresh mint.
- Season to taste with salt and pepper.
- Carve roast and drizzle with sauce.

Lamb in a Fennel Coconut Sauce

Preparation: moderate • Makes 6 servings • Recipe by Chris Knight

This one's got a bit of a Moroccan thing going on with a spicy coconut paste that infuses the braising liquid with a zingy layered taste and a bit of an afterburn. Like the shank, the lamb shoulder is another cut that benefits immensely from a long slow braise.

Coconut Spice Paste:

¾ cup freshly grated coconut (175 mL) or
    ½ cup desiccated coconut (125 mL)

2½ Tbsp. finely chopped fresh ginger,
    peeled (37.5 mL)

1 cup water (250 mL)

1 Tbsp. finely ground fennel seeds
    (15 mL)

2 Tbsp. ground coriander (25 mL)

1½ tsp. Indian red chili powder
    (7.5 mL)

½ tsp. cumin (2 mL)

½ tsp. turmeric (2 mL)

Lamb:

⅓ cup vegetable oil (75 mL)

1 tsp. cumin seed (5 mL)

1 tsp. fenugreek seed (5 mL)

½ tsp. finely ground fennel seed (2 mL)

3 green cardamom pods

one 3-inch cinnamon stick
    (one × 8-cm)

- If using desiccated coconut, you will first need to soak it a bowl of warm water. Cover the coconut, soak for 1 hour, and drain through a sieve before using.

- If using fresh coconut, it will need to be grated, either using a food processor or a hand grater. To open a fresh coconut, use the back (blunt) side of a cleaver. Whack the coconut a few times all around the centre until it cracks open cleanly into two nearly equal halves. Do this over a bowl in the sink to catch the juice as it drains from the cracks.

- In a blender, combine the grated coconut, ginger and ½ cup (125 mL) of water and blend. Then add another ½ cup (125 mL) of water, and the fennel, coriander, chili powder, cumin and turmeric. Blend together until the mixture is thick and paste-like.

- In a 6-quart (6-litre) heavy pot, warm the oil over a medium-high heat until hot but not smoking. Add the cumin, fenugreek, fennel seed, cardamom pods and cinnamon stick and cook until fragrant. Stir in the curry leaves and cook for 1 minute.

- Add the chopped onion and cook until it begins to soften and brown, about 5 minutes.

- Add the chopped tomatoes, and cook until they begin to soften, stirring occasionally, approximately 1 minute.

- Stir in the coconut paste, and season with salt.

- Cook, stirring occasionally for about 5 minutes. Add the lamb and cook for 2 to 3 minutes or until no longer pink. Add 3 cups (750 mL) water, cover and simmer until lamb is tender, about 1½ hours.

10 fresh curry leaves

1 large onion, chopped

3 plum tomatoes, chopped

1 tsp. salt (5 mL)

2½ pounds trimmed boneless lamb
     shoulder, cut into 1½-inch/
     4-cm pieces (1.25 kg)

3 cups water (750 mL)

- Transfer the lamb to a serving plate and cover.
- Simmer the sauce until it thickens.
- Return the lamb to the pot, mix with the sauce and serve.

9 Fish

Salmon Cured with Asian Black Teas

Preparation: easy • Serves between 6 and 10 people • Recipe by Chef Ned Bell

The trick to curing fish is to let it sit for at least 6 hours, overnight being even better. Do this on a Saturday afternoon and serve on Sunday for brunch or as a starter for dinner. Yum. The fish is "cooked" by the salt and sugar while in the frigo.

1 filet salmon (4–5 pounds/2–2.2 kg)

1 cup coarse or kosher salt (250 mL)

¾ cup sugar (175 mL)

1 cup loose black tea leaves steeped in boiling water (250 mL)

1 lemon, thinly sliced

1 Tbsp. whole coriander seeds (15 mL)

1 Tbsp. caraway seeds (15 mL)

1 Tbsp. fennel seeds (15 mL)

- Clean the salmon so that you are left with a whole side with no bones, but with the skin still on. You might have to use tweezers to pull out the pinbones.
- Drain the boiled water from the black tea leaves and reserve the liquid.
- Discard the leaves.
- Place in a non-reactive dish. Cover the fish filet with all the other ingredients and allow to cure in the fridge for at least 6 hours or overnight.
- Remove all the marinating ingredients by scraping the filet. Lie it on a board and slice very thinly. Serve like smoked salmon.

Chef's Tip: *There has been much hand-wringing of late over whether or not farmed salmon is bad for you. Truth is, wild salmon just tastes better. Way better. Ask your fishmonger to get some in for you when it's in season.*

Thai Green Curry Salmon

Preparation: moderate, and luckily involves lots of chopping, which is one of the fun parts of cooking.

Makes 6 servings • Recipe by Chris Knight

Got to love Thai cooking. Fresh ingredients done *à la minute*. This recipe might look complicated, but it's all *mise en place*. The curry paste can be kept for 2 weeks in a tightly sealed jar in the refrigerator or for 2 months in the freezer. It actually gets better the longer you let it set up.

Thai Green Curry Paste:

4 stalks fresh lemon grass, outer leaves discarded and roots ends trimmed

- To make the curry paste, thinly slice the lower four inches (10 cm) of the lemon grass stalks and discard the remainder.
- Place the trimmed lemon grass, chilies, red onion, garlic and galangal or ginger root in the food processor. Add the white pepper, coriander

continued on next page

4 Tbsp. fresh green Thai or serrano chilies
    chopped, seeds and ribs discarded
    (60 mL)

½ cup chopped red onion (125 mL)

8 large cloves garlic, chopped

2 Tbsp. fresh or frozen (and thawed)
    galangal or ginger root (25 mL)

2 tsp. freshly ground white pepper
    (10 mL)

2½ tsp. ground coriander seeds (12.5 mL)

2 tsp. anchovy paste (10 mL)

2 tsp. finely grated lime zest (10 mL)

1 Tbsp. vegetable oil (15 mL)

Salmon:

two 13½ ounce cans unsweetened
    coconut milk, chilled (750 mL)

¼ cup fish sauce (50 mL)

3 Tbsp. firmly packed brown sugar
    (45 mL)

1 Tbsp. fresh lime juice (15 mL)

1 Tbsp. vegetable oil (15 mL)

1½ pounds skinless salmon filet, cut into
    2-inch (5-cm) pieces (750 g)

1 red bell pepper, thinly sliced

½ cup thinly sliced mushrooms
    (125 mL)

½ cup torn fresh basil (125 mL)

seeds, anchovy paste, lime zest and vegetable oil and blend until it reaches a smooth paste consistency. Set aside until needed.

- To prepare the salmon, first remove 1 cup (250 mL) of the cream that has risen to the top of the chilled coconut milk and add it to a large skillet or wok. Bring to a boil and cook for 5–8 minutes until the oil begins to separate from the white solids.

- Add 8 Tbsp. (120 mL) of the curry paste and continue to cook for another 5–8 minutes.

- Add some thin coconut milk a little at a time. If the mixture begins to stick, add the remaining coconut milk slowly until a nice consistency is achieved. Stir in the fish sauce, brown sugar and lime juice and let simmer.

- Place a medium-sized skillet over high heat and add the 1 Tbsp. (15 mL) vegetable oil. Add the salmon pieces and cook until golden brown on all sides but not cooked through. Remove from the heat.

- Add salmon pieces to the skillet with the curry paste and coconut cream. Stir occasionally until the salmon is almost cooked through.

- Add the red pepper, mushrooms and fresh basil.

- Serve with jasmine rice, roasted pine nuts and diced cilantro.

Peppercorn-Crusted Salmon with Pernod

Preparation: easy • Makes 6 servings • Recipe by Chris Knight

Peppercorn combos are sold pretty much everywhere. Lemon balm (sometimes just called "balm"), on the other hand, might require a bit of a search depending on where you live. Flavour-wise it's kind of a cross between lemon and mint and well worth getting a hold of. If you're using salmon steaks, just remove the centre bone, fold the flaps in and tie so you have a sort of salmon disk, which is called a "tournedos" in fancy-schmancy restaurants.

2 Tbsp. pink peppercorns (25 mL)

2 Tbsp. black peppercorns (25 mL)

2 Tbsp. green peppercorns (25 mL)

2 Tbsp. szechuan pepper (25 mL)

6 salmon tournedos or steaks, boned and
    tied, weighing about 6–8 oz each
    (175–250 g each)

10 Tbsp. olive oil (150 mL)

6 shallots, chopped

1½ cups fresh corn kernels (375 mL)

1½ cups Pernod (375 mL)

1½ cups 35% cream (375 mL)

salt and pepper

2 Tbsp. fresh tarragon, chopped
    (25 mL)

2 Tbsp. lemon balm (25 mL)

- Preheat the oven to 350°F (180°C).

- Smash the peppercorns and Szechuan pepper together with a rolling pin in a dishtowel, grind in spice grinder or use a mortar and pestle. Schmucking with a dishtowel is preferable around tax time.

- Crust the outside of the salmon with the peppercorns and sear in a cast iron skillet with some olive oil over high heat.

- Transfer the salmon to the oven to cook for a further 6 minutes or until desired doneness.

- Meanwhile, heat the remaining olive oil in a pan and add the shallots.

- Sauté over medium heat until they are translucent and soft. Add the fresh corn kernels and toss and sauté for 1 minute.

- Deglaze the pan with the Pernod, scraping up the yummy brown bits from the bottom of the pan and reduce for one minute before adding the cream.

- Boil for 30 seconds. Season to taste with salt and pepper and add the tarragon.

- Retrieve the salmon from the oven and serve with the Pernod cream sauce around the plate. Dress the plate with the lemon balm.

Chef's Tip: For optimum flavour, cook the salmon medium rare. To test for doneness, stick a sharp knife gently into the thickest part of the flesh. The flesh turns from translucent to opaque; it should be juicy and just barely opaque. Press gently on the salmon with your finger to test its firmness. With practice you will know just from touch when it is cooked.

Red Snapper Filets in Romaine with Crisp Rice Cakes

Preparation: moderate • Makes 6 servings • Recipe by Chris Knight

Wrapping the fish in Romaine leaves not only looks pretty funky when you serve it—it also keeps the filets nice and juicy. This works well with lots of other types of fish (I'm big on tilapia these days). Rice cakes are a great twist on piling starch on a plate, and they go well with lots of dishes.

8 large romaine lettuces, leaves only

¼ cup chopped fresh parsley (50 mL)

2 Tbsp. chopped fresh mint (25 mL)

2 Tbsp. brown sugar (25 mL)

*1 Tbsp. freshly squeezed lemon juice
     (15 mL)*

1 Tbsp. cider vinegar (15 mL)

1 tsp. curry powder (5 mL)

1 tsp. ground cumin (5 mL)

1 tsp. salt (5 mL)

½ tsp. white pepper (2 mL)

*six 4-ounce red snapper filets de-boned
     (six × 125-g)*

salt and white pepper to season

Rice Cakes:

½ cup wild rice (125 mL)

*2 cups water, boiling and salted
     (500 mL)*

1 large egg

⅓ cup chopped fresh parsley (75 mL)

⅓ cup chopped fresh chives (75 mL)

salt and pepper

- Preheat oven to 400°F (200°C).

- Bring a large pot of salted water to a boil. Add the romaine lettuce leaves and boil until pliable, about one minute.

- Remove the leaves from the boiling water and refresh under cold water. Drain, pat dry and arrange 2 leaves on the bottom of an oiled baking dish.

- Place the parsley, mint, brown sugar, lemon juice, vinegar, curry powder, cumin, salt and white pepper in a blender and purée until smooth.

- Rinse and pat dry the snapper filets. Season with salt and white pepper.

- Place one filet on each of the remaining romaine leaves. Scoop a spoonful of the purée on to each filet. Fold the stem end of the romaine over the fish, tuck in the sides of the leaf and roll up into a fully wrapped parcel. Place the fish packages seam side down in the baking dish. Bake for approximately 8 minutes.

- Meanwhile, prepare the rice cakes. Rinse the rice under cold water and drain. Add it to the boiling salted water. Cook the rice for approximately 30 minutes or until the rice is tender but not open.

- Drain the rice and rinse with cold water to cool. Drain well and place in a bowl. The rice can be made in advance and kept cool in the refrigerator. Bring to room temperature before making the cakes.

- Lightly beat the egg and stir into the rice with the parsley, chives and salt and pepper.

2 Tbsp. vegetable oil (25 mL)

- Heat the oil in a large skillet and add a large scoop of the rice mixture.
- Fry 1 minute on each side until golden.

Chef's Tip: If your romaine leaves are small, wrap the fish in two leaves. Serve the filets along with the rice cakes as soon as the fish is done. There's nothing worse than a cold bit of fish.

Bouillabaisse à la Marseillaise

Preparation: moderate • Makes 6–8 servings • Recipe by Chef Georges Laurier

This recipe is for a classic "Marseillaise" bouillabaisse and calls for such *poisson* as rascasse, loup de mer and St. Pierre. Although chefs have their ways, it's unlikely you'll be able to find these particular fish unless you're planning on a trip to France. Instead, use a variety of firm-fleshed white fish. Check with your fishmonger for suggestions. Marinating the fish overnight adds a lot to the end soup, so do take the time.

Saffron helps give the soup a dark rusty colour and the bouquet garni is essential to give the soup a deep layered flavour. If you don't have fish stock handy, try using a combination of 1 part vermouth, 2 parts bottled clam juice, 2 parts white wine, and 4 parts water.

Bouquet Garni:

3 leek leaves, green part only, 3 inches/ 8 cm

4 sprigs fresh thyme

2 bay leaves

6 sprigs parsley

Bouillabaisse:

6 pounds white rock fish such as rascasse, monkfish, loup de mer, St. Pierre, grondin (2.7 kg)

½ cup chopped onions (125 mL)

1 cup chopped leeks, white part only (250 mL)

½ cup finely chopped garlic (125 mL)

1 cup diced tomatoes (250 mL)

2 tsp. cayenne pepper (10 mL)

½ cup olive oil (125 mL)

salt and black pepper to taste

- Preheat the oven to 375°F (190°C).

- To make the bouquet garni, place the leek leaves flat, add the herbs and tie securely with butcher's twine. Set this to one side until needed.

- To make the bouillabaisse, clean the fish and cut it into large bite-sized pieces. Put the fish into a large stainless steel bowl and add the onions, leeks, garlic, tomatoes, cayenne pepper, bouquet garni and olive oil. Add a good turn of fresh cracked pepper from the mill. Cover and let the fish sit in the refrigerator for at least 5 hours or, preferably, overnight.

- Remove the fish from the marinade. Pour the juices, including any pieces of tomato, leek, garlic etc., into a hot sauté pan, and add the fish stock and salt.

- Bring the stock to a simmer over a medium heat and skim it as impurities rise to the top. Let it simmer for 30 minutes.

- Strain the liquid through a sieve and add the saffron. Let it sit for 5 minutes so that the saffron can steep into the liquid.

- Put the liquid into a saucepan and bring it to a boil over medium heat.

- Add the fish pieces, starting with the firmest and moving toward the softest. Cook them for 2 minutes, then add the lemon zest and juice.

- Remove the fish from the pan and set it aside in a warm place.

12 cups fish stock (3 L) (see page 28)

2 tsp. saffron (10 mL)

1 lemon, zest and juice of

Rouille:

2 egg yolks (if yolks are large, only 1)

¼ cup garlic, finely diced (50 mL)

1 cup olive oil (250 mL)

1 tsp. cayenne pepper (5 mL)

10 threads saffron

6 slices baguette

- To make the rouille, beat the egg yolks together with the garlic.
- Whisk in the olive oil in a steady stream and add the cayenne and saffron. Brush the slices of baguette with olive oil and toast them until golden. Cut a garlic clove in half and rub each toast with garlic.
- Divide the fish among the bowls. Pour the bouillabaisse overtop and float the baguette toasts on top with a dollop of rouille.

Halibut Steaks in Parchment with Mushrooms and Tarragon

Preparation: moderate • Makes 6 servings • Recipe by Chef Michael Bonacini

This recipe calls for cooking "en papillote," which is French for cooking in paper. In this case it's moisture-and grease-resistant parchment paper, available pretty much anywhere. The fish of choice here is the much underrated halibut—a big meaty white fish that holds up well to all sorts of cooking.

6 halibut steaks, 1 inch (2.5 cm) thick,
    6–8 ounces each (175–250 g each)

parchment paper

6 Tbsp. melted butter (90 mL)

3 cups fresh, sliced mushrooms
    (750 mL)

6 fresh tarragon sprigs; tops reserved and
    leaves finely cut

1 lemon, juice of

salt and pepper for seasoning

2 medium-sized zucchini, sliced

3 egg whites beaten

- Preheat the oven to 375°F (190°C).
- Rinse the halibut under cold water and pat dry with paper towel. Set aside.
- Fold a 15- × 13-inch (38- × 33-cm) piece of parchment paper in half crosswise to make a rectangle 13 × 7½ inches (33 × 19 cm).
- Draw a half-heart, beginning and ending at the folded edge, and cut along the line. Repeat this so that you have 6 pieces of parchment ready to go.
- Open each paper and brush one half with some of the melted butter, leaving a 1-inch (2.5-cm) border unbuttered.
- Combine the mushrooms, tarragon leaves, lemon juice, salt and pepper in a bowl. Stir thoroughly to coat the mushrooms.
- Spread the mushroom blend over the buttered portion of the parchment and set a halibut steak on top of each.
- Season the halibut with salt and pepper.
- Arrange the zucchini slices on the fish by slightly overlapping them lengthways along the centre of the fish. Top with the reserved tarragon tops.
- Brush the edges of each piece of parchment paper with egg white and crimp the edges, ensuring they are well sealed. Transfer the paper packages to a baking sheet.
- Bring the sheet to the heated oven and bake until the packages are puffed and light brown, about 12–15 minutes.
- Transfer to dinner plates and serve. Make sure to pinch the top of the parchment and rip open just before serving, for mouth-watering aromatic steam.

Chef's Tip: *Cooking small filets of fish en papillote is a delicious way to enjoy fish without losing any of the flavour. Touch the fish carefully, ensuring you don't tear the parchment. It should feel slightly firm, with a spongy spring.*

Haddock Mousse-Stuffed Trout with Butter Sauce

Preparation: moderate • Makes 6 appetizer-size servings • Recipe by Chef Michael Bonacini

This classic chef-goes-to-town dish features both haddock and trout in a funky counterpoint kind of rolled mousse thing. The ingredients are simple, the prep takes a bit of time, the results are spectacular. Be not afraid, young Skywalker, the Force is with you.

salt and pepper

3 cups fresh spinach (750 mL)

20–24 ounces skinless and boneless centre cut trout filet (625–750 g)

1¾ cups haddock mousse (425 mL)

- Bring a pot of salted water to a boil. Submerge the spinach in the water for 30 seconds. Quickly remove it and dunk it in a large bowl of ice water to stop the cooking process.

- Place the cooled spinach on a towel and pat dry.

- Place the trout between two sheets of plastic wrap and pound it lightly to even out the thickness. Remove only the top piece of plastic wrap

Mousse:

10 ounces skinless and boneless haddock
  filet (300 g)

½ medium onion, diced small

salt and pepper

pinch freshly grated nutmeg

pinch cinnamon

1 cup light cream (250 mL)

2 egg whites

Butter Sauce:

2 Tbsp. butter (25 mL)

6 shallots, minced

1 cup dry white wine (250 mL)

1 cup whipping cream (250 mL)

1 cup concentrated fish stock (250 mL)
  (see page 28)

9 Tbsp. unsalted butter, cold (135 mL)

salt and pepper

¾ tsp. freshly grated nutmeg (4 mL)

2 lemons, juice of

and season the flattened filet with salt and pepper. Cover with the blanched spinach.

- For the mousse, cut the haddock filets into strips and place them in a chilled food processor bowl.
- Add the onion and salt, pepper, nutmeg and cinnamon to taste. Add half the cream and the two egg whites to the mix and give it a couple of turns. Remove and rub through a fine mesh sieve into a chilled bowl and fold in the rest of the cream.
- Take this mixture, also known as forcemeat, and spoon a layer on top of the spinach.
- With the help of the plastic wrap, roll up the fish, making sure to keep the ends of the wrap on the outside at all times. Repeat with your second filet. Tie the ends.
- Place the fish in a perforated pan over boiling water and cover and steam for approximately 10 minutes or until it is just opaque and the mousse is cooked.
- Meanwhile, make the butter sauce. Melt the butter in a large skillet.
- Add the shallots and sauté until tender. Add the dry white wine. When the wine has reduced and the shallots are almost dry, add the cream and the fish stock.
- Beat in the butter, a few squares at a time. Make sure not to let the sauce boil after adding the butter. Season with salt, pepper, nutmeg and finish with fresh lemon juice.
- Spoon the sauce into the centre of each serving plate and remove the cooked trout from the steamer. Cut slices and place the trout on top of the sauce.

Chef's Tip: It is crucial when making mousse that all the ingredients stay very cold, otherwise the mousse could separate. Place your food processor top in the freezer before using.

Grouper with Saffron-Fennel Compote

Preparation: moderate • *Makes 6 servings* • *Recipe by Chris Knight*

This dish is named for the famous American author Truman Compote. Okay, it's not. A compote is sort of a relish, kind of a chutney. In this case it's made with fennel and saffron and is even better if made a day or so in advance.

Grouper can weigh up to 700 pounds, but personally I'd suggest getting something slightly smaller. It's one of those big meaty white fish that holds up to all sorts of cooking techniques. Unlike salmon or cod, the skin on a grouper has to be removed, as it has one mama strong taste. Get your fishmonger to do it for you.

Grouper Marinade:

4 Tbsp. olive oil (60 mL)

2½ tsp. minced garlic (12.5 mL)

1 tsp. crushed and packed saffron threads
(5 mL)

4–5 pounds grouper filets (about 2 filets),
well trimmed and skinned (2–2.2 kg)

salt and pepper

Saffron-Fennel Compote:

4 Tbsp. olive oil (60 mL)

4½ cups fresh fennel bulbs, chopped
(about 2) (1.25 L)

3 cups chopped onions (750 mL)

1 Tbsp. crushed fennel seeds (15 mL)

3 tsp. minced garlic (15 mL)

2 cups dry white wine (500 mL)

1 cup chicken stock (250 mL)

¾ tsp. crushed and packed saffron
threads (4 mL)

- In a large bowl, combine the oil, garlic and saffron. Add the fish and coat both sides. Cover with plastic wrap and refrigerate to marinate (at least 3 hours and up to 1 day).

- In a large, heavy pot, heat the oil over medium heat. Add the fennel, onions and fennel seeds and cook until tender, stirring occasionally, for about 1 hour.

- Add the minced garlic and stir for 30 seconds or so.

- Add the wine, stock and saffron and simmer until thick (approximately 20 minutes), stirring occasionally.

- Preheat oven to 425°F (220°C).

- Place the coated fish, with marinade, on a baking tray, season with salt and pepper and roast the grouper until the fish feels almost firm to the touch (approximately 15 minutes).

- Serve the fish on top of spinach and steamed rice with a spoonful of saffron-fennel compote on top.

Grilled Whole Sea Bass with Bread Crumbs and Anchovies

Preparation: moderate • Makes 6 servings • Recipe by Chris Knight

Bass holds up really well to grilling when done as a whole fish. It has a buttery sweet flesh and gets a crunch from the bread crumbs and a zing from the anchovies.

5 Tbsp. extra virgin olive oil (75 mL)

1 small onion, minced

1 egg

1 Tbsp. anchovy paste (15 mL)

3 Tbsp. chopped fresh parsley (45 mL)

2 tsp. minced fresh cilantro (10 mL))

½ tsp. minced fresh rosemary (2 mL)

½ tsp. minced fresh thyme (2 mL)

1½ cups coarse fresh white bread crumbs (375 mL)

salt and pepper

one 4-pound whole sea bass, cleaned (2 kg)

wooden skewer soaked in water for 20–30 minutes

- Preheat grill to medium heat.
- For the stuffing, heat 3 Tbsp. (45 mL) of the oil in a skillet and sauté the onion until soft. Transfer to a large bowl and let cool.
- Once cooled to room temperature, add the egg, anchovy paste, 2 Tbsp. (25 mL) parsley, cilantro, rosemary and thyme.
- Mix in ¾ cup (175 mL) of bread crumbs and season with salt and pepper.
- Slice two ½-inch (1-cm) deep diagonal cuts on each side of the sea bass, spacing the cuts about 3 inches (8 cm) apart.
- Season the fish cavity with salt and pepper and spoon in the stuffing, being careful not to overstuff the fish. Using a soaked wooden skewer, close the belly.
- Rub the fish with oil and season with salt. Place the fish on the grill and cook for approximately 20 minutes, turning only once.
- While the fish is grilling, add the remainder of the bread crumbs to a skillet with the remainder of the oil and sauté over medium heat until golden brown. Add the remaining parsley.
- Once the fish is cooked, transfer to a platter; remove skewer and sprinkle with bread crumb topping.

Chef's Tip: When grilling the fish, the grill should be hot, clean and well oiled, or you run the risk of the fish sticking. Take half an onion and rub on a hot grill (the oils and acid of the onion help to clean as well as season). Take a well-oiled towel and repeat.

Stuffed Red Snapper with a Port Glaze Sauce

Preparation: easy • Makes 6 servings • Recipe by Chris Knight

Red snapper is low in fat and delicate in taste, and it holds up very well to being cooked whole. Port is a classic base for a glaze and imparts a complicated layered taste that makes the fish sit up and applaud on the plate.

6 red snapper weighing 6–8 ounces each
    (175–250 g each)
sea salt and pepper
6 large sprigs oregano
6 large sprigs thyme
6 pieces lemon grass, cleaned
6 inches fresh ginger (15 cm)
9 apricots
4 Tbsp. olive oil (60 mL)
12 large pieces nori

Glaze:
1½ cups port (375 mL)
⅔ cup tarragon vinegar (150 mL)
3 Tbsp. sugar (45 mL)

- Preheat the oven to 350°F (180°C).
- De-scale each fish. Using a sharp knife, scrape the skin in the opposite direction to the scales, which should flick away from the skin.
- Open each red snapper and de-bone it through the stomach cavity. Or get your fishmonger to do it for you—he can de-scale while he's at it.
- Place the fish skin side down and season the inside with salt and pepper. Lay a sprig of oregano and thyme inside the cavity of each fish.
- Add a clean smashed piece of lemon grass stalk.
- Peel and chop the ginger into small pieces. Add one-sixth to the middle of each fish.
- Cut up the apricots with kitchen scissors and add them to the cavity of each fish. Drizzle with a very small amount of olive oil.
- Lightly score the fish on each side.
- Brush the nori with water to soften it, and then wrap the fish from head to tail in the seaweed.
- Warm 1 Tbsp. (15 mL) of the olive oil in a large ovenproof sauté pan over medium heat. Once hot, slide the fish into the pan, turning as needed until almost cooked, about 6 to 8 minutes.
- Put the fish in the oven to cook through for a further 7 minutes.
- Meanwhile, put the port, vinegar and sugar in a small saucepan over a medium-low heat to reduce. Reduce to a glaze that coats the back of a wooden spoon.
- Retrieve the fish from the oven and serve with the port glaze drizzled overtop. Parsley boiled new potatoes go well with this.

Pan-Fried Pike Fingers with Black Olives and Tomatoes

Preparation: moderate • Makes 6 servings • Recipe by Chef Michael Bonacini

Most people don't realize that pike is the only fish with hands instead of fins. Fishmongers trim the hands and fingers off for aesthetic reasons before selling the fish. Ask your fishmonger for a big bag of pike fingers as they can be stored in the freezer wrapped in snowmobile mitts. Okay, maybe not. The fingers are just big thin slices of the filet, and if you can't get your hands on pike then try another big meaty white fish that will play nicely off the salty olives and tangy tomatoes.

one 3-pound pike, de-boned (1.5 kg)
seasoned with salt and pepper

1 cup all-purpose flour (250 mL)

2 Tbsp. butter (25 mL)

2 Tbsp. olive oil (25 mL)

6 artichoke bottoms, diced and cooked

1 cup mushrooms of choice, sliced (250 mL)

½ cup pitted kalamata olives (125 mL)

⅓ cup good white wine (75 mL)

3 Tbsp. chopped parsley (45 mL)

1 Tbsp. fresh lemon juice (15 mL)

3 tomatoes, diced

- Cut the pike into 3–4-inch (8–10-cm) length strips and dust them with seasoned flour.
- Melt 1 Tbsp. (15 mL) of butter and 1 Tbsp. (15 mL) of oil in a cast iron pan over a medium-high heat and sauté the pike until golden brown, about 5 minutes.
- Remove the pike from the pan and keep it warm.
- Using the same pan, add the remaining olive oil and butter and sauté the artichoke bottoms, then add the mushrooms and cook for 5 minutes.
- Add the olives, white wine, chopped parsley, lemon juice and diced tomatoes. This makes a delicious ragout base for the pike. Place hot ragout over the warm pike.
- Serve immediately.

Chef's Tip: Artichokes require some special attention before cooking. There are two areas of concern. First, they have extremely sharp barbs on the ends of the leaves that must be removed. Second, they tend to discolour when exposed to air. The barbs are simply snipped away with scissors or a sharp paring knife. To keep the artichoke pale and yellow, simply tie a slice of lemon on the exposed surface before steaming. Once steamed, scoop out the hay from the middle of the artichoke and pare down with a knife to the choke.

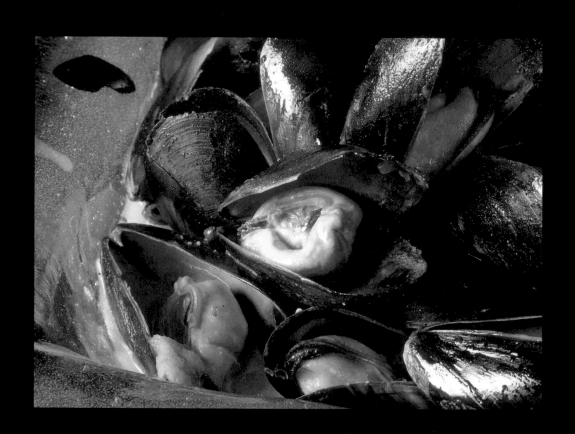

10 Shellfish

Mini Crab Cakes with Roasted Red Pepper Sauce

Preparation: easy • Makes twelve small crab cakes • Serves 6 as an appetizer • Recipe by Chef Michael Bonacini

In a super-sized world of fast food crap, Chef Bonacini has gone the other way and mini-sized these crab cakes to make a great appetizer. No need to get crab legs for this one—the frozen block stuff (not canned) is fine. Just make sure you pick it over once it's thawed, as there are often little bits of shell in there that you really don't want to bite down on.

Crab Cakes:

15 pumpernickel bread slices, toasted

¼ cup mayonnaise (regular or low-fat) (50 mL)

2 tsp. Dijon mustard (10 mL)

1 large egg

1 tsp. lemon zest (5 mL)

1 Tbsp. freshly squeezed lemon juice (15 mL)

1 pound crabmeat, drained and patted dry (500 g)

1 cup fresh white bread crumbs (250 mL)

¼ cup finely chopped green onions (50 mL)

½ tsp. salt (2 mL)

¼ tsp. white pepper (1 mL)

1½ Tbsp. butter (22.5 mL)

2 Tbsp. vegetable oil (25 mL)

- Preheat oven to 375°F (190°C).
- Slice the pumpernickel bread into small squares or rounds. Place on a baking tray and toast lightly in the oven for around 15 minutes.
- Combine the mayonnaise, Dijon mustard and egg in a bowl.
- Grate in the lemon zest and squeeze in the lemon juice.
- Add the crabmeat, bread crumbs, green onions, salt and white pepper.
- Mix the ingredients well.
- Form the mixture into little crab cakes, approximately 2 inches (5 cm) in diameter.
- Place them on a parchment-lined baking sheet and put in the refrigerator to set for 1 hour.
- Add the butter and oil to a large non-stick skillet and heat to medium-high.
- Gently slide a few of the cakes from the baking sheet into the oil.
- The skillet has to be very hot to produce the crispy exterior on the cakes. Do not overcrowd the skillet; it will cause the cakes to steam rather than fry.
- Cook until golden brown and crispy, about 3 minutes on each side. Add more oil if necessary.

Red Pepper Sauce:

4 roasted red bell peppers, chopped

1 cup mayonnaise (regular or low-fat)
(250 mL)

2 Tbsp. fresh tarragon, chopped (25 mL)

2 large cloves garlic, chopped

1 tsp. Dijon mustard (5 mL)

½ tsp. fresh lemon juice (2 mL)

½ tsp. Tabasco sauce (2 mL)

salt and pepper to taste

- For the sauce, add the roasted peppers, mayonnaise, fresh tarragon, garlic, Dijon, lemon juice and Tabasco to a blender. Mix until smooth.

- Season to taste with salt and pepper.

- To serve, place one crab cake on top of each toasted slice of pumpernickel. Slice and top with a small dollop of the sauce.

Asiago and Pasta Crab Cakes

Preparation: easy • Serves 6 • Recipe by Chris Knight

You're going to die when you make this. Not only is this appetizer delicious—it also looks très cool. The recipe calls for semi-firm nutty sweet Asiago cheese, which acts as a great counterpoint to the crab. You can substitute mozzarella or any other cheese that is soft enough to melt easily but hard enough to help bind the cake.

2 Tbsp. unsalted butter or olive oil (25 mL)

2 cloves garlic, finely diced

2 shallots, finely diced

½ pound thin pasta (preferably angel hair) (250 g)

2 eggs, beaten

¼ cup Italian parsley, finely diced (50 mL)

¼ cup fresh cilantro, finely diced (50 mL)

⅓ cup Dijon mustard (75 mL)

10 ounces Asiago cheese, grated (300 g)

2 Tbsp. all-purpose flour (30 mL)

½ red or yellow bell pepper, finely diced

10 ounces good-quality crabmeat, picked over, approx. 1.5 cups (375 mL) (300 g)

salt and pepper to taste

vegetable oil for pan-frying

- Add the butter to a medium-sized skillet and melt over a medium-high heat.

- Add the garlic and shallots and reduce the heat to medium. Cook until nicely brown and caramelized. Watch the heat, or the garlic will burn and you will have to start all over.

- Bring a large pot of salted water to a boil and add the pasta. Cook until *al dente* and drain. *Al dente* is Italian for "Damn! I lost a filling!" Let cool slightly but don't rinse, because you want the pasta a bit sticky.

- Once the pasta is done, transfer the shallots and garlic to a large mixing bowl and add the eggs, parsley, cilantro and mustard. Mix well and add the pasta. Mix some more. Use your hands. Get in there and feel your food. Be sure to wash your hands first though.

- Add the cheese, flour, diced pepper, crabmeat and salt and pepper and mix some more.

- Add just enough vegetable oil to coat a large skillet and bring to medium-high heat until the oil is hot but not smoking. Using your hands, scoop up some of the crab cake mixture and form a patty, just as you would do if you were making a small hamburger (about 2 inches/5 cm wide and 1½ inches/4 cm thick). Slide the crab cake into the oil and cook for about 3 minutes each side or until crispy brown. Continue to add crab cakes to the skillet, but make sure you don't overcrowd or the cakes won't crisp up.

- Transfer the finished cakes to paper towel to drain. Serve with a nice roasted red pepper and balsamic purée and chopped chives.

Crab Flan

Preparation: easy • Makes 6 servings • Recipe by Chef Georges Laurier

To a rookie, a flan sounds like an ominous to-do. Fear not—it's quite simple once you learn the secret of the *bain-marie*, a.k.a. the warm water bath (not for *you*, for the flan!). It keeps the soft moist egg and crab mixture from curdling and hardening. This dish is perfect as an appetizer or as a main course for brunch. The recipe calls for chervil, which has a mild anise flavour and is a member of the parsley family. As with all herbs, try to buy the fresh stuff.

1 pound queen crab leg meat, chopped
    into bite size pieces (500 g)
¾ cup 35% cream (175 mL)
¾ cup 2% milk (175 mL)
3 eggs
3 Tbsp. chopped chervil (45 mL)
1 Tbsp. unsalted butter (15 mL)
kosher salt and black pepper

- Preheat the oven to 300°F (150°C).
- Butter six 1-cup (250-mL) moulds and set them aside.
- Put all but 6 pieces of the crab in a food processor and add the cream, milk and eggs. Blend until it comes together and is smooth. Add salt and pepper to taste. Mix well.
- Put one piece of crab in the bottom of each mould. Cover with the egg and cream mixture. Cover with chopped chervil.
- Put the moulds in a baking dish and fill it to two-thirds full with hot water. Bake the flans in the oven for 15 to 20 minutes.
- Serve immediately.

Chef's Tip: To ensure you don't overcook your flan, test by gently shaking one mould. It should be firm on the outside, and jiggle in the centre. Remember the flan will continue to cook slightly after it has been removed from the oven.

Crab and Shrimp Soufflé with Red Bell Peppers and Tarragon

Preparation: easy • Serves 6 as an appetizer • Recipe by Chris Knight

Okay, this recipe is so a winner. First you got your charred red bell peppers. Then you add juicy shrimp and crab, a bit of tarragon and serve the whole thing up in that wondrous egg cloud known as *le soufflé*.

1 medium red bell pepper

¼ cup grated Parmesan cheese (50 mL)

½ cup crabmeat (125 mL)

½ cup small cooked shrimp (125 mL)

2 Tbsp. fresh whole tarragon leaves (25 mL)

1¾ tsp. salt (9 mL)

pepper

½ cup butter (125 mL)

½ cup all-purpose flour (125 mL)

1 large shallot, minced

⅛ tsp. cayenne pepper (.5 mL)

½ cup whole milk (125 mL)

1¼ cups dry white wine (300 mL)

6 large egg yolks

8 large egg whites

- Place the red bell pepper on a rack under the broiler, approximately 1 inch (2.5 cm) away from the heat. It will take about 10 minutes to brown, and should be turned.
- When the pepper is charred all over, remove from the broiler and place it in a paper bag.
- Close the bag and let the steam soften the pepper. This should take about 10 minutes. Remove the pepper from the bag, hold it by the stem and peel off the skin. Once all the skin is removed, pull the stem away from the pepper and with it will come most of the seeds. Remove any seeds left inside with a teaspoon.
- Preheat oven to 400°F (200°C) and position rack in the centre of the oven.
- Butter one 10-cup (2.5-L) soufflé dish or six 1¼-cup (300-mL) soufflé dishes. Sprinkle with parmesan cheese to coat. (If using the smaller soufflé dishes, place all six on a rimmed baking sheet.)
- Mix together the crabmeat, shrimp, roasted pepper and tarragon in a food processor. Blitz, making sure the seafood mixture is chopped finely. Season with 1 tsp. (5mL) salt and pepper.
- In a large heavy saucepan melt the butter over medium heat. Add the flour, shallot and cayenne pepper and cook without browning until mixture begins to bubble. You must whisk constantly.
- While whisking, gradually pour in the milk, then the wine. Cook until smooth, thick and beginning to boil, about 2 minutes. Remove from heat.
- Mix the egg yolks and ¾ tsp. salt together in a bowl, whisking quickly, and add the mixture to the sauce all at once. Stir in the seafood mixture and season to taste with salt and pepper.

- Beat the egg whites in a large bowl until stiff but not dry. Fold one-third of the egg whites into the soufflé base to lighten. Add the remaining whites. Then transfer the soufflé mixture to the soufflé dish or dishes.

- Carefully place the soufflé in the oven. Bake until puffed and golden. For a large soufflé, bake for about 30 minutes. For smaller soufflé dishes, bake for about 15 minutes.

Chef's Tip: Do not open or close the oven door while soufflés are rising as they'll quickly fall. If soufflés aren't served immediately, they'll fall.

Mussels in Curry Sauce

Preparation: easy • Serves 6 • Recipe by Chris Knight

There are three crimes against culinary humanity: margarine, canned potatoes and overcooked mussels. Mussels only take a couple of minutes, just long enough for them to open and they're ready. All you have to remember is to throw out the ones that are already open before cooking them, and throw out the ones that don't open after the cooking is done. A perfectly cooked mussel is tender, pregnant with juice, and ready to burst when you bite into it.

18 cloves garlic, peeled

12 Tbsp. unsalted butter, room temperature (180 mL)

1½ cups whipping cream (375 mL)

9 tsp. curry powder (45 mL) (see page 27)

8 pounds small mussels, scrubbed and debearded (4 kg)

9 Tbsp. clear cherry brandy or kirsch (135 mL)

- Place the garlic cloves in enough water to cover and boil for 5 minutes to blanch. Remove the garlic and cut the cloves in half. Combine the blanched garlic with room-temperature butter and blend together until it forms a paste. Blend in the whipping cream and curry powder.

- Heat a large skillet and add the curry butter, mussels and cherry brandy or kirsch. Cover and cook for 4–5 minutes until the mussels open. Remove the mussels with a slotted spoon and transfer them to serving bowls. Remember to discard any unopened mussels.

- Serve with lots of crusty bread and enjoy!

Linguine with Clams, Chorizo and White Wine

Preparation: easy • Makes 6 servings • Recipe by Chris Knight

This classic pasta dish is so simple and delicious you'll be making it at least once a month. Remember that your final dish is only as good as the ingredients you use, so don't skimp on the quality of the white wine. Rule of thumb: If it ain't good enough to drink, it ain't good enough to cook with.

2 pounds live clams (1 kg)

3 pounds chorizo sausages (1.5 kg)

6 Tbsp. olive oil (90 mL)

4 cloves garlic

3 tsp. smoked paprika (15 mL)

6 large tomatoes, diced

3 cups good white wine (750 mL)

1½ pounds fresh linguine (750 g)

salt and pepper

- Clean the clams, removing any mud or visible dirt.
- Remove the casing from the chorizo sausages and chop into bite-size slices.
- Heat a pan to medium-high heat with half the olive oil.
- Crush the garlic and add the sausage and garlic to the pan to sauté.
- Take care not to burn the garlic.
- After a couple of minutes, add the smoked paprika, diced tomatoes, white wine and clams. Cover the saucepan and leave to steam for 6 to 10 minutes or until the clams open and the sauce has thickened slightly. Stir occasionally.
- Drop the pasta into a large saucepan of boiling, salted water. Return to the boil and cook for one minute. Drain, toss with olive oil and divide between four plates. Ladle the clam, chorizo and white wine sauce overtop and serve immediately.

Chef's Tip: Do not grate cheese overtop. Most chefs feel cheese has no place on top of seafood pasta. The cheese flavour tends to compete with, as opposed to enhancing, the seafood flavours.

Chorizo is a spicy garlicky sausage common to Spanish and Mexican cooking. You can buy it in any reputable butcher shop and it provides counterpoint to the clams in this dish.

Corn, Shrimp and Chive Fritters

Preparation: easy • Makes 12 small fritters • Recipe by Chris Knight

This recipe works as an appetizer (2 fritters each with a dollop of lemon-chive sour cream) or as a side with your main fish course instead of ho-hum rice or spuds. It's super simple. Make the batter in advance and deep-fry *à la minute.*

canola oil for deep-frying

1 cup fresh corn kernels (250 mL)

½ cup baby shrimp (125 mL)

1 Tbsp. fresh chives (15 mL)

¼ cup buttermilk (50 mL)

1 egg

2½ tsp. baking powder (12.5 mL)

½ cup all-purpose flour (125 mL)

¼ tsp. (pinch) salt (1 mL)

¼ tsp. (a couple of turns) pepper (1 mL)

- Preheat the oil to 375°F (190°C) in a deep fryer or large saucepan.
- Stir together the corn, shrimp, chives, buttermilk and egg.
- In another bowl, sift the baking powder, flour, salt and pepper.
- Add the flour mixture to the corn mixture to make the batter.
- Drop the batter into the hot oil by the tablespoonful. Cook for 2 to 3 minutes, until puffy and golden. Drain on paper towels and sprinkle immediately with salt.

Chef's Tip: *Drop one fritter in to test its flavour and adjust if necessary. Never overcrowd your deep fryer. Your fritters will just fall apart and you'll end up serving nachos with velveeta as an appetizer.*

Matane Shrimp Chowder

Preparation: easy • Makes 6 servings • Recipe by Chef George Laurier

Matane shrimp are tiny, sweet little guys from the cold, deep waters of the Gulf of St. Lawrence. You always get them pre-cooked and frozen, so they go in the chowder near the end just to warm through. If they're not available where you are, any small shrimp (36–45 count) will do. The sourdough bread bowls aren't essential, but they do make for a novel way of serving.

6 small sourdough bread loaves

¾ cup vidalia onions, diced (175 mL)

¾ cup leeks, white part only, finely chopped (175 mL)

¾ cup carrots (175 mL)

¾ cup celery root, diced (175 mL)

3 Tbsp. butter (45 mL)

6 cups shellfish stock (1.5 L)

2 sprigs fresh thyme

2 bay leaves

¾ cup corn kernels (175 mL)

1½ cup 35% cream (375 mL)

12 ounces Matane or baby shrimp (375 g)

¾ cup chopped herbs (chives, parsley, coriander, chervil, etc.) (175 mL)

pepper and sea salt (grey salt)

- Cut the top off each of the loaves, about a quarter of the way down.
- Using your fingers, pull the bread out from inside the loaf so as to leave a hollowed-out bowl. Make sure you leave enough bread inside to contain the soup! Open the kitchen door and feed the bits of bread to the squirrels.
- Sweat the onion, leek, carrot and celery root with butter in a large pot over medium-low heat. The veggies should not brown, just soften and turn translucent ("sweating" as opposed to sautéing), for about 4 minutes.
- Add the shellfish stock, thyme and bay leaves. Simmer for about 5 minutes over a low heat.
- Add the corn kernels and the cream. Simmer for another 5 minutes.
- Add the shrimp and herbs and take the saucepan off the heat.
- Season to taste and serve by ladling into the bread bowls.
- Put the top back onto each bowl and serve.

Chef's Tip: If you don't have any seafood stock handy, substitute with 1 part vermouth, 2 parts bottled clam juice, 2 parts white wine and 4 parts water.

Coriander and Pumpkin Seed-Crusted Scallops

Preparation: easy • Makes 6 appetizers • Recipe by Chris Knight

Three nice crusted scallops on a plate with a bit of fennel and some good-quality olive or chive oil as a drizzle is a quality restaurant starter. Try and get "dry" scallops, meaning ones that haven't spent time in a phosphorous soaking bath, which gives off a filmy white goo when you cook them. Blah.

3 Tbsp. coriander seeds (45 mL)

5 Tbsp. pumpkin seeds (70 mL)

1 tsp. salt (5 mL)

1 tsp. pepper (5 mL)

18 large scallops

2 Tbsp. olive oil (25 mL)

- Preheat the oven to 375°F (190°C).
- Put the coriander seeds into a dry non-stick pan over a medium heat. Fry them until they smoke and release their aroma. Watch them closely because this doesn't take much time.
- Put the pumpkins seeds on a baking tray and roast in the oven until they are golden brown in colour and begin to release their aroma, around 10 minutes.
- Once cooled, crush the coriander and pumpkin seeds with the salt and pepper in a mortar with a pestle. Do it in batches if you have to and transfer to a bowl.
- Brush the scallops with a little olive oil and dip them to coat in the roast spice mixture.
- Heat the remainder of the olive oil (just enough to cover the surface of the pan) in a non-stick pan over a high heat. Once hot, turn the heat down to medium-high. Add the scallops and sear. Turn them once after a crust has formed, maybe a minute or so.
- Turn off the heat to finish the cooking, about 1 minute.
- Serve immediately with a radish salad with fennel, grapefruit and avocado.(see page 211)

Chef's Tip: Nothing is worse than an overcooked scallop. Resist the urge to cook them for more than a minute or so per side. You want a nice crust on the outside and just warmed through in the middle.

Inky Fried Squid

Preparation: medium • Makes 6 servings • Recipe by Chris Knight

Okay, so not everyone is going to be able to get their hands on squid with the ink sacs intact. This recipe works just as well without. The black squid ink just adds a funky cool colour to the dish. One more reason why you need a good fishmonger in your life. A nice store-bought spicy-sweet Thai dipping sauce would go nicely with this.

vegetable oil for frying

12 squid, 4 ink sacs intact

⅓ cup all-purpose flour (75 mL)

pinch salt

2 Tbsp. olive oil (25 mL)

2 eggs

⅔ cup club soda (150 mL)

all-purpose flour, for dredging

sea salt and chives for serving

- Clean the squid, keep the ink sacs aside, discard the beak and cut the squid into bite size pieces. Pat dry.
- Put the flour, salt and oil into a mixing bowl. Separate the eggs and add the yolks to the bowl, reserving the whites.
- Slowly pour in the club soda, beating with a whisk. The mix should resemble a thick pancake batter. Mix the ink sacs with a very small amount of water and add to the batter so that it changes colour.
- Beat the egg whites to soft peaks. Fold into the batter in thirds, stirring gently after each addition.
- Heat the oil to 375°F (190°C).
- Dip the squid in some flour and shake off the excess.
- Dip in the inky batter and fry immediately. Serve sprinkled with sea salt and chives.

Chef's Tip: The egg whites should be at room temperature before beating. Take care not to let any of the yolk get into the whites. Never beat egg whites until they look flaky, as they will not hold air. If this happens, add another white and whisk until creamy and glossy.

11 Pasta

Fava Bean Agnolotti with Curry Emulsion

Preparation: moderate • *Makes 6 servings* • *Recipe by Chef Michael Bonacini*

Agnolotti is Italian for "priest's cap," which will make sense after you've made a couple of these outstanding pasta pouches stuffed with a fava bean mascarpone sort of thing. The pasta is served with a thick and creamy spicy curry sauce.

Fava Bean Filling:

18 1-inch (2.5-cm) ramps or green onions

2–3 pounds fresh fava beans (1–1.5 kg)

¾ cup fresh bread crumbs (175 mL)

⅓ cup mascarpone (75 mL)

2 tsp. sage (10 mL)

2 tsp. thyme (10 mL)

kosher salt to taste

freshly ground pepper to taste

½ pound pasta dough (see page 34) (250g)

- In a large pot of boiling salted water, blanch the ramps or green onions. Cook until bright green and tender crisp. Refresh in ice water, drain and pat dry. Reserve.

For the Filling:

- Shell the fava beans and peel the skins from the beans (peeling the beans before cooking them prevents gases from being trapped between the bean and the skin that could cause discolouring).

- Remove the small germ at the side of each bean. You need 1½ cups (375 mL) of beans for the filling; reserve any extra beans for another use.

- Blanch the beans for approximately 5 minutes, or until tender, and immediately transfer to ice water to chill. When they are cold, drain them and spread on paper towels to drain thoroughly.

- Place the beans in a food processor with the bread crumbs. Blend until they come together and form a ball.

- Add the mascarpone, sage and thyme. Process again with on and off turns until the mixture is combined. Season to taste with salt. You will have 1–1¼ cups (250–300 mL) of filling—enough to fill 48 agnolotti.

- Refrigerate the mixture to cool.

To make the agnolotti:

- Roll the pasta dough on the thinnest setting of your pasta machine to approximately ¹⁄₁₆ inch (2 mm). Roll the pasta into four rectangles approximately 12 × 5 inches (30 × 12 cm). Cut the pasta evenly with a knife to create 48 squares, 2 × 2 inches (5 × 5 cm) in size.

Curry Emulsion:

2 tsp. curry powder (10 mL)

2 Tbsp. chopped green onions (25 mL)

¾ cup plus 2 Tbsp. vegetable stock,
    chicken stock or water
    (200 mL)

¼ cup heavy cream (50 mL)

¼ cup crème fraîche (50 mL)
    (see page 25)

1 cup unsalted butter, cut into chunks
    (250 mL)

kosher salt and freshly ground black
    pepper

18 1-inch (2.5-cm) pieces garlic sprouts or
    garlic chives

- Place the filling in a pastry bag fitted with a ½-inch (1-cm) plain tip.
- Pipe the filling in the centre of the pasta squares and leave a ¾-inch (2-cm) border.
- Fold the pasta over to make a triangle. Seal the edges with your finger by pressing down lightly and at the same time removing any air bubbles. You should have 48 small triangles with little balls of filling protruding when finished.
- With one hand, pick up each triangle and wrap the long base (the side where you have folded the pasta over with no seam) around your thumb and pinch, to seal both ends.
- Repeat until all the agnolotti are formed.

To complete:

- For the curry emulsion, toast the curry powder in a small saucepan over medium heat until it is fragrant, maybe 2 minutes or so.
- Stir in the green onions and heat for another minute. Add ¾ cup (175 mL) of stock or water, cream and crème fraîche. Bring to a simmer and cook until the liquid is reduced to ½ cup (125 mL).
- Swirl in the butter. When the butter is melted, transfer the sauce to a blender. Add the remaining 2 Tbsp. (25 mL) of stock and blend for 30 seconds to emulsify the mixture. Season with salt and pepper. Strain into a wide pan.
- Place the agnolotti in a large pot of lightly salted boiling water and boil until *al dente* (cooked with a slight resistance) for approximately 4 to 5 minutes.
- Drain the agnolotti in a colander.
- Add the agnolotti and ramps to the curry emulsion and toss over low heat to coat with sauce.
- Divide the agnolotti and ramps among six serving dishes and garnish the top of each with 3 garlic sprouts. Serve immediately.

Chef's Tip: *Ramps are also known as* wild leeks *and have sort of a leek-onion-scallion thing going on. They hit the market late March through April. They keep refrigerated for about a week and can be used raw, cooked or pickled. For me, a makeshift table piled high with bunches of ramps at the outdoor farmer's market is the true sign that spring is really here.*

Goat Cheese and Fresh Herb Cappelletti
with Asparagus and Brown Butter

Preparation: difficult • Makes 6 servings • Recipe by Chris Knight

I was sort of torn about whether or not to include this recipe. Don't get me wrong, it's a good one. The tangy cheese and herb pasta combo works extremely well with the woodsy asparagus and nutty brown butter. It's just that EVERYBODY is doing goat cheese these days. It's friggin' everywhere! You can't swing a dead cat without hitting some salad or pasta or stuffing that has goat's cheese in it. Have you ever seen a goat? They're like a fifth the size of cow. A cow can give milk until the goats come home, but a poor little goat needs a day off now and then. Anyway, if you're going to go chèvre it might as well be with this knockout recipe.

Filling:

1½ pounds fresh goat cheese, room
    temperature (750 g)

1 Tbsp. finely chopped garlic (15 mL)

¼ cup dry white wine (50 mL)

2 Tbsp. extra virgin olive oil (25 mL)

2 lemons, grated zest of

¾ cup finely chopped mixed fresh herbs
    (parsley, chervil, basil, chives,
    tarragon, and thyme, etc.) (175 mL)

2 Tbsp. fine fresh white bread crumbs
    (25 mL)

salt to taste

1 large egg yolk, beaten lightly

1½ pounds pasta dough (see page 34)

- To make the filling, combine the goat cheese, garlic, white wine, olive oil and lemon zest in a mixing bowl.
- Mix together thoroughly and gradually introduce the bread crumbs and the finely chopped herbs. Mix well and refrigerate overnight to allow herbs to infuse. Season with salt and pepper to taste.
- Place a large pot of salted water on to boil.
- Roll out half the pasta dough to a 12- × 10-inch (30- × 25-cm) rectangle. Repeat with the remaining dough. The pasta should be no thicker than 1⁄16 inch (2 mm).
- Using a knife and a ruler gently cut out 6 rows of five 2-inch (5-cm) squares on each pasta sheet.
- In the centre of each square, place a small amount of the filling and gently fold over to create triangles.
- Using the large lightly beaten egg yolk and your fingers, press down on the sides of the triangle to create an egg yolk seal. Once the sides have been sealed, fold the long tips of the triangle over each other to create a hat-like shape.
- Gently place the cappelletti into the boiling water and cook for 3–5 minutes, until they begin to float and become tender. Then carefully, without tearing, strain them with a slotted spoon.

continued on next page

Sauce:

1 pound asparagus, blanched and cut
    into 1-inch (2.5-cm) pieces (500 g)

¾ cup unsalted butter (175 mL)

salt and pepper to taste

½ cup freshly grated Parmesan cheese
    (125 mL)

1 cup torn basil for garnish (250 mL)

Parmesan cheese for garnish (optional)

- Store the cappelletti on a greased baking tray and cover with plastic wrap while you prepare the sauce.
- Blanch the asparagus in a pot of boiling salted water for approximately 1 minute.
- Refresh in a bowl of ice water. Pat dry.
- Heat the butter in small saucepan over moderate heat. Whisk sporadically until the butter solids turn light brown.
- Sprinkle in some salt and pepper and add the asparagus. Toss gently to coat.
- Add the cooked cappelletti. Continue to toss gently and completely coat the pasta with butter. Add the Parmesan cheese and toss to coat again.
- Plate the pasta, sprinkle with a touch more Parmesan and season with salt and pepper. Garnish with fresh torn basil and more Parmesan if desired.

Chef's Tip: When making fresh pasta, keep the dough covered with a damp towel. Place the cappelletti on a tray lined with cornmeal or flour to prevent sticking.

Spaghetti with Caviar and Champagne Sauce

Preparation: easy • Makes 6 servings • Recipe by Chris Knight

They say the best things in life are the simplest. Here is a perfect example of how a few excellent ingredients combine to make a rich, creamy, sweet AND simple dish. Now remember, as in all cooking, the final dish is only as good as the ingredients you use. This is definitely a special occasion dish, so don't skimp on the champers or the fish eggs!

1¾ cups clear vegetable stock (425 mL) (see page 30)

1½ cups champagne (375 mL)

2 sprigs thyme

2 shallots, finely chopped

big pinch freshly grated nutmeg

1¾ cups double cream (425 mL)

2 Tbsp. white wine vinegar (25 mL)

salt and pepper

1½ pounds fresh spaghetti (750 g)

3 Tbsp. olive oil (45 mL)

3 Tbsp. butter, chilled (45 mL)

6 ounces Sevruga caviar (175 g)

- Bring the stock, champagne, thyme, shallots and nutmeg to a boil.
- Reduce the heat to a simmer and reduce the liquid by three-quarters.
- Remove from the heat and strain through a fine mesh sieve.
- Whisk in the cream and vinegar and season lightly with salt and pepper.
- Plunge the spaghetti into a large saucepan of salted boiling water.
- Cook until *al dente*, drain, and toss with the olive oil and butter.
- Stir the spaghetti into the warm cream sauce and top with caviar. Serve immediately.

Chef's Tip: Caviar should never look greasy or pulpy. It shouldn't feel sticky or ooze liquid. Sevruga caviar is one of the smallest caviars, with delicate eggs sporting a dark grey colour. It's very tasty.

Scallops in a Spicy Broth with Soba Noodles

Preparation: easy • Makes 6 servings • Recipe by Chris Knight

Soba noodles are made from the bark of the Japanese miniature Soba tree. It stands only 8 inches (20 cm) tall and it takes twenty years for the bark to grow again, making soba bark powder only slightly less expensive than truffles or saffron.

Okay, that's not actually true. In fact, soba noodles are made from buckwheat and regular wheat flour, giving it that nice brown colour. Be careful though, as the noodles can turn to mush if overcooked even a little bit. There is another variety you can buy in Asian grocery stores that is made with powdered green tea leaves. Very cool.

Anyway, please buy your scallops from a reputable fishmonger and ask for "dry" scallops if you can (see page 172). And unless you're a high-end restaurant with great connections, most scallops you buy will have been frozen at one point, so don't let anyone fool you with a "fresh" one.

1 pound soba noodles (500 g)

2 Tbsp. extra virgin olive oil (25 mL)
   (plus extra for tossing pasta)

2 cups torn fresh shiitake mushrooms,
   stems removed (500 mL)

6 cups chicken stock (1.5 L)
   (see page 27)

salt and pepper

1½ cups snow peas (375 mL)

18 large sea scallops

¼ cup chopped and packed fresh cilantro
   (50 mL)

¼ cup chopped and packed fresh parsley
   (50 mL)

Spice Mixture:

6 small cloves garlic

1 Tbsp. dry-roasted coriander seeds
   (15 mL)

2 tsp. coarse sea salt (10 mL)

3 Tbsp. chopped fresh ginger (45 mL)

1 Tbsp. dried chilies (15 mL)

- Add the soba noodles to a pot of unsalted water and cook at a boil for 3 minutes.
- Drain the noodles and run them under cold water until chilled to stop the cooking process. Reserve in a colander.
- Toss with olive oil to prevent sticking.
- Grind the spice mixture ingredients in a mortar and pestle until the mixture is fine in texture.
- Heat the olive oil over medium heat until it is hot, but not smoking.
- Add the spice mixture and stir for 30 seconds until fragrant.
- Add the shiitake mushrooms and stir for another 30 seconds.
- Add the stock and season with salt and pepper. Simmer for 2 to 3 minutes.
- Add the snow peas and remove from the heat.
- Ladle some of the stock mixture into a separate skillet and bring to a simmer. Add the scallops and cover. Let the scallops cook for 30 to 45 seconds then remove from heat and let sit, covered, for approximately 2 minutes.
- Boil some water in a kettle. Pour over the noodles while they are still in the colander to reheat them. Drain the noodles thoroughly and divide them between 6 soup bowls. Spoon the scallops and sauce overtop. Divide the stock, snow peas and mushrooms between the bowls and garnish with fresh cilantro and parsley.

Crispy Fried Noodle Cake

Preparation: moderate • Makes 6 servings • Recipe by Chef Caroline McCann-Bizjak

If you're like me, you're tired of the same old spuds or pasta or rice as a side for a Tuesday night dinner. Well, check this one out. It's not a lot of work and is a nice change up from the same ol' same ol'. The crispiness is a nice counterpoint to a piece of fish or a some sliced pork tenderloin. Yum.

1 pound dried spaghetti (500 g)

1 cup onion, diced (250 mL)

2 Tbsp. unsalted butter (25 mL)

3 large eggs

1 cup heavy cream (250 mL)

1 cup grated mozzarella (250 mL)

¼ pound smoked ham, diced (125 g)

1 cup flat-leafed finely chopped parsley (250 mL)

1 tsp. salt (5 mL)

2 tsp. pepper (10 mL)

¾ cup clarified butter (175 mL) (see page 23)

¼ cup olive oil (50 mL)

1 Tbsp. minced garlic (15 mL)

1 Tbsp. balsamic vinegar (15 mL)

4 large tomatoes, chopped coarsely

3 Tbsp. torn fresh basil (45 mL)

- Preheat oven to 350°F (180°C).
- Cook the pasta in a large pot of boiling salted water until al dente.
- Add the onion and the unsalted butter to a large frying pan and sauté over medium heat until the onion is golden brown, approximately 5 minutes.
- Whisk together the eggs and cream in a large bowl and add them to the frying pan.
- Stir the mozzarella, ham and parsley into the frying pan and season with salt and pepper. Add the pasta.
- Combine the contents by tossing the pasta and sauce thoroughly.
- Grease a medium springform pan along the interior with room-temperature butter.
- Pour the pasta mixture into the pan, which will then be set on a baking tray. Press down to pack in the mixture.
- Place the baking tray in the middle of the oven and bake for approximately 1 hour and 15 minutes, or until the centre of the top layer is firm when touched.
- Leave the baking dish with pasta to cool on a rack for 30 minutes.
- Refrigerate to chill for at least 3 hours, or up to 24 hours.
- Once cool, pass a sharp knife around the pan in order to cleanly separate the pasta cake from the sides of the pan.
- Transfer on to a working surface and cut in twelve wedges.
- Place four wedges in a hot skillet over medium heat with 4 Tbsp. (60 mL) of clarified butter.

- Cook until crispy and golden brown on all sides, flipping as each side turns brown. You will have to do this in batches of four. The pan must be hot and not overcrowded.

- Repeat with the remaining eight wedges, cooking four per batch.

- To make the sauce, heat ¼ cup (50 mL) of olive oil in a small skillet at medium to high heat. Allow the oil to get very hot but not smoking.

- Add the garlic and sauté until fragrant.

- Add the balsamic vinegar and chopped tomatoes, and season with salt and pepper.

- Stir occasionally and let it cook for 2 minutes. Remove from heat and add 3 Tbsp. (45 mL) fresh basil.

- Ladle the sauce over the noodle cake.

- Serve and enjoy.

12 Veggies

Tomato Basil Sauce

Preparation: easy • Makes 6 cups (1.5 L) of sauce • Recipe by Chris Knight

Most pre-made pasta sauce is good for only one thing: laboratory rats. Check the ingredients on the back. Chances are you'll find lots of salt and sugar and an assortment of stabilizers and preservatives … mmmmm … mondocraptomate! Just like Mom used to make! Check this recipe out: 6 ingredients plus S and P. I promise you a better taste than anything you buy in a jar.

¼ cup olive oil (50 mL)

6 cloves garlic, minced

1 medium onion, diced

1 Tbsp. granulated sugar (15 mL)

1 cup chopped fresh basil (250 mL)

4 pounds plum tomatoes, seeded and chopped (2 kg)

salt and pepper

- Preheat oven to 375°F (190°C).
- Heat the oil in a large ovenproof skillet over medium-high heat until hot.
- Add the garlic and onion and reduce the heat to medium. Cook for 5 minutes, or until the onion has become translucent but not browned.
- Add the sugar and half the basil and sauté for 1 minute longer.
- Add the tomatoes and stir some more. Transfer the sauce to the oven and cook for 40 minutes, uncovered.
- Remove from the oven and stir in the rest of the basil. Adjust seasoning with salt and pepper.
- Serve with your favourite pasta and a big fruity red wine.

Chef's Tip: This sauce is best made in the height of tomato season. The tomatoes should be ruby red and ripe for best results. The sauce can be frozen for times when tomatoes are not at their best.

Stuffed Roasted Tomato with Goat Cheese Fondant and Crispy Basil

Preparation: easy • Makes 6 appetizers • Recipe by Chef René Rodriguez

Don't feel intimidated by the number of ingredients in this recipe ... it's really just a bunch of chopping and stuffing. But what a combination! The macerated raisins and figs with herbs stuffed into a juicy plump roasted tomato and that *chèvre fondant* (which means goat cheese sauce in Anglais) make for a killer appetizer.

3 Tbsp. sultana raisins (45 mL)

2 large figs, chopped

¼ cup red port (50 mL)

3 Tbsp. golden raisins (45 mL)

2 Tbsp. finely chopped orange rind (25 mL)

1 Tbsp. finely chopped lemon zest (15 mL)

¼ cup Sauternes (50 mL)

2 Tbsp. chopped fresh fennel (25 mL)

3 Tbsp. pine nuts (45 mL)

1 Tbsp. finely minced garlic (15 mL)

2 Tbsp. finely minced shallots (25 mL)

2 Tbsp. chopped walnuts (25 mL)

2 Tbsp. sherry vinegar (25 mL)

¼ cup extra virgin olive oil (50 mL)

1 Tbsp. chopped mint (15 mL)

1 Tbsp. chopped tarragon (15 mL)

2 Tbsp. chopped celery (25 mL)

1 vanilla bean (scraped)

3 Tbsp. fresh white bread crumbs (45 mL)

1 tsp. sugar (5 mL)

salt and pepper to taste

6 medium vine-ripened tomatoes

- In a small stainless steel bowl, soak (macerate) the sultana raisins and figs with the port for two hours.

- In a separate stainless steel bowl, soak (macerate) the golden raisins, orange rind and lemon zest with the Sauternes for the same two hours.

- In a large non-reactive bowl, combine all the remaining ingredients except the tomatoes, goat cheese, cream and basil and set the bowl aside.

- Preheat the oven to 350°F (180°C).

- Drain the port from the figs and the Sauternes from the raisins and add the fruit to the bowl. Mix well.

- Remove the tops from the tomatoes and reserve. Scoop out the inside of the tomatoes using a small spoon. Stuff well with the fruit mix and place the tomato tops back on the tomatoes. Bake in the oven for 20–25 minutes or until slightly tender and still holding their shape.

- Remove the tomatoes from the heat and set aside for a few minutes.

continued on next page

To serve:

¾ cup goat cheese (175 mL)

¼ cup heavy cream (50 mL)

salt and pepper

8 basil leaves

olive oil to taste

- Mix the goat cheese, cream and a few drops of water in a food processor. Blend until smooth and season with salt and pepper. Spoon this mixture (fondant) onto the centre of each plate, place 1 tomato on top and garnish with torn basil leaves and a few drops of extra virgin olive oil.

Tomato Tarte Tatin

Preparation: easy • Makes 6 appetizers • Recipe by Chef Caroline McCann-Bizjak

Hey, guess what? For this one, you get to make a gastrique! HONEY, GET IN HERE! I'M MAKING A GASTRIQUE! Gastrique is the devilish French technique of adding vinegar (liquid and tart) to sugar just as it becomes caramel (syrupy and sweet), adding a zing to this funky take on the classic tatin.

4 Tbsp. olive oil (60 mL)
   (plus extra for drizzling)
4 large onions, sliced
1 cup chicken stock (250 mL)
   (see page 27)
1 Tbsp. white wine vinegar (15 mL)
salt and pepper to taste
⅓ cup granulated sugar (75 mL)
½ tsp. sherry vinegar (2 mL)
12 oven-dried tomato halves
   (see page 24)
12 ounces prepared puff pastry (375 g)
18 Niçoise olives, pitted

- Preheat oven to 325°F (160°C).
- Place the garlic cloves (skins still on) in a small ovenproof skillet. Drizzle with some olive oil and cover with foil. Roast in preheated oven until tender and fragrant, about 15 minutes.
- Heat the 4 Tbsp. (60mL) olive oil in large pan. Add the onions and allow them to sauté slowly until golden and translucent.
- Add the chicken stock and the white wine vinegar and allow the mixture to continue cooking until all the liquid has evaporated. By this time the onions should be a rich golden colour. Season to taste with salt and pepper.
- Put the sugar in a pot with 1 Tbsp. (15 mL) of water and allow the mixture to caramelize (the sugar will turn a nut-brown colour) over a medium-high heat.
- Remove the pot from the heat and add the sherry vinegar to the caramel. Swirl the pan until the liquids are combined. The sugar is hot so take extra care. This is your gastrique.
- Pour the caramel into four 1-cup (250-mL) ramekins. Allow the caramel to cool for a minute. Put two halves of dried tomato into each ramekin. Top with the onions.
- Preheat oven to 425°F (220° C).
- Roll out the puff pastry to ¼ inch (5 mm) and cut into rounds slightly larger than the ramekins. Place the pastry rounds over the onions.
- Tuck the pastry slightly inside the ramekins. Transfer to the oven and bake until the pastry is puffed and golden, about 15 minutes.

continued on next page

- Turn the tarts upside down onto plates. The pastry should be on the bottom. You may need to run a knife around the ramekins to loosen them.
- Top with a roasted garlic clove, decorate with olives and serve warm.

Chef's Tip: Puff pastry is many layers of pastry with butter between each layer. The pastry rises by the process of lamination. If it gets too warm, it will not rise and will have a slightly undercooked appearance and taste, so keep it as cold as you can. If it is warm after rolling out the circles, simply place in the refrigerator until chilled.

Tomato Zabaglione

Preparation: moderate • Makes 6 servings • Recipe by Chef Caroline McCann-Bizjak

Looking for a little something to wow those food-snob neighbours? Here it is. Zabaglione, also known as Sabayon, is a classic Italian foamy dessert. In this case, Chef has turned it on its ear by incorporating tiny sweet tomatoes into the mix. The dessert not only looks stunning, but one mouthful of the creamy sweet foam coupled with the perfectly odd pairing of fruit, tomatoes and chocolate will set your taste buds to gaga.

2 Tbsp. sour cherry extract (25 mL)

¼ cup granulated sugar (50 mL)

4 egg yolks

1 cup 35% cream (250 mL)

¼ cup shaved semi-sweet chocolate (50 mL)

6 tiny pear tomatoes

1 cup blueberries (250 mL)

chocolate curls for decoration

- Mix the cherry extract and sugar in a stainless steel bowl.
- Whisk in the egg yolks.
- Place the bowl over a pot of simmering water. Whisk constantly until the mixture is very light and fluffy and there is no liquid at the bottom of the bowl. It should hold its shape for a moment when you drop some from the whisk.
- Whisk over a bowl of ice to chill down immediately.
- Whip the cream and fold into the mix.
- Fold in the shaved chocolate.
- Chop the tomatoes very finely. Add half the chopped tomatoes and half the blueberries. Chill.
- To serve: In the bottom of a martini glass or glass ramekin, layer the blueberries, then the zabaglione. Top it off with more berries and the remainder of the chopped tomatoes.
- Sprinkle with chocolate curls.

Chef's Tip: If pear tomatoes are not available, substitute with heirloom tomatoes. They also have a distinct sweetness.

Garlic Marmalade

Preparation: easy • Makes 2 cups (500 mL) • Recipe by Chef Georges Laurier

Good Chefs know that often it's the little extra on the plate that elevates a dish to Oh-My-God-I-Think-I've-Died status. A simply grilled piece of quality fish or beef becomes the stuff of legends when served with just the right sauce or drizzle or, in this case, marmalade. Think lamb chops or pork tenderloin with a dollop of this sweet-garlicky marmalade on the side. Yum. You can prepare it in advance, as it will keep, refrigerated, for about 10 days.

¼ cup extra virgin olive oil (50 mL)

6½ ounces chopped garlic flower (185 g)

3 Tbsp. sugar (45 mL)

2 Tbsp. chopped fresh thyme (25 mL)

2 Tbsp. chopped chives (25 mL)

3 Tbsp. red wine (45 mL)

⅓ cup red wine vinegar (75 mL)

salt and freshly ground pepper to taste

½ cup chopped pistachio nuts (125 mL)

- Heat the olive oil in a small stainless steel pot. Add the garlic flower, sugar and chopped herbs.
- Cook for about 5 minutes at medium temperature, until fragrant.
- Add the red wine, vinegar, salt and freshly ground black pepper. Cook for another 2 minutes.
- Finally, add the pistachios and mix well.

Chef's Tip: Garlic flowers are available only in the summer months. They have a distinct sweet mild garlic flavour.

Roasted Garlic Compound Butter

Preparation: easy • Makes 1½ cups butter (375 mL) • Recipe by Chef Georges Laurier

All "compound" means is adding something to the butter, whether lemon zest or herbs or, in this case, roasted garlic. If you're doing the dinner party thing, make this the day before to let the flavours set up.

1 whole head garlic

2 Tbsp. olive oil (25 mL)

1 cup unsalted butter, room temperature (250 mL)

¼ cup chopped organic parsley, cleaned and stemmed (50 mL)

salt and freshly ground black pepper to taste

- Preheat oven to 300°F (150°C).
- Cut the garlic head in half and place both halves, exposed sides up, on a baking tray.
- Pierce the exposed surfaces with a fork and drizzle with the olive oil.
- Cover the tray with foil, and bake until the garlic is soft and the sweet perfumes are distinct. Bake for approximately 30 minutes. Let cool, then peel.
- In a mixing bowl, mix the butter until it is soft. Add the peeled roasted garlic.
- Mix with a wooden spoon until the garlic is evenly distributed. Add the chopped parsley, salt and pepper.
- Roll in the form of a cigar and wrap in plastic. Place in refrigerator.
- When the butter has chilled for 3 hours slice in rounds.
- Use as garnish on vegetables, grilled meats and warm breads.

Chef's Tip: *To remove the garlic from the head, simply grab the closed end of the garlic bulb and squeeze gently. The garlic cloves will pop out of their skins.*

Twice-Baked Fancy Potatoes with Saffron

Preparation: easy • Makes 6 servings • Recipe by Chris Knight

Even in these crazy no-carb days, everyone needs a nice baked potato once in a while. So if you're going to treat yourself to a spud, it might as well be something special. In this recipe you bake the spud, scoop out the insides and add butter and milk for creaminess, peas and pancetta for taste and texture, and saffron for a brilliant rusty red orange colour, THEN you bake 'em again!

6 large russet potatoes, cleaned with skin on

6 Tbsp. unsalted butter, melted (90 mL)

salt and pepper to taste

½ cup unsalted butter, softened (125 mL)

1 cup whole milk (250 mL)

1 Tbsp. saffron (15 mL)

¾ cup cooked green peas (175 mL)

½ cup diced pancetta (125 mL)

- Preheat oven to 400°F (200°C).
- With a fork, prick the potatoes, then place on a baking sheet. Bake in the middle of the oven for 1 hour, or until tender.
- When the potatoes are just cool enough to handle, halve lengthways and scoop out flesh into a bowl, making sure to leave ¼ inch (5 mm) of potato around the shells.
- Place the potato shells on a baking sheet, brush the insides with the 6 Tbsp. (90 mL) melted butter and season with salt and pepper. Bake in the oven for approximately 15 minutes or until golden brown.
- Meanwhile, put the potato flesh through a ricer. Stir in the unsalted butter and mix until it has completely dissolved.
- Over medium heat, add the milk to a saucepan and bring to simmer.
- Add the saffron and continue to simmer over low heat until fragrant.
- Add the warm milk to the riced potatoes and season with salt and pepper. Mix in the cooked green peas.
- Remove the golden brown potato shells from the oven and fill them with the mashed potato mixture. Place them back on the baking sheet and cook for another 10 minutes.
- Meanwhile, in a small skillet cook the diced pancetta until crispy.
- Sprinkle on top of the fancy potatoes.

Chef's Tip: *A ricer is a large kitchen tool that resembles a large garlic press. Cooked vegetables are pressed through tiny holes that resemble rice. It makes the final purée extra smooth. It is well worth buying. However, if you don't have one, just use a potato masher.*

Sweet and Mashed Potato Napoleons au Gratin

Preparation: moderate • Makes 4 servings • Recipe by Chris Knight

I love new ways to serve the same old starch component to a meal. It's amazing how making two types of spuds (sweet and regular) instead of one and then stacking them turns a plate from really good to really great.

3 pounds yellow flesh potatoes (1.5 kg)

3 large sweet potatoes

2 Tbsp. olive oil (25 mL)

salt and pepper

1 cup kalamata olives (250 mL)

1 red bell pepper

1 yellow pepper

1 cup whole milk (250 mL)

6 Tbsp. unsalted butter (90 mL)

3 cloves garlic, minced

¾ cup fresh white bread crumbs (175 mL)

¾ cup chopped parsley (175 mL)

¼ cup Parmesan cheese (50 mL)

You will need 4 napoleon tubes for this recipe.

- Preheat oven to 350°F (180°C).

- In a large pot, cover the yellow flesh potatoes, peels on, with cold salted water and bring to a boil. Let boil for 10 minutes. Reduce heat and simmer until potatoes are tender, maybe 5 minutes or so.

- Using a knife or a mandolin, slice the sweet potatoes to ¼-inch (5-mm) slices. Use your napoleon tube like a cookie cutter and press into a round of sweet potato. This will create the perfect size of round potato.

- Repeat until all the sweet potatoes are done. You will need 12 rounds.

- Brush the sweet potato rounds with oil and season with salt and pepper. Place on a baking tray lined with parchment and roast in the oven until slightly tender. Cook for approximately 10 minutes.

- Remove the pits from the kalamata olives and slice thinly. Finely dice the red and yellow pepper to resemble confetti.

- Once the yellow flesh potatoes are cool enough to handle, peel and place in a bowl.

- In a small saucepan combine the milk and 2 Tbsp. (25 mL) of the butter; simmer until butter is completely melted. Add to the warm potatoes and mash until smooth.

- Place the minced garlic and the remaining butter in a hot skillet and sauté for a few seconds until fragrant.

- Add the bread crumbs, and cook until light and golden. Remove from the heat and stir in ½ cup (125 mL) parsley and the Parmesan cheese.

- Place the four napoleon tubes on a baking sheet lined in parchment. The parchment will ensure that the napoleons are easy to remove when they are done.

continued on next page

To assemble:

- Place a roasted round of sweet potato in the bottom of each napoleon tube.

- Place a 1-inch (2.5-cm) layer of mashed potato on top and smooth out with a spoon.

- Sprinkle half of the diced peppers on the mashed potato.

- Place another round of sweet potato on top.

- Repeat with mashed potato as above.

- Evenly distribute half the olives over the potatoes.

- Place the final sweet potato round on top.

- Top with the toasted bread crumbs.

- Bake the potato towers in the oven until cooked through and golden on top, approximately 10–15 minutes.

- Transfer each tube to serving plates. Remove the casing by running a knife around the tube. Garnish plates with the remaining olives, parsley and diced peppers.

Chef's Tip: *Napoleon tubes are stainless steel and come in a range of sizes. If you don't have the tubes, you can make your own with the same size (14-ounce/398-g) clean tin can.*

Potato Confit en "Sous-Vide"

Preparation: easy • Makes 6 side dish servings • Recipe by Chef René Rodriguez

"Sous-vide" is a French culinary term meaning "in vacuum." We have a rather less elegant name for it in English—it's called vacuum-packed. Yup, good old vac-packed, as in those horrible cold cuts or industrial one-bag dinners. Yuck! However, here we apply the principle of vacuum-packing with mouth-watering results. In this case we add potatoes and duck fat to a baggie and poach them in a water bath. Yummers!

3 large Yukon gold potatoes

1 cup duck fat (softened) (250 mL)

3 cloves garlic, whole

1 tsp. salt (5 mL)

pinch white pepper

3 Tbsp. shaved Parmesan cheese (45 mL)

2 tsp. ground porcini mushrooms (10 mL)

truffle oil to drizzle

- Bring a medium pot of water to a simmer.
- Peel the potatoes and cut each into 4 wedges.
- Turn the potato wedges into a barrel shape about 3 inches (8 cm) long and 1 inch (2.5 cm) thick. Not comfortable doing this? No problem, just leave them as wedges.
- Put the potatoes in a large zip-lock bag with the duck fat, garlic and seasoning and expel any excess air from the bag.
- Seal it and place it in the simmering water. Cook for 35 minutes, or until the potatoes are tender.
- Drain the fat from the bag and serve the potatoes with shaved Parmesan, ground porcini mushrooms and a few drops of truffle oil.

Chef's Tip: You can get rendered duck fat at any reputable butcher. If none is available, you can always substitute bacon fat. The truffle oil drizzle is a great touch, but don't pass on this dish if you don't have any around.

Scalloped Sweet Potatoes with Leek and Blue Cheese

Preparation: moderate • Serves 6 as a side dish • Recipe by Chef Ned Bell

If you're like me and think really bad buffet when you hear "scalloped potatoes," then you have to try this recipe. The combo of the stinky blue cheese with leeks dances in your mouth when served up with slices of achingly soft sweet potato. Nutmeg is the secret ingredient, as it has this flavour enhancer thing going on like it was Mother Nature's MSG.

1 Tbsp. butter for buttering pan (15 mL)

3 large sweet potatoes

4 leeks

2 Tbsp. olive oil (30 mL)

salt and freshly ground black pepper
    to taste

⅓ cup clarified butter (75 mL)
    (see page 23)

2 tsp. freshly grated nutmeg (10 mL)

1½ cups Danish Blue cheese, crumbled
    (375 mL)

1 cup milk (250 mL)

- Preheat oven to 350°F (180°C).
- Generously butter a large rectangular shallow baking dish (11 × 7 × 2 inches /28 × 18 × 5 cm).
- Peel the sweet potatoes and slice them into ⅛-inch (3-mm) thick rounds using a mandolin. Submerge in water to halt discolouration and set aside.
- Cut the green tops off the leeks on a diagonal and discard. Cut the white part of the leeks in ⅛-inch (3-mm) diagonal slices. Wash in a bowl of cold water, then gently shake to remove excess water and place in colander to dry. Repeat washing several times if there is still any dirt.
- Heat a large skillet with the olive oil. Add the leeks to the pan and sauté just to slightly soften, about 2 minutes. Cool.
- Drain the sweet potato slices and pat dry with a towel.
- Place a layer of overlapping sweet potatoes on the bottom of the buttered baking dish. Sprinkle with salt and pepper.
- Cover the potatoes with a layer of leeks (about half of them). Brush lightly with some clarified butter and sprinkle with the freshly grated nutmeg.
- Crumble ¼ cup (50 mL) of blue cheese on top. Add another layer of potatoes, leek, butter, nutmeg and cheese. Add one more layer of potato slices and top with the remaining cheese.
- Pour the milk overtop and finish with more generous sprinkles of clarified butter. Cover with aluminum foil and bake for 20 minutes.
- Remove foil and bake for another 20 minutes, until the cheese is nicely browned and the potatoes are cooked through.

Chef's Tip: *A mandolin is a helpful tool in the kitchen. It is a hand-operated machine with an adjustable blade for thick or thin cutting. It cuts with precision and keeps vegetables uniform.*

Barley "Risotto"

Preparation: moderate • Makes 6 servings • Recipe by Chef Georges Laurier

I once sat through an achingly pompous dinner-table debate among three prominent national food writers about how risotto can't be risotto unless it's made with Italian *Arborio superfino*. Yah yah. There's nothing more precious than a foodie know-it-all. What makes this recipe interesting is the use of barley instead of Arborio. You get asparagus stock, by the way, from simmering the tough woody ends of the asparagus stalks in a bit of water.

6 roma tomatoes

⅔ pound asparagus, chopped (350 g)

*6 cups vegetable stock (1.5 L)
(see page 30)*

3 Tbsp. olive oil (45 mL)

1 large onion, finely chopped

2 Tbsp. garlic, finely chopped (25 mL)

1½ pounds barley (750 g)

4 vine-ripened tomatoes, diced

*2 medium zucchini, chopped in ½-inch
(1-cm) dice*

*1½ cups freshly grated Parmesan
(375 mL)*

salt and black pepper

⅓ pound asparagus tips (170 g)

3 cups reduced asparagus stock (750 mL)

5 Tbsp. chopped fresh basil (75 mL)

- With the roma tomatoes, prepare a tomato concassé (see page 25).
- In a pot of boiling water, cook the asparagus until bright green and still crisp. Remove and plunge in ice water. Pat dry and reserve for garnish.
- In a medium-sized saucepan warm the vegetable stock.
- Heat the olive oil in a heavy-bottomed pan over a medium-high heat.
- Add the onion and garlic and cook until golden, about 3 minutes.
- Add the barley and sauté for 1 minute.
- Add the vine-ripened tomatoes and stir well, reduce the heat to low and let the flavours mingle for a minute or so.
- Add ½ cup (125 mL) of warm vegetable stock and continue stirring until the liquid has been absorbed.
- Constantly stirring, repeat this process of adding the liquid slowly to the barley.
- When the barley is almost cooked, add the zucchini and continue to cook until barley is *al dente* (when it offers a slight resistance when bitten into).
- Stir in the parmesan and season with salt and pepper.
- Place the barley risotto in a bowl, garnish with additional asparagus tips, tomato concassé, reduced asparagus stock and fresh basil.

Chef's Tip: To clean asparagus, hold each spear at both ends and bend gently. Where the asparagus tip snaps is where the tough woody part of the asparagus begins.

Roasted Onions with Chive Oil

Preparation: easy • Makes 6 side servings • Recipe by Chef Tim McRoberts

Onions are related to lilies. Shallots are sort of onions but more closely resemble garlic because of their segmented cloves. Garlic is also related though it bears no resemblance in taste or looks to either, or to a lily for that matter. A leek does, however, look like a green onion, which is also called a scallion, though not all scallions are green onions. Confused? I am. Think of them all as variations on a theme and when combined, as in this dish, they make for a rich, complex side dish that heightens the taste of whatever main is lucky enough to be plated alongside.

16 green onions, trimmed

2 large leeks, trimmed and washed

12 small-sized yellow onions, skinned and
    cut in quarters

8 shallots, peeled

12 pearl onions, skinned

8 cloves garlic, halved

olive oil for drizzling, approx. 3 Tbsp.
    (45 mL)

salt and pepper

1 bunch chives

½ cup canola oil (125 mL)

- Preheat oven to 350°F (180°C).
- Put the cleaned green onions on a baking sheet lined with parchment, drizzle with olive oil and salt and pepper and roast until tender, about 10 to 12 minutes. Do the same thing with the leeks.
- Put the yellow onions, shallots, pearl onions and garlic on another tray, drizzle with olive oil and season with salt and pepper. Roast for 15 to 18 minutes, turning occasionally, or until tender and caramelized.
- Cut up the chives with a pair of scissors and add them to the bowl of a food processor. Add the canola oil and a pinch of salt to taste. Whiz until the oil has a creamy consistency.
- Serve the roasted onions warm, drizzled with the chive oil.

Chef's Tip: Onions have a high sugar content. When roasted, the sugary juice is released and, with heat, turns to caramel.

Onion Demi-Glace

Preparation: moderate • Makes 2 cups (500 mL) • Recipe by Chef René Rodriguez

Here is a vegetarian twist on the classic demi-glace sauce. The sweet Vidalia onions and the dark toasted bread make for a rich complex sauce that is surprisingly like the beef-based version.

2 Tbsp. butter (25 mL)

1 cup diced porcini or shiitake mushrooms (250 mL)

2 cups cold water (500 mL)

1 piece dark-toasted white bread

salt and pepper

2 Tbsp. canola oil (25 mL)

2 large Vidalia onions, peeled and cut in half

4 Tbsp. turbinado sugar (60 mL)

1 head garlic, spilt in half

¼ cup sherry vinegar (50 mL)

1 bottle red Bordeaux wine (750 mL)

1 tsp. coriander seeds (5 mL)

1 bay leaf

1 tsp. black peppercorns (5 mL)

2 sprigs thyme

2 Tbsp. dark soy sauce (25 mL)

- In a small pot, over medium-low heat, melt the butter and sweat (cook with no colour) the mushrooms for 2 minutes.

- Add the 2 cups (500 mL) of cold water and simmer for 30 minutes. You should be left with 1½ cups (375 mL) of mushroom stock.

- Add the toasted bread and remove the pan from the heat. Let cool for 20 minutes. Strain, season with salt and pepper and set stock aside.

- Heat the canola oil in a medium non-reactive, ovenproof saucepan over medium heat. Place the onion pieces flat side down and cook for approximately 15 minutes. Flip the onions halfway through for a nice caramelized colour on both sides.

- Add the sugar and garlic and continue to cook until light caramel forms. Add the sherry vinegar.

- Deglaze with the red wine and add the coriander seeds, bay leaf, peppercorns and thyme. Bring to a low simmer and reduce by half.

- Preheat oven to 350°F (180°C).

- Add the mushroom stock to the saucepan and cover with foil. Transfer to the oven to cook for another 1½ hours in the oven. Check on the mixture; if it's getting too dry add some water.

- Strain the cooked sauce through a fine sieve into a clean saucepan. Press on the solids to release all the flavour.

- Place the sauce over medium-low heat and simmer.

- Add the dark soy sauce and reduce until the sauce coats the back of a spoon.

- Use hot, or cover and chill. It will keep for 4 days refrigerated.

Chef's Tip: *When you add bread to a sauce it acts as a thickener. Meat demi-glaces have bones with gelatin to thicken them.*

Raw Sugar is what's left after the molasses has been yanked out of sugarcane. Turbinado sugar is raw sugar that's been steam-cleaned to get rid of impurities. In a pinch, good old-fashioned brown sugar always works in the same quantity.

Balsamic Onion Marmalade

Preparation: easy • Makes 1½ cups (375 mL) • Recipe by Chef Tim McRoberts

I love this recipe. The more I cook the more I realize that the best meals are the ones that feature the best ingredients simply prepared. Take a nice chop or a chicken breast with a few spices and grill it. Roast a roast. Braise a shank. It's all about letting the flavour and texture of what you're cooking shine through, rather than burying it under a cloying sauce or crust. A little dollop of this onion marmalade with a veal chop or grilled sea bass (not the endangered kind of course) or thinly sliced leg of lamb highlights the protein without overpowering it.

2 Tbsp. peanut oil (25 mL)

4 medium onions, finely chopped

⅓ cup sugar (75 mL)

⅔ cup balsamic vinegar (150 mL)

1 tsp. freshly grated nutmeg (5 mL)

salt and pepper to taste

- Heat the peanut oil in a saucepan over a moderate heat. Add the onions and allow them to cook gently until they are soft, about 20 minutes.
- Add the sugar and reduce the heat. Cook until the onions appear dry, then add the balsamic vinegar and the nutmeg.
- Reduce the heat to low and allow the onions and vinegar to cook until dry, about 1 hour. Stir occasionally.
- Serve warm or store in the refrigerator for several weeks.

Chef's Tip: Balsamic vinegar is Italian vinegar made from white Trebbiano grape juice. It gets its dark colour from being aged in various styles of barrels and woods. The best way to choose your balsamic vinegar is much the same as you choose wine—by taste.

Fried Artichokes and Frisée Salad
with Lardons and Raspberry Vinaigrette

Preparation: moderate • Makes 6 servings • Recipe by Chef Caroline McCann-Bizjak

If you've only ever had marinated artichoke hearts from a jar, are you in for a treat! The only tough part of this recipe is getting to the choke way down inside all those spiny leaves. Buy a couple of extra to practice on. It's a breeze once you get the hang of it. The crispy fried chokes are served piping hot on salad greens and are offset by the smoky saltiness of the double-smoked bacon (available from any self-respecting butcher) and the tart sweetness of the raspberry vinaigrette. Enjoy.

6 baby artichokes

3 lemons

6 ounces double-smoked bacon,
*   cut in thin strips (175 g)*

2 tsp. butter (10 mL)

2 tsp. grapeseed oil (10 mL)

1 cup olive oil (250 mL)

salt and pepper

Vinaigrette:

⅓ cup raspberry vinegar (75 mL)

¾ cup olive oil (175 mL)

2 tsp. sugar (10 mL)

salt and pepper

6 cups frisée, cleaned and dried (1.5 L)

- Clean the artichokes by removing the tough outer leaves, and pare down the bottom of the chokes with a sharp knife. Scoop out the hay in the choke, although most baby artichokes will have little or none.

- Squeeze the juice of 2 lemons over the artichokes to prevent discolouration. Make sure you cover the artichokes evenly.

- In the meantime, fry the lardons (double-smoked bacon) in the butter and grapeseed oil until they become crispy. Drain them on a piece of paper towel and reserve for later.

- Heat the olive oil in a large skillet. Fry the artichokes until golden in colour (about 5 minutes) and drain on paper towel until ready to use. Slice into quarters.

- Mix the raspberry vinegar with the olive oil and sugar in a small jar. Add salt and pepper to taste.

- Toss the frisée with the raspberry vinaigrette, warm bacon and the artichokes. Season to taste and serve immediately.

Chef's Tip: Cooking artichokes without liquid to start helps prevent discoloration.

Radish Confit

Preparation: easy • Makes 2 cups • Recipe by Chef René Rodriguez

Put this on a plate with a big honkin' steak next time the boys come over for a red meat fest. Try this with everything from pork to salmon and watch the eyes pop on people who think radishes are too peppery.

2 cups simple syrup (500 mL)

1 pound red radishes, sliced into thin half-moons (500 g)

1 Tbsp. minced ginger (15 mL)

1 cup cranberry juice (250 mL)

¼ tsp. dried crushed chilies (1 mL)

¼ tsp. salt (1 mL)

- To make simple syrup, place 1 cup (250 mL) sugar and 1 cup (250 mL) water in a saucepan. Bring to a boil over medium heat. Cook until the sugar has dissolved.

- Place all the ingredients in a non-reactive saucepan and simmer until you're left with a syrup-like consistency and all the radishes are glazed.

- Cool and serve.

Radish Salad with Shaved Fennel, Grapefruit and Avocado

Preparation: easy • Makes 6 servings • Recipe by Chris Knight

No watermelon radishes? No problem, just substitute with regular ones. Find yourself a good greengrocer, though, and ask about getting in seasonal goodies like radish and tomato varietals.

9 large red radishes thinly sliced

5 watermelon radishes, thinly sliced

1 avocado, diced

1 Tbsp. jalapeño pepper, minced (15 mL)

1 cup grapefruit segments (250 mL)

½ cup thinly sliced fennel (125 mL)

4 Tbsp. fresh lemon juice (60 mL)

½ cup olive oil (125 mL)

1 Tbsp. granulated sugar (15 mL)

1 Tbsp. finely minced lemon grass (heart of lemon grass only) (15 mL)

2 Tbsp. chopped cilantro (25 mL)

½ tsp. coarse salt (2 mL)

pepper to taste

½ cup olive oil (125 mL)

- Put the radishes, avocado, jalapeño, grapefruit and fennel in a large non-reactive mixing bowl.
- In a separate bowl, whisk together the lemon juice, olive oil, sugar, lemon grass and cilantro and season with salt and pepper.
- Toss the dressing with the radish salad and divide the salad among four plates.

Chef's Tip: To prepare avocado, cut the avocado lengthways and separate the halves by gently twisting. To release the seed, hit gently with the blade of a sharp knife, skew the knife slightly and lift the seed out. If the avocado is ripe the skin should peel off easily.

Stuffed Roasted Poblano with Walnut Sauce and Pomegranates

Preparation: moderate • Serves 6 as an appetizer or as a side dish • Recipe by René Rodriguez

This makes for a very interesting appetizer. The heat of the pepper plays against the sweetness of the dried fruit while the creaminess of the mascarpone and crunch of the walnuts provide texture contrasts. If you can't find poblano peppers, then large jalapeños will do in a pinch. Don't sweat the plantains if you can't find any.

3 Tbsp. olive oil (45 mL)

½ cup leek, finely chopped (125 mL)

2 cups mesclun greens (500 mL)

⅓ cup small diced plantains (75 mL)

6 large poblano peppers

1½ cups diced soft dried fruits (golden raisins, apricots, prunes, sultanas) (375 mL)

½ cup chopped walnuts (125 mL)

1 cup mascarpone cheese (250 mL)

¼ cup thinly sliced kumquats (50 mL)

1 canned chipotle, chopped

½ tsp. salt (2 mL)

pinch granulated sugar

Walnut Sauce:

½ cup sour cream (125 mL)

3 Tbsp. walnut oil (45 mL)

1 Tbsp. sherry vinegar (15 mL)

salt to taste

Garnish:

½ cup pomegranate seeds (125 mL)

- Preheat the oven to 375°F (190°C).

- In a medium-sized skillet heat 1 Tbsp. (15 mL) of olive oil, add the leek and cook until tender and translucent, maybe 5 minutes or so. When the leek is cooked, add the mesclun greens and cook until just wilted. Let cool.

- In another sauté pan heat 1 Tbsp. (15 mL) of olive oil. Place the diced plantains in the hot pan and cook until golden brown and slightly crispy. Cool.

- Make a small slit along the length of the peppers and remove the seeds and veins, leaving the peppers whole.

- Rub the peppers with a little oil and roast them in the oven until charred, about 20 minutes. Remove them from the oven, place in a bowl and cover with plastic wrap. Let sit 10 minutes.

- Peel off the pepper skins using rubber gloves.

- Combine the dried fruits, walnuts, mascarpone, kumquats, chipotle, leek and mesclun mixture, and plantains in a non-reactive bowl and season with salt and sugar. Mix the filling well, stuff the peppers with the mixture and return to the oven to cook for another 15 minutes. Remove them from the oven and set aside for a few minutes.

- For the walnut sauce, mix the sauce ingredients together in a small bowl. Set each pepper on a serving plate, spoon the sauce overtop and garnish with pomegranate seeds. Serve with sweet potato purée (Sweet and Mashed Potato Napoleons au Gratin, see page 199) on the side.

Mushroom Ragout with Lardons and Roasted Garlic

Preparation: easy • Makes 6 appetizers • Recipe by Chef Michael Allemeier

Different 'shrooms will give this dish a variety of tastes and textures so mix it up. I love this on top of a BBQ'd steak or next to a nice sliced pork roast.

1 head garlic

6 large whole Portobello mushroom caps

2 pounds mixed mushrooms, including some of the following: button, shiitake, oyster and chanterelle (1 kg)

2 Tbsp. olive oil (25 mL)

6 ounces double-smoked bacon, cut into ¼ inch (5 mm) pieces (170 g)

salt and pepper

2 Tbsp. butter (25 mL)

1½ cups crème fraîche (375 mL) (see page 25)

½ cup parsley, chopped (125 mL)

- Preheat oven to 325°F (160° C).
- Preheat grill to 375°F (190° C).
- Place the whole head of garlic on a baking tray and drizzle with olive oil. Place in the oven and leave to roast for at least 30 minutes.
- Meanwhile, clean and prepare the mushrooms.
- Set aside the whole Portobello caps for later use. Remove any dirt with a mushroom brush and cut off the woody stems.
- Cut the button mushrooms into halves or quarters depending on their size. Tear the other mushrooms apart into bite-sized pieces.
- Heat a skillet with 1 Tbsp. (15 mL) of the olive oil and add the lardons (bacon pieces). Once crispy and the fat has been rendered, remove them and set aside.
- In the same pan with the bacon fat add the mushrooms, starting with the densest ones that take longer to cook. Cook them for a couple of minutes, tossing all the time. If you need more fat, add a small knob of butter. Cook until desired doneness. Season with salt and pepper.
- Lightly oil the portobello caps. Place them on the preheated grill with the gill side up.
- Cook until nice grill marks are achieved. Season with salt and pepper.

  Remove the garlic head from the oven and chop off the top with a pair of scissors. Squeeze the roasted garlic into the pan with the mushrooms.
- Add the crème fraîche and chopped parsley. Stir well and serve in a grilled portobello mushroom cap and finish with the crispy bacon.

Mushroom and Chèvre Tart

Preparation: easy • Makes 6 appetizers • Recipe by Chris Knight

We call this a "tart" but there's no pastry involved. Instead the meaty thick portobello serves as the vessel for the cheese and tomato. Pretty neat, huh? When the cheese melts and gets all gooey over the tomato, you cut into the mushroom and smell the garlic. The whole thing is set off by the acidic sweetness of the balsamic. Dinner guests will speak of you in hushed reverent tones.

4 cloves garlic, minced

½ cup olive oil (125 mL)

salt and pepper to taste

6 large portobello mushroom caps

2 large vine-ripened tomatoes

Six 1-ounce slices mozzarella (6 × 25-g)

3 large shallots, thinly sliced

1¼ cups chèvre (goat cheese) (300 mL)

¼ pound mixed baby greens (125 g)

balsamic vinegar to taste

- Preheat oven to 350°F (180°C).
- Combine the minced garlic with the olive oil in a bowl, season with salt and pepper to taste and mix well.
- Place the mushroom caps in this garlic oil and coat.
- Transfer the coated mushrooms caps to a roasting pan, gill side up. Bake in the centre of the oven for 10 to 12 minutes or until tender.
- Remove from oven and let cool.
- Slice the tomatoes into ¼-inch (5-mm) rounds.
- Flip the cooled portobello caps over in the roasting pan. Top each mushroom with a slice of mozzarella and shallots.
- Lay a slice of tomato on top, along with a generous layer of chèvre and season with salt and pepper to taste.
- Bake in the oven for 5 to 6 minutes or until the mozzarella cheese is melted and the vegetables are cooked through.
- Remove from oven and plate with mixed baby greens drizzled in balsamic. Serve immediately.

Chef's Tip: When buying portobello mushrooms, look under the cap and make sure the gills are firm and have no bruises. Portobellos are the elder of the crimini mushroom and carry lots of moisture. That is why it is wise to roast gill side up. It will hold in all the mushroom juice.

Polenta Lasagne with Vegetable Bolognese

Preparation: moderate • Makes 6 servings • Recipe by Chef Georges Laurier

Oh man, you are so going to love this one. Lasagna sure, but you use creamy polenta instead of noodles! And the rich-textured bolognese sauce will make your vegetarian friends go weak at the knees.

Polenta:

6 cups water (1.5 L)

2 cups polenta (500 mL)

salt to taste

1 Tbsp. extra virgin olive oil (15 mL)

Bolognese Sauce:

2 Tbsp. olive oil (30 mL)

1 onion, peeled and chopped, small dice

1 carrot, peeled and chopped, small dice

1 celery stalk, chopped, small dice

salt and pepper

1 clove garlic, peeled and minced

12 ounces mixed mushrooms (shiitake, oyster, button, wild mix), chopped (375 g)

1 Tbsp. chopped fresh thyme (15 mL)

2 cups chopped tomatoes, peeled (500 mL)

1 cup tomato juice (250 mL)

Parmesan cheese to garnish

- Bring the water to a boil in a large saucepan over a high heat. Gradually pour in the polenta in a steady stream, stirring all the while with a wooden spoon.
- Reduce heat to low. Stir polenta constantly, until it is no longer grainy and it pulls away from the sides of the pot, about 20 minutes.
- Add salt to taste and 1 Tbsp. (15 mL) olive oil. Remove from the heat.
- Pour the polenta out onto a baking tray lined with parchment paper and spread evenly with a spatula to form a layer ⅓ inch (8 mm) thick. Leave it to set and cool. Keep in mind you are going to cut the polenta into 3 equal pieces.
- Meanwhile, prepare the sauce. Heat 1 Tbsp. (15 mL) of the olive oil in a large non-stick skillet over a medium-high heat.
- Add the onion, carrot and celery and cook until the vegetables begin to soften. Season with salt and pepper.
- Add the garlic and stir for a minute. Add the mushrooms and thyme and cook until the mushrooms are soft, about 3 minutes. Stir well.
- Add the tomatoes and ½ cup (125 mL) of the tomato juice. Leave the mixture to simmer very gently for 5 minutes. If it looks like it is getting too dry, add extra tomato juice. Season again with salt and pepper.
- Preheat oven to 350°F (180°C).
- Once the polenta has set, cut it into equal slabs to fit the dish you will use to make your lasagne.

continued on next page

- Put a layer of sauce in the dish, followed by a layer of polenta. Repeat this process until all the polenta has been used (3 layers) and finish with a layer of sauce.

- Cook the lasagne in the oven for 20 minutes or until the polenta is warmed through again.

- Garnish with large shavings of Parmesan.

Chef's Tip: *When cooking polenta it is important to stir constantly. The Italians take their polenta very seriously, adding it slowly grain by grain while stirring with a wooden stick.*

Carrot Pudding

Preparation: moderate • Makes 6 servings • Recipe by Chef Georges Laurier

This recipe calls for using a ricer on the carrots. If you don't own one it's well worth the investment. They make the silkiest veggie purée. You can also use six 1-cup (250-mL) ramekins instead of a big baking dish if you'd like.

1 Tbsp. softened butter for lining baking
    dishes (15 mL)

1½ cups dark rum (375 mL)

½ cup raisins (125 mL)

2 pounds steamed carrots (1 kg)

1 cup unsalted butter (250 mL)

1½ cups rice flour, sifted (375 mL)

1½ tsp. baking powder (7.5 mL)

3 large eggs, separated

½ cup granulated sugar (125 mL)

1 tsp. salt (5 mL)

- Butter a 16-inch (40-cm) square baking dish and set it aside.
- Pour the dark rum in a saucepan and cook over low heat for 3 minutes.
- Add the raisins to the hot rum and remove from the heat. Let the mixture cool for 20 minutes at room temperature.
- Press the steamed carrots through a ricer into a large bowl. Let cool.
- Melt the cup (250 mL) butter and set aside to cool.
- In a medium bowl sift together the rice flour and baking powder.
- In a large bowl, beat the egg yolks and whisk in the sugar until well combined.
- Add the melted butter and carrot pulp.
- Whisk in the rice flour, salt and baking powder mix.
- Using a slotted spoon, remove the raisins from the rum and add them to the mix. Season with salt.
- Place the rum back over low heat and reduce to 1 cup (250 mL).
- Preheat the oven to 400°F (200°C).
- In a separate bowl, whisk the egg whites into stiff peaks.
- Fold them into the carrot pudding in three stages. Pour the mixture into the buttered baking dish.
- Bake the pudding for 10 minutes then lower the oven temperature to 350°F (180°C).
- Continue to cook the pudding for another 30–40 minutes until it is spongy to the touch and the edges are slightly browned. The interior should be moist.
- Serve with warm rum drizzled overtop.

Rutabaga, Carrot and Butternut Squash Purée with Honey-Dipped Pecan Crust

Preparation: moderate • Makes 6–8 servings • Recipe by Chef Tim McRoberts

Imagine this one next Thanksgiving instead of boring old mashed potatoes! The rutabaga, carrot and squash combine for a root veggie orgasmatron heightened by the nutmeg, star anise and sugar, then mellowed with the cream. The honey pecan crust provides a crunchy texture counterpoint to the purée.

½ pound carrots, peeled, cut into medium dice (250 g)

2 pounds butternut squash (1 kg)

2 pounds rutabagas (1 kg)

1 cup chicken stock (250 mL) (see page 27)

salt and pepper

1 tsp. cinnamon (5 mL)

½ tsp. fresh nutmeg (2 mL)

½ tsp. ground star anise (2 mL)

2 Tbsp. granulated sugar (25 mL)

½ cup 35% cream (125 mL)

1 Tbsp. butter for buttering ramekins (15 mL)

1 cup crushed honey pecans (250 mL)

- Preheat oven to 350°F (180°C).
- Steam the peeled carrots until tender, about 5 minutes. Remove and drain well.
- Peel and seed the butternut squash. Cut into 1-inch (2.5-cm) cubes.
- Peel the rutabaga and cut into 1-inch (2.5-cm) cubes.
- Arrange the cubes in a baking dish. Add 1 cup (250 mL) chicken stock and season with salt and pepper. Cover with foil and bake in preheated oven until tender, approximately 15–20 minutes.
- Once cooked, drain off any excess chicken stock.
- In a large food processor add all the cooked vegetables and blend. Add the spices, sugar and cream and season with salt and pepper.
- Place the mixture into eight 1-cup (250-mL) buttered ramekins, and top with honey pecans.
- Return to preheated oven and bake for 20 minutes or until nice and caramelized.

Chef's Tip: *To make your own honey pecans, take 1 cup (250 mL) of pecans and toss with ¼ cup (50 mL) of warm honey. Place on baking tray lined with parchment. Heat oven to 325°F (160°C) and roast until nuts are fragrant, approximately 7–10 minutes.*

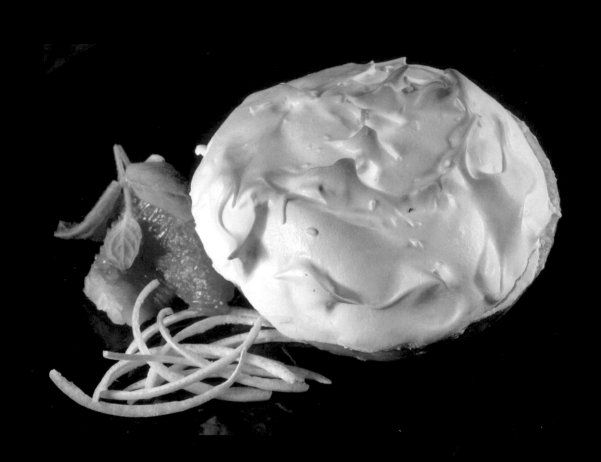

13 Fruit

Cranberry Eggs Benedict

Preparation: moderate to difficult • Makes 6 servings • Recipe by Chef Caroline McCann-Bizjak

Eggs Benny on a lazy Sunday morning with the *New York Times* and a big pot of strong coffee is my kind of heaven. What's fun about this recipe is that it calls for cranberry muffins instead of the English variety, and a workaday hollandaise sauce gets a jolt from cranberry juice. Try this and you'll never go back to the original.

Cranberry Muffins:

1½ cups all-purpose flour (375 mL)

¾ cup granulated sugar (175 mL)

¼ tsp. salt (1 mL)

1½ tsp. grated lemon zest (7.5 mL)

2 tsp. baking powder (10 mL)

½ cup whole milk (125 mL)

½ cup melted butter (125 mL)

1 large egg, lightly beaten

1 cup of fresh or frozen cranberries
    (if using frozen, thaw first) (250 mL)

Cranberry Hollandaise Sauce:

½ cup sparkling white wine (125 mL)

¼ tsp. black peppercorns (1 mL)

½ cup cranberry juice (125 mL)

3–4 egg yolks

1 cup clarified butter (see page 23)
    (250 mL)

fresh lemon juice to taste

salt and pepper to taste

- Preheat oven to 350°F (180°C).
- Begin by making the muffins. In a large mixing bowl, mix the flour, sugar, salt, lemon zest and baking powder until well combined.
- Make a well in the centre. Add the milk, melted butter and the egg.
- Mix until combined and smooth.
- Fold in the cranberries.
- Scoop into 6 paper-lined extra large muffin cups.
- Bake in preheated oven for 20 to 25 minutes or until a toothpick inserted in the middle comes out clean.
- Meanwhile prepare the hollandaise sauce. In a saucepan over moderate heat, combine the sparkling wine, peppercorns and cranberry juice.
- Let the mixture reduce to 2 Tbsp. (25 mL). Strain and cool.
- Add the reduction to the egg yolks in a stainless steel bowl. Whisk to combine.
- Set the bowl over a pan of slightly simmering water.
- Whisk until the eggs are thickened and frothy.
- Add the clarified butter gradually in a thin stream, whisking constantly.
- Continue adding the butter and whisking until the sauce is thickened and all the butter is incorporated. Remove from heat.
- Add the lemon juice and adjust seasoning with salt and pepper.
- Adjust the consistency by adding more cranberry juice or water.

Cranberry Eggs Benedict:

4 cups water (1 L)

1 tsp. white vinegar (5 mL)

12 medium-sized eggs (12)

6 ounces Atlantic smoked salmon (175 g)

salt and pepper

- To poach the eggs, heat the water to a simmer in a skillet. Add the vinegar.
- Crack one egg at a time into a small cup or bowl and slowly slide into the water.
- Poach until the whites are solid, but the yolks are still soft, approximately 3 minutes.
- Remove the eggs with a slotted spoon and drain on kitchen towel.
- Cut the cranberry muffins in half.
- Place 1 ounce (25 g) of Atlantic smoked salmon on each half.
- Set one poached egg on each muffin half and drizzle with a generous amount of hollandaise sauce.

Chef's Tip: Problem-solving techniques when making hollandaise

If the sauce becomes too hot, the egg yolks will begin to scramble. Add a small amount of cold water and whisk. Another solution is to whisk the broken sauce into a fresh egg yolk. You will have to strain this after it has cooked.

Rosemary and Grapefruit Granite with Ice Wine Jelly

Preparation: easy • Makes 6 servings • Recipe by Chef Tim McRoberts

Granite has regained popularity as a palate cleanser since the return of the multi-course tasting menu. The ice wine jelly is a nice touch that looks a lot more complicated than it really is. Hey, you don't have to tell anyone.

2½ cups water (625 mL)

1½ cups granulated sugar (375 mL)

3 sprigs rosemary

6 cups fresh grapefruit juice (1.5 L)

1 Tbsp. grapefruit zest, finely chopped (15 mL)

3 sheets gelatine

1 cup ice wine (250 mL)

- Add the water, sugar and two sprigs of the rosemary to a saucepan and simmer slowly, until a syrup has formed and the herb has infused its flavour. You will know when it is infused, as the syrup will take on a greenish colour and give off a pine aroma. Remove from heat.

- Strain through a fine mesh sieve and cool.

- Add the fresh grapefruit juice to the syrup with the zest and some chopped rosemary for a speckled appearance.

- Pour the mixture into a shallow pan and place in the freezer for 40 minutes.

- After 40 minutes scrape the mixture with a fork as the crystals develop. Repeat for at least 5 hours, scraping every 40 minutes.

- Soak the gelatine in the ice wine to soften.

- Place in a small saucepan and heat gently to dissolve the gelatine.

- Pour the mixture into the bottom of 6 champagne glasses. Place in the refrigerator. The gelatine ice wine should take 1 hour to set.

- To serve, spoon in the grapefruit and rosemary granite mixture on top of the ice wine jelly base in the wine glass. Decorate with a sprig of rosemary.

- You will have extra granite. Cover well and save in freezer for up to ten days for another occasion.

Chef's Tip: Serve in between courses to refresh palates. It also works well as a light summer dessert. 3.5 sheets of gelatine are equal to 1 envelope of powdered.

Pear and Fig Strudel

Preparation: difficult • Makes 6 servings • Recipe by Chef Michael Bonacini

I love strudel. Actually, I love saying strudel like I was an old German guy: SHHHTRRROOOODOOL! They taste pretty good too. This version is easy and decadent (much like myself) with its double whammy of figs and pears. Serve it up with a nice glass of port at the end of dinner.

Strudel Filling:

¼ cup unsalted butter, room temperature (50 mL)

3½ cups (approx. 3 large) firm, ripe pears, peeled, cored, cubed (875 mL)

1 cup granulated sugar (250 mL)

1½ pounds fresh figs, stemmed, each cut into 6 wedges (750 g)

Strudel Pastry and Bread Crumb Mixture:

¼ cup filberts (50 mL)

½ cup dry white bread crumbs (125 mL)

¾ cup unsalted butter, melted (175 mL)

1½ tsp. ground cinnamon (7.5 mL)

¼ cup vanilla-infused sugar (50 mL) (sugar with a vanilla bean stored in it)

8 frozen phyllo sheets, thawed

Garnish:

fresh mint sprigs

icing sugar

- Prepare the filling first.
- Generously butter a large baking sheet.
- Place the cubed pears on the baking sheet in a single layer. Sprinkle with the sugar and roast in the oven.
- Stir occasionally and cook until tender and beginning to brown around the edges, approximately 20 minutes.
- Transfer the baked fruit and any juices to a medium bowl and let cool.
- Add the fig wedges to the cooled pear mixture and combine. Set aside.
- To make the bread crumb mixture, place the filberts on a baking tray. Roast in the oven at 350°F/180°C until fragrant and golden brown. Let cool. Rub with a damp kitchen towel to remove skins. Set aside.
- Place the cooled toasted filberts into a mini processor or spice mill and blend until fine. Remove and place in a small bowl.
- Add the bread crumbs, 3 Tbsp. (45 mL) vanilla sugar and cinnamon. Set aside.
- Melt the ¾ cup (175 mL) of butter in a small saucepan.
- Line a baking tray with parchment.
- Lightly dampen a kitchen towel.
- Lay the phyllo flat on a work table and cover with the damp towel to stop it from drying out.
- Lay one phyllo sheet on the work table with the short side toward the edge of the work surface.
- Brush the sheet with melted butter and then sprinkle with ⅛ of the bread and filbert mixture.

continued on next page

- Place a second phyllo sheet on top and brush it with butter.

- Sprinkle again with bread crumbs and filberts.

- Repeat the process with two more phyllo sheets, creating a four-layer structure. Do this with the other four sheets.

- With a spoon, spread a 3- × 6-inch (8- × 15-cm) strip of half the pear and fig mixture on the short side of the pastry. Leave a 3-inch (8-cm) border around the short side.

- Dust ½ Tbsp. (7.5 mL) vanilla sugar and ¼ tsp. (1.25 mL) of the cinnamon over the fig/pear mixture.

- Fold the long sides of phyllo in over the filling, enclosing the filling halfway (making an envelope). Roll the strudel, carefully tucking in the sides when necessary, to the end of the pastry. You will have a roll when finished.

- Brush the top and the exposed sides with melted butter.

- Repeat for the other strudel.

- Place the rolled strudels on a baking sheet with the seam facing down.

- Bake in the centre of the oven at 325°F/160°C for approximately 20 minutes. Let cool for 10 minutes.

- Sprinkle with icing sugar and garnish with mint.

Grilled Pineapple with Tequila-Brown Sugar Glaze and Ginger-Lime Mascarpone Mousse

Preparation: moderate • Makes 6 servings • Recipe by Chef Michael Bonacini

Some *South of The Border* going on in this one. Except for the mascarpone, which is Italian. So it's a sort of Mexican-Italian dessert. Except for the Grand Marnier, making it a Mexican-Italian-French recipe. Except for the vanilla that might come from Madagascar, which makes it ... ah, forget it. All you need to know is that it's delicious.

Ginger-Lime Mascarpone Mousse:

1½ cups apple juice (375 mL)

¼ cup cold water (50 mL)

1 (¼-ounce) package unflavoured gelatine (60 mL)

½ cup granulated sugar (125 mL)

1-inch piece fresh ginger, peeled and sliced (2.5-cm piece)

2 limes, grated zest and juice of

2 Tbsp. Grand Marnier (25 mL)

2 cups mascarpone (500 mL)

1 cup heavy cream, whipped to soft peaks (250 mL)

Grilled Pineapple:

¾ cup tequila (175 mL)

¾ cup (packed) golden brown sugar (175 mL)

1½ tsp. vanilla extract (7.5 mL)

¼ tsp. ground cinnamon (1 mL)

¾ large pineapple, peeled, cored, cut into pieces

- Line six 1-cup (250-mL) ramekins in plastic wrap, leaving enough surplus to cover the top once full.
- Begin with the mousse. In a medium saucepan reduce the apple juice to ¾ cup (175 mL).
- Fill a small wide-mouthed bowl with ¼ cup (50 mL) cold water. Sprinkle the gelatine over evenly.
- Let the gelatine bloom for 5 minutes. It will look like a big jelly candy.
- To the reduced apple juice add the sugar, ginger, lime zest and lime juice. Heat to a simmer.
- Whisk in the bloomed gelatine.
- Warm slightly to dissolve gelatine. Remove from heat.
- Stirring occasionally, bring the mixture to room temperature. Gradually stir in the Grand Marnier.
- Strain this liquid through a cheesecloth-lined bowl and discard the solids.
- Slowly and gently stir the mascarpone into the gelatine mixture. Do not whisk, as it could cause the mascarpone to separate.
- Whisk the whipping cream to soft peaks. Fold into the mascarpone mixture in three additions.
- Pour the mousse into the plastic-lined ramekins and put in the fridge to set for 4 hours.

continued on next page

- For the pineapple, preheat grill to medium-high 375°F (190°C).
- Combine the tequila, brown sugar, vanilla and cinnamon in a bowl and mix until the sugar dissolves.
- Oil the grill and place the pineapple rings on it. Using a pastry brush, baste the pineapple with the tequila mixture.
- Grill the pineapple until brown, turning occasionally (approximately 10 minutes).
- To serve, transfer the pineapple from the grill to serving plates.
- Remove the mousse ramekins from the refrigerator and, using the plastic wrap as a guide, carefully pull them from their moulds.
- Place one on top of each hot pineapple ring. Serve immediately or the mousse will melt.

Chef's Tip: You can make the mousse and have it set in a bowl. Carefully quenelle the mousse and place on top of the pineapple. Quenelles are usually made with 2 spoons, but for a creamy mousse it is best to do an oval quenelle. Place a large soup spoon in hot water. Hold the spoon on an angle with the bottom slightly up. Place the spoon at the far side of the mixture, dip down approximately halfway in the mixture and drag the spoon toward you.

Fig Tatins with Vanilla Mascarpone

Preparation: moderate • Makes 6 servings • Recipe by Chef René Rodriguez

Conventional culinary wisdom holds that the classic apple tatin is so named for a couple of spinster sisters (family name Tatin) who lived in the Loire. What is not so well known is that the sisters were actually a couple of cross-dressing Knights of the Templar Order who were safeguarding the Holy Grail in their cold cupboard behind the canned beets. Okay, maybe I made the last bit up, but the sister thing is apparently true. In this recipe, figs are centre stage in place of apples and are given a new-world jolt with a nice splash of ice wine.

Tatins:

12 large figs (stems removed and
   cut in four)

⅓ cup plus 2 Tbsp. ice wine (100 mL)

1 tsp. pure vanilla extract (5 mL)

1 Tbsp butter, for greasing (15 mL)

2 Tbsp. granulated sugar (25 mL)

six 3.5-inch (9-cm) diameter circles
   puff pastry

1 Tbsp. butter, melted (15 mL)

Vanilla Mascarpone:

1 cup mascarpone cheese (250 mL)

1 vanilla bean, seeds of

1 Tbsp. plus 1 tsp. honey (20 mL)

- Preheat oven to 400°F (200°C).

  Begin by preparing the tatins.
- Toss the figs with the ice wine and vanilla in a stainless steel bowl.
- Spread some butter on the bottom of six 4-inch (10-cm) ramekins, sprinkle with sugar and arrange the figs skin side down in a fan pattern in the ramekins.
- Place a circle of puff pastry on top of each one and tuck in slightly.
- Brush the tarts with the melted butter.
- Bake in the preheated oven for 12 minutes. The pastry should be puffed and golden brown.
- Let the tart tatins cool for 5 minutes before turning them upside down onto a plate.

  Meanwhile, prepare the mousse.
- Add the mascarpone, vanilla seeds and honey to a bowl and stir gently until well combined.
- Make a mascarpone quenelle (see page 228) and place one on top of each warm fig tatin.

Chef's Tip: *Mascarpone is a very rich Italian cheese. Its high butter content means that when it is overmixed it will separate, so stir the ingredients carefully.*

A Terrine of Summer Fruits

Preparation: difficult • Makes 6–8 servings • Recipe by Chef Ned Bell

If this is the first terrine you've ever made then it will be difficult, only in that most people feel intimidated by playing with gelatine. Once you have your first one under your belt, you'll wonder why you were ever freaked in the first place.

Fruit:

1 cup small strawberries (250 mL)

¾ cup raspberries (175 mL)

½ cup mixture of blackcurrants, redcurrants and blueberries (125 mL)

Gelatine:

5 sheets gelatine (5)

1½ cups sparkling rosé or white wine (375 mL)

5 Tbsp. granulated sugar (75 mL)

1 Tbsp. fresh lime juice (15 mL)

You will also need one 2-pound (1-kg) loaf tin, 7½ × 4¾ × 3½ inches (19 × 12 × 9 cm) deep, preferably non-stick.

If you don't have a non-stick loaf tin, line a bread pan with plastic wrap. Be sure to smooth out any wrinkles.

- First, prepare the fruit. Remove the stalks and pick out only nice firm berries. Make sure you use only baby spring strawberries.
- Soak the gelatine sheets in cold water for 5 minutes or until soft.
- Heat half the wine until it starts to simmer.
- Whisk in the sugar and gelatine.
- Make sure that the gelatine and sugar have dissolved.
- Add the remaining wine and the lime juice.
- Set the liquid aside to cool slightly.
- Arrange the fruit in the tin, with the prettiest and smallest fruit on the bottom, as these will be on the top when the terrine is turned out.
- Pour all but ⅔ cup (150 mL) of the cooled liquid over the fruit and cover with a sheet of plastic wrap.
- Place the terrine in the refrigerator for 2 hours, or until it has set.
- When the terrine has set, top with the remaining liquid. If the remaining liquid has set, gently reheat it.
- Cover with plastic wrap and return to the refrigerator overnight to set.
- To serve, turn out the terrine by dipping the tin very quickly in hot water and inverting it onto a plate. Cut slices with a slightly warm knife. Serve with Greek yogurt or fresh cream.

Chef's Tip: Use only small fruit. If you have to cut larger fruit it will bleed into your wine-gelatine mixture and form pockets of liquid.

Millefeuille of Apple, Walnut and Roquefort

Preparation: moderate • Makes 6 servings • Recipe by Chris Knight

Millefeuille is French for something like "a thousand leaves" as in a thousand leaves of delicate sweet flaky pastry. This one goes from moderate to easy if you decide to go with store-bought pastry dough. Make sure you use a serrated knife to cut the finished dessert.

Flaky Pastry:

1 cup unsalted butter (250 mL)

2 cups all-purpose flour (500 mL)

pinch salt

2 Tbsp. fresh lemon juice (25 mL)

Egg Wash:

1 egg

1 Tbsp. whole milk (15 mL)

Filling:

1 cup walnuts (250 mL)

6 Granny Smith apples

½ cup orange juice (125 mL)

3 Tbsp. granulated sugar (45 mL)

½ cup raisins (125 mL)

1 tsp. cinnamon (5 mL)

8 ounces Roquefort (250 g)

Begin with the pastry.

- Wrap the butter in tinfoil and put it in the freezer for an hour.
- Sift the flour and the salt together.
- Remove the chilled butter from the freezer.
- Holding the butter in the foil, dip it in the flour, then grate it coarsely into the flour.
- Mix the flour and butter with a fork until it looks evenly distributed.
- Sprinkle in the lemon juice. Bring the dough together with your hands, adding water if necessary.
- Wrap the dough in plastic wrap and set aside in the refrigerator for 30 minutes to rest.
- Roll out the dough 1 inch (2.5 cm) smaller than the size of your baking tray.
- Cut the pastry into three wide strips, approximately 10 × 3 inches (25 × 8 cm).
- Place the three strips on a baking tray lined with parchment paper.
- Prick the surface of the pastry with a fork.
- Brush with the egg wash.
- Refrigerate the pastry for 20 minutes.
- Preheat oven to 375°F (190°C).
- Bake the pastry in the preheated oven for 10 to 12 minutes, or until golden brown. Let cool.

- Place the walnuts on a baking sheet and roast in oven until fragrant. Let cool.
- Peel and core five of the apples, and chop them into 1-inch (2.5-cm) cubes. The pieces don't have to be perfect, just roughly the same size.
- Put the apple pieces in a saucepan with the orange juice, sugar, raisins and cinnamon.
- Cook over medium heat until soft. The texture should be rough but without any large lumps.
- Cut the Roquefort into very thin slices.
- Put one strip of the pastry down on a large serving plate.
- Add a layer of apple and raisin mixture, crumble on some walnuts and add a layer of Roquefort. Add a second layer of pastry and repeat.
- Finish with a top layer of pastry and decorate with pieces of sliced apple and walnuts.

Grapefruit Alaska

Preparation: moderate • Makes 6 servings • Recipe by Chris Knight

When I think of traditional baked Alaska, I think of some very white people dressed in very loud plaid, having dinner at a golf and country club sometime in the mid-70s. Kind of like Ted Knight (no relation) in a *Caddyshack* sort of thing. This recipe is not that recipe. It is, however, a sweet yet tart dessert surprise for your next backyard BBQ dinner party on a lazy summer evening.

3 large pink grapefruits

1 cup plus 3 Tbsp. granulated sugar (295 mL)

6 large scoops vanilla ice cream (approx. 1 pint) (½ L)

4 large egg whites

- Cut the grapefruits in half by slicing along the equator.
- Level the round edge of each grapefruit half so they won't roll around.
- Use a grapefruit knife to cut out the flesh.
- In a large bowl combine the flesh and any juices.
- Add 3 Tbsp. (45 mL) of sugar.
- Carefully remove and throw away inner membranes from the grapefruit halves. With the rinds still intact, there should be six hollow cups.
- Distribute the sugar and grapefruit mixture equally between the cups.
- Scoop perfectly round large scoops of ice cream into the cups and place in freezer. Chill for 40 minutes.
- Using an electric mixer, whisk the egg whites slowly until frothy.
- Slowly add 1 cup (250 mL) of sugar and raise speed to high.
- Whisk until whites transform into smooth silky white peaks.
- Preheat oven to 450°F (230°C).
- Remove the grapefruit cups from the freezer just before dessert is to be served.
- Top with a generous amount of meringue.
- Cover the entire surface, creating a sealed mound.
- Place the cups on a baking sheet and bake in the middle of the oven for 5 minutes, or until the meringue is golden. Serve immediately and enjoy!

14 Desserts

Cœurs à la Crème

Preparation: easy • Makes 6 servings • Recipe by Chef Georges Laurier

Cœurs à la Crème means "hearts of cream." The reason why it's so named will become quite obvious as you read this simple recipe.

1 cup unsalted cream cheese (250 mL)

1½ cups sour cream (375 mL)

6 Tbsp. berry sugar (90 mL)

2 large egg whites

cheesecloth

Sauce:

1 cup ripe raspberries (250 mL)

1 cup redcurrants (250 mL)

2 Tbsp. granulated sugar (25 mL)

¼ cup double cream (50 mL)

4 moulds, approx. ¾ cup/175 mL

- Combine the cream cheese, sour cream and berry sugar thoroughly in a mixing bowl.

- Whisk the egg whites with your hand blender (make sure the blades are very clean first) until they are stiff.

- Fold by thirds into the cream mixture.

- Place the mixture in a suitably sized square of cheesecloth, and place this in a sieve over a bowl. Liquid should accumulate in the bottom of the bowl. Drain overnight in a cool place.

- The following day, at least an hour before you want to serve the *cœurs*, pile the mixture into individual moulds (traditionally heart-shaped) and let sit in the refrigerator to set.

- Save a few of the best-looking raspberries and redcurrants for a garnish. Make a fruit purée by putting the raspberries in a food processor and mixing until liquid. Remove the redcurrants from their stems with a fork and add them to the raspberries. Add the sugar to taste, as redcurrants can sometimes be rather tart. Push the mixture through a fine-meshed sieve into a bowl.

- Serve the *cœurs à la crème* by turning them out onto a plate decorated with the fruit purée and double cream. Pile the whole berries on top.

Chef's Tip: Run out of cheesecloth? You can always use a sheet of J-cloth—just make sure it's a new one.

Herb Cheesecake with Parmesan and Rosemary Crust

Preparation: moderate • Makes 6 servings • Recipe by Chef Michael Allemeier

Wasn't sure whether to list this one as a dessert, an appetizer or a side dish! When you think about it, Parmesan and rosemary work pretty well together in a crust. As for a light fluffy cheese filling, why not garlic and herbs? Try this once and it will undoubtedly find a regular place in your cooking repertoire.

Base:

⅓ cup unsalted butter (75 mL)

1 cup grated Parmesan cheese (250 mL)

1 cup dried white bread crumbs (250 mL)

1 Tbsp. fresh rosemary, minced (15 mL)

Filling:

10 cloves garlic, unpeeled

⅓ cup olive oil (75 mL)

1½ pounds cream cheese (750 g)

1 cup crème fraîche (250 mL)
   (see page 25)

3 large eggs

3 Tbsp. all-purpose flour (45 mL)

salt and pepper

1 Tbsp. fresh chervil, chopped (15 mL)

1 Tbsp. fresh basil, chopped (15 mL)

1 Tbsp. fresh oregano, chopped (15 mL)

1 Tbsp. fresh parsley, chopped (15 mL)

½ cup red pepper, finely diced (125 mL)

2 egg whites, room temperature

- Preheat the oven to 350°F (180°C).
- Line a 9-inch (23-cm) cake tin with removable base with a circle of parchment paper.
- For the crust, melt the butter in a small saucepan.
- In a medium bowl, mix together all the dry ingredients for the crust.
- Add the melted butter and mix to form a crumbly mixture.
- Press the crumbs into the bottom of the prepared cake tin. Line the tin with tinfoil, at least 3 sheets. The cheesecake is going to be baked in a water bath, so you want to make sure it is sealed well. Chill the crust.
- Roast the garlic cloves with the olive oil in a small pan in the oven for 15 to 20 minutes or until they are soft. Set them aside to cool.
- Reduce the oven temperature to 325°F (160°C).
- Once cool, squeeze the garlic out of its skin into the bowl of a food processor. Add the cream cheese, crème fraîche, 3 eggs, flour, salt and pepper to the bowl.
- Add the herbs and pulse once or twice with on and off turns.
- Remove the cheese mixture and place in a large bowl.
- Fold in the diced red pepper.
- In a separate, clean bowl, beat the egg whites until stiff peaks form.
- Add the egg whites in three additions to the cheese mixture.
- Pour the cream cheese mix into the chilled crust.

continued on next page

- Place the cheesecake in a roasting pan filled with 1½ inches (4 cm) of water.

- Bake in oven for 50 minutes.

- Do not remove the cheesecake from the oven but turn the oven off and allow the cheesecake to rest there for a further hour.

- Remove the cheesecake from the oven and set aside on a wire rack to cool.

Chef's Tip: *To bake a cheesecake perfectly, with a smooth, crack-free surface, a water bath is essential. To test when a cheesecake is cooked, pick it up and gently shake it with a back and forth motion. The rim of the cake should be firm and the centre will jiggle slightly. The cake will continue to cook with its own internal heat while resting.*

Chocolate and Rum Tartellette

Preparation: moderate • Makes 6 servings • Recipe by Chris Knight

Okay, so this one has BOTH chocolate AND rum. Need I say more? You need another reason to make this? Hmmm ... how's this for rationalization? Chocolate is one of life's few natural pleasures. It is as good as sex. It's better than sex. Plus you got rum, which makes it feel like sex. Perfect.

2 Tbsp. butter (25 mL)

3 Tbsp. cocoa powder (45 mL)

Pastry:

2⅓ cups pastry flour (575 mL)

⅓ cup granulated sugar (75 mL)

½ tsp. salt (2 mL)

1 cup unsalted butter, chilled (250 mL)

1 vanilla pod, scraped (retain seeds)

2 egg yolks

1–2 Tbsp. 35% cream (15–25 mL)

Filling:

6 egg yolks

3 Tbsp. granulated sugar (45 mL)

2 cups whole milk (500 mL)

8 ounces dark chocolate (72%) cocoa,
 finely chopped (250 g)

3 Tbsp. dark rum (45 mL)

3 Tbsp. finely ground blanched almonds
 (45 mL)

six 4-inch (10-cm) tart tins with
 removable bottoms

- Butter the tart pans and cover with sifted cocoa powder.
- To make the pastry, mix the flour, sugar and salt together.
- Add the butter and vanilla until the consistency is like cornmeal. In a small bowl, whisk together the egg yolks and 1 Tbsp. (15 mL) of cream and add to the flour mixture. Mix together until combined. If the dough is too dry, add the extra Tbsp. (15 mL) of cream. Wrap in plastic and let the dough rest in the refrigerator for 30 minutes.
- Meanwhile, prepare the chocolate filling. Whisk the egg yolks and sugar in a mixing bowl. Warm the milk in a saucepan. Melt the chocolate over a pot of simmering water.
- Add a little milk to eggs to temper and slowly add the remaining milk. Whisk in the warm chocolate.
- Flambé the rum and add it to the warm mix.
- Roll the pastry dough out on a lightly floured surface to ⅛ inch (3 mm) thickness. Cut out 6 circles, 2 inches (5 cm) larger than the tart pans. Line the pans with the pastry and refrigerate for 30 minutes.
- Preheat oven to 375°F (190°C).
- Once the crust has chilled, prick it all over with a fork. Line the tart pans with parchment paper and fill with pie weights or dried beans.
- Bake for 15 minutes (dough should be cooked through with no browning) and remove the weights/beans and paper.
- Add the ground almonds to the chocolate mix and fill the tarts ¾ full. Place in oven and bake for 10 minutes. Chill for 4 hours.
- Garnish the tarts with fresh fruit compote, candied orange peel, chocolate curls and fruit coulis.

Chocolate and Rum Cream Sauce

Preparation: easy • Makes 3 cups sauce (750 mL) • Recipe by Chris Knight

This sauce is a perfect accompaniment for the Chocolate and Rum Tartellette (page 239).

1½ cups icing sugar (375 mL)

1½ cups water (375 mL)

¾ cup maple syrup (175 mL)

9 ounces dark chocolate (72% cocoa),
 chopped finely (275 g)

¾ cup 35% cream (175 mL)

1½ Tbsp. dark rum (22.5 mL)

1 vanilla bean (seeds only)

- Put the sugar, water and maple syrup in a saucepan and bring to a boil.
- Stir gently over a medium heat for 3 minutes.
- Remove from the burner and add the chocolate, stirring until it is melted.
- Slowly add the cream, rum and vanilla bean seeds. Mix well.
- Use as a garnish on ice cream, pie and fresh fruit.

Chocolate and Pecan Molten Cake

Preparation: moderate • Makes 6–8 servings • Recipe by Chef Georges Laurier

What's better than a nice piece of chocolate cake after a lovely dinner? A nice piece of chocolate cake with a warm gooey middle that oozes out onto the plate with the first cut of an eager fork. The trick to achieving the molten middle is to chill the cakes before putting them in the oven. That way the outside bakes completely while the middle just gets gooey.

Moulds:

eight 4-inch (10-cm) ramekins or 4-inch (10-cm) baking rings

2 Tbsp. unsalted butter, melted (25 mL)

3 Tbsp. all-purpose flour (45 mL)

3 Tbsp. powdered pecans (45 mL)

1½ Tbsp. icing sugar (22.5 mL)

1½ Tbsp. cocoa powder (22.5 mL)

Cake:

2 egg yolks

2 whole eggs

1 cup granulated sugar (250 mL)

7 ounces dark chocolate, chopped finely (72% cocoa) (200 g)

½ cup unsalted butter (125 mL)

½ cup plus 1 Tbsp. all-purpose flour (140 mL)

½ cup whole pecans, roasted (125 mL)

- Butter the ramekins or rings, dust with a mixture of flour, pecans, icing sugar and cocoa powder and set aside.

- In a mixing bowl, whisk the egg yolks and whole eggs with 1 cup (250 mL) of sugar until the ribbon stage (see below).

- Melt the chocolate with the butter in a metal bowl set over a pot of simmering water. Let cool slightly.

- Whisk in the flour. Slowly add the fluffy eggs to the warm chocolate and combine.

- Incorporate well but be gentle so as not to deflate the eggs.

- Fill the ramekins ¾ full. Sit a whole pecan in the middle of each one. Refrigerate for 1 hour or just until slightly firm. This is to ensure the cake has a liquid centre.

- Preheat oven to 400°F (200°C).

- Cook for 8 minutes maximum. The middle should be slightly liquid.

- Garnish the cake with fresh fruit compote and fruit coulis.

Chef's Tip: Ribbon stage means that when the whisk is pulled out of the mixture it leaves a ribbon trail of egg and sugar that will sit on the mix a few seconds. Some chefs warm the sugar and eggs gently before whisking.

Caramel Pudding with Two Sauces

Preparation: easy • Makes 6 servings • Recipe by Chef Michael Allemeier

Man, this is sooooo easy. Plus you get to do a *bain-marie* (water bath) twice: once for the pudding and once for the chocolate sauce. Please, you can thank me later.

Pudding:

½ cup butter (125 mL)

1⅓ cups brown sugar (325 mL)

6 egg yolks

½ cup 35% cream (125 mL)

½ cup whole milk (125 mL)

Caramel Sauce:

½ cup brown sugar (125 mL)

2 Tbsp. water (25 mL)

¼ cup butter (50 mL)

⅓ cup 35% cream (75 mL)

Chocolate Sauce:

½ cup semisweet dark chocolate (125 mL)

½ cup 35% cream (125 mL)

1 Tbsp. butter (15 mL)

six 1-cup ramekins (250-mL)

- Preheat the oven to 350°F (180°C).
- Beat the butter and sugar together in a bowl until pale and creamy.
- Add the egg yolks and beat well.
- Whisk in the cream and milk.
- Fill the ramekins with this mixture.
- Place the ramekins in a baking tray and fill with enough water to come halfway up the sides (*bain-marie*). Bake for 20 minutes or until custard has set.
- Remove from the water bath and cool. Once cool, refrigerate for 1 hour or up to a day.
- To make the caramel sauce, stir together the sugar, water and butter over a low heat until the sugar has melted and is smooth.
- Add the cream and allow the sauce to simmer until it has thickened, about 5 minutes.
- For the chocolate sauce, melt the chocolate over a *bain-marie*.
- In a small saucepan over medium heat, warm the cream slightly.
- Add the cream to the melted chocolate and stir in the butter.
- Serve the puddings in their ramekins with both sauces poured overtop.

Cinnamon Pear Pies

Preparation: easy • Makes 6 servings • Recipe by Chef Michael Allemeier

Pies is a bit of a misnomer for this one, as they're individually made in ramekins. Whatever. The end result is a lovely warm little dessert featuring the classic taste combo of cinnamon and pear.

3 pears, peeled

1½ cups granulated sugar (375 mL)

2 cinnamon sticks

3 cups water (750 mL)

For the filling:

⅓ cup all-purpose flour (75 mL)

¾ tsp. baking powder (3.75 mL)

1 cup fine sugar (250 mL)

3 Tbsp. butter (45 mL)

3 eggs, separated

1½ cups ground almonds (375 mL)

⅓ cup 35% cream (75 mL)

¾ tsp. vanilla extract (4 mL)

six 1-cup baking cups (250-mL)

- Preheat the oven to 350°F (180°C).
- Cut each pear in half and use a melon baller to scoop out the core.
- Put the pears, sugar, cinnamon sticks and water in a pan over a low heat for 15 minutes or more, until the pears are just soft.
- Set them aside to cool in their juice.
- Sift together the flour and baking powder.
- In a separate bowl, mix the sugar and butter until light and fluffy.
- Add the egg yolks, ground almonds, cream and vanilla.
- Stir in the flour and baking powder.
- In a separate bowl beat the egg whites until they form soft peaks. Fold them into the batter in three additions.
- Fill the 6 baking cups with the mixture and put a pear half on top of each. Press it down until it is one-third submerged.
- Bake for 20 minutes until the filling is firm.
- Serve warm with ice cream.

Lemon Meringue Pie with Candied Lemons and Hazelnut Crust

Preparation: moderate • Makes one lovely pie • Recipe by Chris Knight

Lemon meringue pie is possibly the ultimate in down home North American comfort food. The crust in this one is given a certain *je ne sais quoi* by including crushed hazelnuts. What? Make your own pie dough when you can get stuff from the freezer section of a grocery store? Hey baby, anyone can spoon filling into an industrial crust. *You* are a cooking god. *You* are the cat's ass of culinary doowop. *You* make your own crust!

The candied lemons are a nice touch and you should make an extra big batch. They keep well and can be used with lots of other non-lemon desserts.

Candied Lemons:

5 lemons

2 cups granulated sugar (500 mL)

2 cups water (500 mL)

Pie Crust:

⅓ cup hazelnuts, toasted (75 mL)

2½ cups all-purpose flour (625 mL)

1 tsp. salt (5 mL)

2 tsp. granulated sugar (10 mL)

¾ cup plus 3 Tbsp. butter, cut into small pieces (220 mL)

3 Tbsp. shortening (45 mL)

ice water

Filling:

1½ cups water (375 mL)

1 cup granulated sugar (250 mL)

½ cup fresh lemon juice (125 mL)

- Scrub the skin of the lemons very well with a hard brush. Slice the lemons very thinly. Layer them on a flat wire basket and lower into a saucepan.
- Add the sugar and water and slowly bring the syrup to a simmer. Place a round of wax paper over the lemons and allow to simmer for 10 to 15 minutes.
- Remove from the heat and leave the lemons in the syrup for 24 hours. Lift the fruit from the syrup and drain.
- Place slices on a rack and allow to dry overnight.
- For the pie dough, grind the hazelnuts in a food processor until fine.
- Add the flour, salt and sugar
- Add the butter and shortening until the mixture resembles coarse meal.
- Add ¼ cup (60 mL) ice water in a slow and steady stream through the feed tube, pulsing until the mixture holds together. If necessary, add more ice water, 1 Tbsp. (15 mL) at a time. Form a disk and wrap in plastic. Refrigerate for 1 hour.
- Roll out the dough between two sheets of waxed paper to fill the 8-inch (20-cm) deep dish pie plate. Pierce the crust with a fork and crimp the edges. Chill for a further 15 minutes. Line the crust with foil.
- Preheat the oven to 400°F (200°C).

6 large egg yolks

5 Tbsp. cornstarch (75 mL)

2 Tbsp. grated lemon peel (25 mL)

pinch salt

2 Tbsp. unsalted butter (25 mL)

Meringue:

7 large egg whites

½ tsp. cream of tartar (2 mL)

¾ cup granulated sugar (175 mL)

one 8-inch (20-cm) deep-dish pie plate

- Add pie weights and blind bake for 15 minutes. Remove the pie weights and remove the foil and bake for a further 20 minutes, or until golden.

- Meanwhile, whisk the water, sugar, fresh lemon juice, egg yolks, cornstarch, lemon peel and salt together over a low heat until the filling begins to thicken and bubbles rise to the surface.

- Whisk in the unsalted butter and pour the filling into the baked crust.

- Using a hand beater, beat the egg whites until foamy. Add the cream of tartar and one Tbsp. (15 mL) of sugar.

- Gradually beat in the remaining sugar in a slow and steady stream, until stiff and glossy peaks form (about 8 minutes).

- Put the meringue over the lemon filling and make sure that it seals with the pie crust at the edges. Bake the pie for 10-15 minutes until golden brown.

- Serve with slices of candied lemons on the side.

Chef's Tip: When making meringue, whisk your whites with sugar over a pot of simmering water just to warm. Continue to whip as recipe indicates. The whites will whip better and hold longer when whisked warm.

Chocolate Noodles with Fruit Sauce

Preparation: difficult • Makes 6–8 servings • Recipe by Chef Michael Bonacini

If you're going to go to all the trouble of making your own pasta, it might as well be something you can't buy in the store ... like chocolate noodles ... and serve them up with a sweet boozy sauce! Unfortunately, if you don't have a pasta maker there really is no other way of making this. This is the freshest of fresh pasta, by the way. Once cut into individual linguine-width noodles, it can keep for maybe a couple of hours at room temperature on a parchment paper-lined baking sheet, tightly covered in plastic wrap.

Noodles:

2 cups all-purpose flour (500 mL)

1 cup cocoa powder (250 mL)

¾ cup icing sugar (175 mL)

1 vanilla bean

5 eggs

2–4 Tbsp. water, or as required
(25–60 mL)

2 Tbsp. melted butter (25 mL)

Sauce:

2 mangoes

½ cup white wine (125 mL)

½ cup water (125 mL)

1 cup fresh apricots (250 mL)

½ cup granulated sugar (125 mL)

1 Tbsp. apricot brandy (15 mL)

Whipped Cream:

½ cup whipping cream (125 mL)

5 tsp. granulated sugar (25 mL)

- Pour the flour, cocoa powder, and icing sugar into a sieve and gently shake into a small pile directly onto the work surface.
- Split the vanilla bean and scrape the contents onto the pile.
- Make a well in the centre of the dry ingredients.
- Crack 5 eggs into a bowl and beat them together. Pour the eggs into the well. With a fork, start mixing the eggs into the mixture, gradually stirring in the flour mix from the borders.
- If the dough is too tough, add a little water as required. Knead the dough for about 10 minutes until smooth.
- Wrap the dough in plastic wrap and let rest for 30 minutes.
- Roll out the dough to ¼ inch (5 mm). Run through a pasta machine, gradually reducing the setting. Cut the noodles to about ⅛ inch (2 mm) thick (like linguine) and place them on a cloth to dry for about 2–3 hours.
- Immerse the noodles into lightly salted boiling water and cook until *al dente*. Toss with melted butter.
- Separate the mango flesh from the skin and pit. Place in a pot with the white wine, water, apricots and sugar and let reduce by half (it should be thick and syrupy).
- Strain the sauce through a sieve into a fresh saucepan. Add the apricot brandy and let cool.
- Whip the cream and sugar into soft peaks. Fold into the cooled sauce.

crunchy candied nuts for garnish,
store-bought

- Place the noodles in bowls and spoon a generous scoop of sauce and a dollop of whipped cream on top.

- Garnish with crunchy candied nuts.

Chef's Tip: *To knead the dough, press it down bit by bit with the heels of your hands. Re-form the dough and repeat. The dough is ready when it feels silky smooth.*

Hazelnut Caramels

Preparation: easy • Makes 81 caramels • Recipe by Chris Knight

It's almost criminal that something so easy should be so delicious. If the kids are going to eat candy, it might as well be the good stuff you made yourself without preservatives and stabilizers and other such crap, right?

1 cup unsalted butter (250 mL)

1¼ cups packed golden brown sugar
    (300 mL)

1 cup granulated sugar (250 mL)

1¼ cups light corn syrup (300 mL)

1½ cups sweetened condensed milk
    (375 mL)

1 vanilla bean, split lengthways

1 cup crushed hazelnuts, husked
    (250 mL)

coloured cellophane for wrapping

- Line a 9-inch (23-cm) square baking pan with a piece of foil, folding it over the sides.

- Using your hands, butter the foiled pan thoroughly and set it aside.

- Over a low heat, melt the butter in a medium-sized saucepan. Combine the brown and white sugars, corn syrup and sweetened condensed milk. Continue to cook until the sugars have dissolved. Stir continuously, being careful not to burn the sugar.

- Split the vanilla bean lengthways, extract the seeds and add them to the pot. Add the pod to the mix as well.

- Attach a candy thermometer to the pot, to ensure the correct temperature of candy. Bring the mix to a boil and stir frequently. Cook for 10–15 minutes then remove the vanilla bean pod and discard.

- Continue to cook while stirring the candy mixture until thermometer reads 240°F (115°C).

- Start to move quickly here so that the candy does not cool too much before you have finished with it. Remove the candy from heat and stir in crushed hazelnuts. Pour the candy into the prepared pan. Do not scrape the sides of the saucepan.

- Soak your pan while it is still hot to ease the cleaning process.

- Let the candy cool for 1 hour, then butter a heavy knife and score 8 lines lengthways and 8 lines crosswise.

- Using the foil, pull the candy out of the pan. Using the buttered knife, cut through the caramel. Wrap caramels in coloured cellophane, like a store-bought candy only ten times better!

Hard Maple Taffy

Preparation: moderate • Makes 1 pound (500 g) candy • Recipe by Chef Georges Laurier

Remember this stuff from when you were a kid? It's the only treat I know of that strengthens your teeth, what with all the pulling and chewing. It might seem a little odd to use corn syrup and maple extract as well as maple syrup, given we make the best maple syrup in the world. But the recipe requires the thicker consistency of the corn syrup to get this to work.

½ cup grade A pure maple syrup (125 mL)

1¼ cups granulated sugar (300 mL)

¼ cup light corn syrup (50 mL)

6 Tbsp. water (90 mL)

salt (pinch)

baking soda

½ cup heavy cream (125 mL)

2 Tbsp. unsalted butter, cut into small bits and softened (25 mL)

½ tsp. pure maple extract (2 mL)

¼ cup canola oil (50 mL) for oiling the equipment

parchment paper

- You will also need to have a well-oiled large (20 × 20 inches/ 50 × 50 cm) marble slab or another heatproof work surface, a well-oiled bench knife, well-oiled scissors and a candy thermometer.
- Line two large baking sheets with parchment paper.
- Using a 3- or 4-quart size (3–5-litre) saucepan, pour in the maple syrup and cook over a low heat until it reduces to ¼ cup (50 mL), approximately 10 minutes.
- While stirring with a wooden spoon, add the sugar, corn syrup, water, salt and baking soda and cook until the sugar is completely dissolved, 8–10 minutes.
- Increase to a medium heat and continue to cook the mixture, without stirring, until the candy thermometer reads 240°F (115°C).
- Carefully add the cream, butter bits and maple extract. Let this boil until the thermometer reads 260°F (126°C).
- Remove the pan from the heat and immediately pour the mixture onto the oiled work surface. Do not touch the candy as it will be extremely hot. Let the mixture cool for 5 minutes. Using the well-oiled bench knife, fold the edges of the candy in toward the centre to form a 4- × 2-inch (10- × 5-cm) loaf.
- Flip the loaf over continuously with the knife until it is just cool enough to handle. Oil hands and pick up the taffy. Work over a heatproof surface.
- Be careful, because candy taffy will be cooler on the edges than in the centre. Pull ends of taffy away from each other and bring oiled hands together to fold in half. The taffy will cool and harden quickly as it is pulled.

- Release one hand and pick up folded end of taffy. Holding the ends, continue to pull the folded taffy and twist into a rope. It will turn into a golden-streaked ribbon.

- Continue pulling and twisting until the taffy begins to feel firm and starts to harden. When it begins to harden, place onto the work surface and pull until it is 20 inches (50 cm) in length.

- With the oiled knife, cut the taffy into fourths. Twist and pull each piece into an even 8-inch (20-cm) "rope," approximately ¼ inch (5 mm) in thickness.

- With oiled scissors cut the taffy candy into ¾ inch (2-cm) pieces and arrange in one layer on the parchment-lined baking sheets. Be sure that the pieces do not touch each other.

- Let the taffy stand at room temperature until it is hard, about 1 hour.

- Taffy can be wrapped in wax paper or candy wrappers or laid between sheets of parchment paper in an airtight container. It will keep at room temperature for up to two weeks.

Chef's Tip: *If you live at a high altitude, make sure you know the temperature your water boils at. Note the difference between this and 212°F (100°C), and subtract the difference from the candy temperature given in this recipe. To test, simply boil a pot of water and read the temperature.*

Milk Chocolate-Coated Sponge Candy

Preparation: moderate • Makes 6 servings • Recipe by Chris Knight

Yes, yes, I know it *looks* like a chocolate-covered sponge, but did they really have to be so literal? I mean, cottage cheese doesn't look like a cottage. Whatever you call it, this treat is gloriously light with a chewy finish.

1 cup granulated sugar (250 mL)

1 cup light corn syrup (250 mL)

1 Tbsp. distilled white vinegar (15 mL)

1 Tbsp. baking soda, sifted (15 mL)

1 pound milk chocolate, divided (500 g)

1 Tbsp. melted butter (15 mL)

- Line a 9-inch (23-cm) square pan with 2-inch (5-cm) sides with foil and extend foil over sides. Butter the foil very generously with the melted butter.

- In a heavy large, deep saucepan, combine the sugar, corn syrup and vinegar. Stir over a medium heat until sugar dissolves.

- Swirling pan occasionally, cook the mixture until the candy thermometer reads 310°F (155°C), approximately 18 minutes.

- Remove from heat, immediately add the sifted baking soda and stir quickly until well combined. Mixture will foam vigorously. Be extra careful here, as the hot sugar is going to rise.

- Pour the hot mixture into the prepared pan and cool completely for 1 hour. Don't be tempted to touch the foam or it will deflate.

- Using the foil as an aid, lift the candy from the pan and fold down the foiled sides. Cut or break candy into pieces.

- Chop the chocolate finely and melt in a double boiler or *bain-marie* to 110°F (43°C). Remove from the heat.

- Stirring constantly, bring the temperature down to 85°F (29°C) then reheat to 86°F (30°C). Never heat the chocolate past 112°F (44°C).

- Dip the sponge candy into the chocolate and set on a baking rack to cool.

Chef's Tip: It is important to work quickly when adding the baking soda. The longer you stir, the more the mixture deflates. You must use a pot with high sides. The mixture will expand to six times its volume in a matter of seconds with hot sugar. Never let water come in contact with your chocolate or it will seize.

Cranberry Moussapolooza

Preparation: difficult • Serves 6–8 • Recipe by Chris Knight

This one takes a while to make. The techniques aren't complicated, there are simply a lot of steps to the recipe. If you're having a party or a big dinner, you can make the chocolate cake and cranberry compote the day before. The chocolate granache is best made the day of. Trust me, it's well worth the effort.

Chocolate Cake:

3 Tbsp. melted unsalted butter (45 mL)

¾ cup unsalted butter, room temperature (175 mL)

6 ounces chopped semisweet chocolate, chopped finely (175 mL)

9 large egg yolks

1 cup sugar (250 mL)

4 large egg whites

½ cup of roasted walnuts, chopped (125 mL)

three baking pans, about 8 inches (20 cm) in diameter

Cranberry Compote:

1½ cups frozen cranberries (375 mL)

½ cup granulated sugar (125 mL)

¼ cup water (50 mL)

1 tsp. minced orange zest (5 mL)

3 Tbsp. orange liqueur (45 mL)

- Preheat the oven to 350°F (180°C).

- Brush the bottoms and sides of the baking pans with the melted unsalted butter. Line the bottoms with parchment paper. Brush the parchment with melted butter.

- Melt the ¾ cup (175 mL) of butter and chocolate in a bowl set over a pot of simmering water (*bain-marie*). Stir continuously to achieve a smooth consistency. Let cool slightly.

- Beat the egg yolks and sugar in a large bowl until they triple in volume.

- In a separate bowl, beat the egg whites into soft peaks.

- Fold the melted chocolate into the egg yolk mixture.

- Fold the egg whites in three additions into the chocolate-yolk mixture.

- Separate the batter evenly into the three prepared pans. Bake in the oven for 20–25 minutes or until a toothpick can be inserted easily and comes out clean. Set the cakes aside to cool in their respective baking pans.

- Combine the cranberries, sugar, water and orange zest in a saucepan over moderate to high heat. Bring to a boil, then lower the heat. Simmer for 5–6 minutes, stirring occasionally. The sauce will develop a syrupy consistency and the cranberries will pop. Add the orange liqueur and stir. Refrigerate until cooled.

- Pour the 2 cups (500 mL) of 35% cream into a saucepan and bring to a boil. Place the chocolate in a medium bowl and pour the hot cream overtop. Let the chocolate sit and melt for a couple of minutes. Stir the melting chocolate and warm cream together until fully incorporated and smooth. Let cool slightly.

continued on next page

Chocolate Ganache:

2 cups 35% cream (500 mL)

*1½ pounds chopped semisweet chocolate
(750 g)*

1 cup 35% cream (250 mL)

- In a separate bowl whisk 1 cup (250 mL) of 35% cream to medium peaks and reserve. Divide the ganache into two bowls. To one bowl, add half the cranberry compote, whipping cream and toasted nuts. Chill.

- Cover the second bowl of plain ganache with plastic and leave at room temperature.

- To assemble the cake, gently turn the first cake upside down onto the bottom of a 9-inch (23-cm) diameter tart pan. Remove the parchment. Slide into place on the presentation plate and lightly spread some chocolate-cranberry mix on top of it, creating an even foundation. Be careful not to apply too much pressure.

- Slide the second cake upside down onto this first layer. Peel off the parchment paper and spread the remaining chocolate cranberry mix evenly. Turn out your third cake as before and place it on top.

- Using a small metal offset icing spatula, apply the plain ganache to the sides and top of the cake.

- Fill a pastry bag with a star tip and add some plain ganache. Pipe a decorative ring along the borders of the top layer. Spoon the balance of the plain cranberry compote inside the ganache ring. Refrigerate the cake for 2 hours.

  OR

- Warm the ganache and drizzle overtop of cake (this produces a great shiny chocolate glaze).

Chef's Tip: *When using ganache to ice the cake, dip your spatula in hot water and dry off with paper towel. Glide the warm spatula and smooth out any bumps. For ease of assembly, place the cake layers in the freezer for 10 minutes. This will allow you to move them easily without breaking them.*

Index